WING DANCER

STORMWALKER
BOOK 7

ALLYSON JAMES

JA / AG PUBLISHING

CHAPTER ONE

The peace of my azure-skied evening was shattered when a gleaming gray pickup flew across the intersection at the Crossroads, tore through the dirt parking lot, and aimed straight for my hotel.

Behind the truck raced at least a dozen motorcycles, the riders with heads down in determination. Behind *them* came law enforcement—deputy sheriff, town police, state highway patrol. They all barreled past Barry's bar, which shares the lot with my Crossroads Hotel, and gunned toward my front door.

I'd stepped outside to enjoy the cool March evening after a busy day. It was starting to get hot, the brutal desert summer on its way, but for now, dawn and dusk were paradise. It was my habit to take a short walk once the guests had headed out for dinner or settled in at the saloon, to savor the weather and reflect on my upcoming nuptials to Mick. A dragon and a Stormwalker marrying in the human way had potential pitfalls.

The pickup showed no signs of slowing down. In mere

seconds, it would plow right through the window-lined wall
of the saloon, which I'd just had repaired after my recent
showdown with an ultra-powerful mage.

My guests in the saloon turned toward the source of the
noise, eyes widening as the vehicles rushed at them. I heard
the magic mirror, suspended over the bar, scream.

Oh, honey! Stop them!

I spread my arms as I faced the pickup, as though that
would have any effect. I was about five foot two and not
very large, not like Mick, who could have simply turned
dragon, picked up the truck, and redirected it. Mick,
though, wasn't here.

The twilit sky was beautifully clear. The few clouds
hanging far away over the San Francisco Peaks wouldn't be
useful to a Stormwalker, because I need an active gale to
work magic. I had other magic, the horrific powers of
Beneath, but those were only for dire emergencies, like the
end of the world or battling the mage who'd destroyed my
saloon the last time.

If I didn't temper the Beneath magic with a storm, I
could implode the hotel, leaving a smoking pit in its place.

If the dude in the truck—I could see it was a man—
plowed into my hotel, there would be a lot of carnage. I
didn't recognize the pickup, had no idea who the guy was,
why half a motorcycle gang was chasing him, or why the
bikers weren't breaking off their pursuit and fleeing all
those cops.

The hotel was warded by Mick's dragon magic and my
Stormwalker powers, mixed with a good witchy dose from
Cassandra Bryson, the hotel's manager. Those wards could
stave off even the strongest magical attack, but would it

make any difference to a Silverado slamming straight into it?

I called a ball of Beneath magic from the depths of my psyche, tamped down the nausea that it caused, and balanced the glowing orb on my palm.

"Stop!" I yelled.

The truck barreled on, the bikers chased the pickup, and the cops kept coming, sirens blaring. The truck would hit the windows any second now.

Throat constricting in panic, I popped the ball of magic onto the ground between the Silverado and the wall of my saloon.

Dust exploded where the ball hit, sending up a wall of gravel that spattered in all directions. I ducked as bits of rock and dirt grated into me. Pebbles smacked the saloon's windows, and every single one of them blossomed into a network of cracks.

The truck swerved at the very last minute, its tires blasting me with another wave of stinging gravel as it roared around to the back of my hotel.

The bikers parted to flow around both sides of the building, and the cop cars followed with an equal split.

I struggled to my feet and then ran after the vehicles. I charged around the part of the hotel that held my private living quarters, past the large juniper tree where two crows perched to watch the spectacle, and into the red-orange earth of desert beyond.

The land here was cut by the remains of a railroad bed, which had been raised about six feet from the scrub-dotted desert floor long ago to carry lumber from Flagstaff and surrounding areas down through the folds of mountains to the Valley. It had been one of many railways snaking through the state, abandoned now, rails and ties long gone.

At present, it was used as a hiking path into and out of Magellan, the nearest town. The man in the pickup was trying to make his truck climb the too-steep incline.

The pickup's wheels slipped and slid in the soft red earth, but did the guy stop? No. Whoever he was, he kept his foot on the accelerator, tires spinning as the truck struggled up the side of the bed.

Finally, the pickup lost all traction and whined in place. The tires spun, slowly digging a shallow grave for the truck and its driver.

The bikers halted with another spray of gravel. The police cars and law enforcement motorcycles also skidded to a stop, men and women pouring from them, vested up, guns out of holsters.

Then there was me, trotting behind them, yelling at the top of my voice for someone to tell me what was going on. No one answered, of course.

I recognized Emilio Salas, the assistant chief of police from Magellan, as well as Deputy Paco Lopez. There was Deputy Maria Abarca, who'd moved here from Los Angeles when Sheriff Jones made a big push to recruit more women into his department. Not in token jobs—Nash said women should be given the same opportunity as men to participate in all aspects of law enforcement. Some admired him for this while others criticized him, but Nash ignored them all. He'd be happy if every man, woman, and child on the planet were special-forces trained.

Of Sheriff Jones himself there was no sign. He had to be out of the county doing something very important, because there was no other way he wouldn't have been leading that chase.

The law enforcement vehicles aimed headlights and spotlights on the truck. Lopez and Abarca approached it together, with Salas behind them, all three stalking forward with extreme caution. The bikers, as pissed off as they were, had moved back to let the cops do their jobs.

I jogged to a biker I recognized as one of Barry's regulars. "What the hell is going on?"

The biker turned his reflective sunglasses on me, showing deep blue dusky sky streaked with intense pink. "That dude is in deep shit," the man growled.

"Why? What did he *do*?"

"Screamed past us, throwing dust in our faces, while we were sitting outside at Dusty's. Gave us all the finger and then took off."

Dusty's was a bar on the 66 in Flagstaff, east of the touristy areas, where a lot of Barry's regulars went when they sought the coolness of high altitude in the summertime. Dusty's wasn't usually a dangerous place, but could get rough, especially if the bikers took offense. Big, big mistake.

"He flipped you off, and twenty guys decided to go after him?"

"It's the principle of the thing, Janet." The biker's cheeks became concave as he sucked in a breath of irritation. "He nearly caused three wrecks on the 66 before he hit the freeway. I don't know why he thought he could hide out *here*. The Crossroads is *ours*."

The truck continued to roar as the man inside jabbed at the accelerator, but he only managed to become more and more embedded.

"Maybe if you stand down, he'll stop," I suggested. "He probably thinks you're going to kill him."

"We thought about seriously injuring him." The biker glowered. "Then we picked up all the damned cops."

"Gee, I can't imagine why." I widened my eyes at him, but the biker only looked away, shaking his head.

People were coming out of the hotel to see what was up, including Cassandra, tidily dressed in her business suit and pumps. She walked across the gravel toward me, but no dirt would dare stick to her pristine shoes.

Every cop except Lopez, Abarca, and Salas had shielded themselves behind their vehicles, weapons drawn.

The crows in the tree, one soot black, the other with a mixture of black and white head feathers, continued to watch the humans with corvid disdain.

"Stop the engine and put your hands on the wheel," Lopez ordered the man in the truck.

No response. The guy kept gunning the engine, to no purpose.

Cassandra stopped next to me. She shielded her eyes against the glare of headlights, then made a flickering motion with her fingers and whispered a word.

Instantly the truck's motor died.

"Someday you're going to have to teach me how to do that," I murmured to Cassandra.

She lowered her hand. "It's practice."

Cassandra was being modest. She was one of the most powerful Wiccans I'd ever met.

Even with the truck dead, the man inside didn't move. I couldn't see him well, but the aura I glimpsed was human. He wasn't demon, mage, dragon, or Changer—simply an ordinary person who'd decided to jump into his truck for whatever reason and go on a rampage. He possibly had an insanely high level of alcohol or other recreational substance running through his body.

Lopez, Salas, and Abarca were taking no chances. They'd split up, guns ready, with a deputy on each side of the truck and Salas at the tailgate. They stood well back from the doors, in case the guy made a sudden move or came out with a weapon.

The bikers surged closer. Soon, the truck would be surrounded. I worried that one of the bikers might simply shoot the man through his windshield, despite the cops, end of problem.

Another siren split the air. A large black F250 hurtled around the end of the hotel, a red light spinning on its roof. Sheriff Jones, at last.

Nash drove right through the crowd, the bikers scrambling out of his way. He slammed his brand-new truck to a halt without hitting any people or other vehicles, and leapt out, the truck's door swinging. He wore civilian clothes of a gray T-shirt, jeans, and hiking boots, as though he'd been out for a walk when he got the call.

Without a vest, his weapon holstered on his hip, he stormed straight to the truck, passing Lopez and Abarca who stared at him in consternation.

Nash ripped open the door of the truck and glared at the driver. "What the hell are you doing?" he bellowed. "Come on out of there."

The man inside didn't move. I inched closer and realized that he was older, his hair a mix of gray and white, his face lined. He glared back at Nash with as much rage as the sheriff gave him and didn't budge.

"I said, get *out*." Nash stated this in a tone that had most perps on their knees, begging for mercy. "I *will* arrest you. Maybe a night in a cell will give you time to think about things."

"Oh, I have plenty of time to think," the man snapped, his voice free of alcoholic slur. "A cell would be a step *up* from where I've been."

Nash reached for his hip, but instead of going for his pistol, he dipped his hand into his pocket and pulled out a cell phone.

"I'll call her," he warned.

I blinked and glanced at Cassandra, who also looked puzzled. *Call who?*

"You are a shit." The man at last slid from the driver's seat and landed in front of Nash. "But you know all about incarceration, don't you?"

The two men squared off. They were of similar height and build, the older guy slimmer. Both had sharp gray eyes, blunt faces, and beaky noses. The older man had a regularity of features that made him attractive, or would have if his face wasn't so crumpled by his scowl.

"I'm doing it," Nash said. "I'm calling Cousin Ada."

The man smacked Nash's phone out of his hand. I distinctly heard plastic crack on the rocks at the base of the railroad bed.

"That's it." Nash had the guy facing the truck in a flash, handcuffs glinting. The truck's driver snarled invective, but Nash clicked on the cuffs. He turned the older man around and marched him to the passenger side of Nash's waiting pickup. "In you go, Grandad."

I realized with a jolt that Nash wasn't calling the man a derogatory name because of his age. Nash was addressing him in the way he always had, probably since he'd been a tiny kid—as hard as was to picture Nash as a boy.

"Son of a bitch," the biker whispered.

We all watched Nash shut the door on the older man, stalk to the driver's side of the truck, and slide in. Without a word to his deputies or anyone else, he expertly turned the pickup, avoiding all other vehicles, and took off in a spatter of gravel.

The law enforcement officers of various branches holstered their weapons, looking around as though they weren't certain how they'd come to be there. The abandoned truck hung on the side of the railroad bed, silent and empty.

"Well, damn." Deputy Lopez appeared at my side, his expression a mixture of perplexity and amusement. "This is going to be one hell of a report."

The biker I'd talked to had faded back, and others joined him. Bikes were pushed quietly to the main parking lot, some men heading into Barry's bar, others starting up and nonchalantly rolling to the highway before the deputies, town cops, and highway patrol thought about going after *them*.

"I didn't know Jones even *had* a grandfather," Lopez went on. "I thought Nash just spawned out of a crack in the ground."

"That's a dangerous thing to say around here," I reminded him.

Lopez looked alarmed. It was true that in Magellan, any number of unholy things could come out of fissures in the ground. He gave me a wary nod and strolled away to join Abarca, who was efficiently noting something on an electronic tablet.

I left the now-subdued scene, the crows turning their heads to follow my path, and walked around the hotel with Cassandra. There we halted and gazed forlornly at the ruined windows of the saloon.

Cassandra let out a sigh. "I'll call our repairman." She strode calmly into the hotel, shoulders squared.

I entered behind her to the cool interior of the lobby, lights already on for the evening. The guests inside the saloon had drifted back to their tables, discussing the incident and calling on Carlos, the bartender, for more alcohol. At least this time the damage hadn't been worse than nicked windows.

I veered toward the office, intending to bury my head in my hands and groan, when one of our ward's alarms went off, signaling the arrival of a very dangerous magical person.

Adrenaline shooting high, I dashed through my private hall to the back door, running past the cops still surrounding the empty truck. I scrambled up the railroad bed, digging my toes into the soft dirt, and slithered down the other side.

Behind me, the crows flapped into the air, croaking harshly, to become black specks on the darkening sky.

Sure, abandon me now, I muttered to myself. The crow without any white in its feathers cawed her deprecation.

I held my magic in close reserve as I headed out across the desert to intercept the newcomer.

CHAPTER TWO

H e walked across the darkening desert from the
direction of the shallow canyon that cut across the
land, where he'd probably descended. He was dressed in his
usual black suit and long duster coat, looking utterly
comfortable in them. The night was cooling rapidly, but it
was still warm for so much clothing.

The man's long black hair was in a neat ponytail, which
accentuated the sharp bones of his face. He had dark skin
and dark brown eyes that became very black when he forgot
he was in human form instead of dragon.

I had to admit that Drake was attractive, and I understood why my half-sister Gabrielle had once made a play
for him. She'd then dumped him for Colby, who actually
has a sense of humor, as well as a warm heart.

Drake halted about twenty feet from me and waited for
me to approach. As I neared him, I saw that he was
carrying what looked like a bowling bag. An ordinary, blue
canvas bag, made for a single ball, with a yellow starburst
stitched into one corner.

I stared at the incongruous bag so hard that I nearly ran into Drake, who had to steady me with a firm hand.

"I need to speak to you, Janet."

I hadn't figured he'd flown out here from the dragon compound for a singalong.

Drake as dragon was satiny black, with no markings at all. When he turned human, his wings became a spreading tattoo on his back, its inked ends rising up his neck to embrace his cheeks.

He was a beautiful dragon and a handsome human, but he'd only stare at anyone who told him so. Drake had no ego about his looks.

About his intellect, on the other hand … Drake believed he was more intelligent than anyone else on the planet. Probably off the planet too, if he thought about it.

"All right, then," I said. "Speak."

Drake frowned, never pleased with my glib tone. "Inside. Where we can be private."

"In the hotel? I have a number of guests at the moment." I spread my arms to indicate we stood on empty land. "There's no one out here."

"That does not mean no one can listen," Drake said. "You or your manager can make certain we aren't overheard inside. Or seen."

He had a point. The desert was quiet, but any number of animals who flew or skittered by might be Changers, and there were other beings who could hide in the dark.

I was intrigued by Drake's need for privacy but still wary. "I need your promise that you won't try to burn down my hotel or destroy anything or anyone in it. I've already had one incident today, and I don't need Cassandra passing out when she receives yet another repair bill."

Drake lifted his brows, but he didn't ask about the incident. Shit happened at my hotel all the time. If it didn't involve him, he wasn't interested.

"You have my word," Drake said.

I didn't have to ask for a handshake or a contract written in blood to believe him. If Drake vowed to keep his flames to himself, he would. He was the most painfully honorable being I'd ever met, even when he was doing his best to kill me.

"All right, then." I turned away and started walking back to the hotel. Drake followed in utter silence.

The night had cooled, the breeze growing sharper. We could experience some serious wind out here, gusting up to fifty miles per hour on any given day. Drake's long coat didn't seem so foolish as the evening temperature steadily dropped. The bowling bag was still weird, though, unless he'd used it for carrying his clothes. I'd expect Drake to have a fine leather suitcase for that, monogrammed, with a brass lock and a little key.

Amber lights swept the darkness on the other side of the railroad bed. A tow truck had arrived to retrieve the pickup, chains rattling as a man hooked up the tow rig. I wasn't surprised to see the name *Hansen* blazed on the side of the large red truck. Fremont, my plumber, had a sideline in hauling stranded vehicles to the local garage.

The state troopers and county deputies had departed, leaving Emilio Salas in charge of cleanup. He was laughing about something with Fremont, and when he saw us climbing down the bank, he turned his engaging smile on me.

"Can you believe it, Janet?" he asked. "Jones's *grandfather*. This truck is stolen, too. Reported missing from an assisted living place in Flagstaff. Apparently, the keys were left in it, so Jones Senior jumped in and took off." Salas shook with more laughter. "Wonder if the sheriff will really lock his old grandad in a jail cell."

"I wouldn't put it past him," I said. Nash didn't tolerate lawbreaking from anyone. Kind of like Drake, who stood silently behind me, uninterested in the weird things humans got up to.

Fremont ducked out from behind the tow truck, finished hooking up the other vehicle. "Crazy, huh, Janet? This is a beautiful pickup. Hope the old guy didn't damage it too much."

"I'm sure the owner hopes not too. How are things with you?"

Fremont was a genuinely nice guy, with a kindness that was worth far more than Drake's dark attractiveness. Fremont's hair was thinning on top, and his face couldn't be described as more than plain, but his smile was winning. He'd recently fallen for a lady named Flora, a minor witch who worked at my hotel.

"Can't complain." Fremont gave me a modest shrug. "If you see Flora inside, will you tell her I'll be a little late tonight? Have to get this to the impound in Flat Mesa."

"Sure, but can't you text her?" I could never keep track of my own phone, but normal people like Flora and Fremont seemed to manage to.

Fremont grimaced. "Texting is so impersonal, isn't it? We can use devices to connect to people around the world, but it's no substitute for talking face-to-face."

No wonder Flora liked him. "I'll tell her. Good night, Fremont. Salas."

"Night, Janet." Fremont went back to check his tow connection.

Salas, still beaming, bade me a good night. He sent a quizzical glance at Drake, who stood beside me in total silence. I shook my head to indicate I couldn't explain Drake and started for the hotel. Drake crunched through the gravel behind me.

I started to lead Drake to the back door, to my private suite, but he stopped me. "No. Somewhere your magic mirror won't listen and where Micalerianicum's aura hasn't permeated."

"Mick warded the entire hotel," I said in impatience. "His aura has *permeated*, as you say, everywhere."

"Not as deeply as in your bedchamber. He is your mate, after all."

It still weirded me out to hear Mick and I referred to as *mates*. Not partners, lovers, or boyfriend and girlfriend, but mates. Like we were wolves. I supposed one day I'd get used to it.

The turquoise, onyx, and silver ring I wore gave a little throb. Mick had put a bit of his own essence into it, a piece of his true name, something dragons trusted no one with. The ring tingled sometimes, when I thought of him, letting me know he was all right.

"Fine," I said. I didn't really want Drake in the bedroom where Mick and I made sweet love, anyway. "My office."

I led the way through the back door and along the narrow hall past my bedroom and into the hotel itself.

When we emerged into the lobby, I saw with dismay that the Horribles, guests who'd arrived this past Saturday, had filed out of the saloon. The youngest daughter, Allie, who was in her thirties, wobbled in a spin in the middle of the room, nearly crashing into the sculpture of the black stone coyote that stood on its pedestal near the stairs.

"Did you see all those bikers?" she bellowed at her collective family—parents, three grown daughters, and assortment of husbands—who were plopping onto sofas and chairs. "I used to hang out with bikers—remember? And the guy with the square beard who puked all over our living room that one time?" She screamed with laughter. "Way before I met you, honey," she said to a lanky young man with long, thin legs bared by Bermuda shorts.

The husband, instead of greeting this tale with a long-suffering expression, burst out laughing. "You've told me that story a million times."

"Allie puked as much as any of them," her eldest sister Yvonne said. "Especially when she was smoking weed."

"I never did any weed. That was *you*." Allie pointed at Yvonne. "Don't you remember?"

"Let's go to the diner," another of the husbands said with restlessness. He hadn't sat still since he'd arrived. "We can tell them all about the thousand bikers surrounding the hotel."

"That guy in the truck almost ran into us," Allie said, her eyes growing wide. "I would have died if he'd gone through the window. I bet I would have died. Mom, do you think I would have died?"

The middle daughter hopped out of her chair, cutting off whatever their rather weary mother was going to say. "If we're going to the diner, we have to change. What do you wear to a small-town diner? Should I wear my jeans? I brought some cowboy boots—oh, wait, no I didn't. Are there any stores still open? I need some cowboy boots."

"What you have is fine," the mother said firmly. "Come on. Let's go up and see what we can find."

"Hurry back," one of the husbands said in a suggestive tone as the women all rushed the staircase, bumping into each other in their haste.

The father of the family, a slender man with gray hair and a trim white beard, lolled back in his chair, eyes closed. A soft snore emitted from his lips.

As I led the way to my office, the three husbands stared in blatant envy at the elegantly dressed Drake, who ignored them completely.

Cassandra sat behind the reception counter, pretending to study her laptop, but the tightening of the lines around her eyes betrayed her annoyance with our guests.

We'd labeled the family "The Horribles" about five minutes into their stay. They were ordinary humans, nothing magical about them, but I worried they'd scare away all our supernatural customers who came to the Crossroads for a little peace. The Horribles had arrived for the weekend but soon professed love for the out-of-the-way hotel in the out-of-the-way town and decided to stay for a week. Sadly, we'd had the room, and Cassandra did not want to turn down a lucrative opportunity.

I gave Cassandra Fremont's message to pass to Flora if she saw our maid before I did. Cassandra nodded and greeted Drake politely. He returned the greeting with as much cordiality. Cassandra was one human Drake respected.

I ushered Drake into my office, removed the shard of magic mirror that sat on my desk, and took it out to Cassandra. "He wants to be private," I whispered to her when she gave me a look of amazement.

"Not fair!" the mirror wailed. "Drake's so pretty."

"Deal with it," I told the mirror, returned to the office, and shut the door.

Mick and I had taken shards of the original mirror, which hung broken in its frame in the saloon, to use as communication devices. More reliable than a satellite phone, though only to those it was bound to. Mick and I had awakened the magic mirror one night, and it had latched on to us. Mirrors were very, very powerful talismans, but I still debated whether us stumbling upon it had been good luck or bad.

I couldn't trust that the mirror wouldn't broadcast whatever Drake said to me to other magical people in the building. A handy thing if Drake put me in danger, but the mirror also might decide to let others eavesdrop just to be a pain in the ass.

Drake moved to the long window and closed the slats of the wooden shutter, blotting out the brightening moonlight. I turned on the lamp on my desk, illuminating my closed laptop and the photo of my dad, stiff and unsmiling, in its silver frame. Pete Begay hated having his picture taken. He'd only let me snap that one because he loved me.

"What's this all about?" I asked Drake.

Drake turned to the desk and set the bag on top of it. I was right—it was a bowling bag, one large enough for a single ball and accessories, zipped shut.

"I need you to keep this for me," he said.

"Your favorite ball?" Nervous laughter bubbled inside me. I couldn't imagine Drake donning bowling shoes and tearing up the lanes in Santa Fe.

"It is not a ball," Drake said tightly. "It is an item of great delicacy."

Better and better. Why couldn't a powerful dragon like Drake take care of something fragile? My suspicions rose. He would only come to me if he couldn't trust other dragons—or anyone else, for that matter—about this.

I couldn't take the suspense anymore. I undid the wide zipper and peered inside the bag.

Tucked into the foam recess meant to hold a heavy bowling ball was an oval object made of what looked like jade. Its color was pale, with only a hint of green. Bands of gold encircled the white jade piece, and tiny green jewels were embedded where the bands intersected. I hoped they were simply sparkling green stones, but I suspected that they were real emeralds.

"You're trusting me with a Fabergé egg?" I asked. "A really big one." The original Fabergé eggs were about the size of ostrich eggs. This was a foot in diameter and eighteen inches tall. "Is this from your hoard?" I had a worrying thought. "Or did you steal it from someone else's?"

Dragons could fight each other to the death over a small necklace, Mick had once told me. I didn't need to get between dragons battling over a trinket.

"It is not a Fabergé egg." Drake was losing patience with me. "It has nothing to do with a deceased Czarist Russian jeweler. This is a *dragon* egg. It needs to stay somewhere safe, and this is the most secure place on earth I could think of."

CHAPTER THREE

I stared at the jade and gold object, dumbfounded. "A *dragon* egg? You mean there's a baby dragon in there?" I hesitantly touched the oval. It felt like jade, smooth and cool, but under my hand, it wobbled the tiniest bit.

"Yes, as you say, there is a baby dragon in there." Drake's expression told me he'd had to talk himself long and hard into bringing it to me, and now he was starting to regret his choice.

"But ..." My mouth hung so far open it was drying out. I closed it. "It's encased in gold bands. How is the kid supposed to get out?"

"Female dragons always decorate their eggs. A hatchling dragon is plenty strong enough to break through gold wire."

"Wire studded with emeralds." I touched one, feeling its smooth facets. "What happens to those?"

Drake's mouth hardened. "It eats them, along with the rest of the shell. This is important, Janet. This egg needs to be guarded. Your hotel, with its wards against creatures of evil and other dragons, is the only stronghold around. I do not always agree with you, but you are powerful, and you can be … kindhearted."

It cost him much to admit that last adjective, I could see. I figured what Drake meant was that as badass magical as I could be, I wasn't looking to kill everyone around me and take over the world.

"Let's slow down a second." I leaned on my hands on the desk, unable to fully look away from the egg. Not only was it beautiful, but it fascinated me. "Why did you feel the need to leave the egg somewhere safe? Why can't a dragon look after it? Where is its mother?"

"The mother is dead," Drake said flatly. Pain flickered in his eyes. "I managed to get the egg away before anyone else discovered it."

This sounded less okay by the minute. "Dead?" I softened my voice, pity for the little dragon filling me. "Poor kid. Who was she? It wasn't Aine, was it?" I named the female member of the dragon council, who pretty much told all other dragons what to do. I hadn't heard that Aine had died, but I didn't keep up with dragon council business.

"No, not Aine." Drake's tone told me I was ignorant for even thinking such a thing. "Cesnialangus lived on a remote island, far out to sea. She preferred that. I don't know who killed her—I assume another dragon, but I don't know which one." This troubled him. "The egg was hidden, but I heard it calling."

"Okaay." I sensed nothing from the egg, and usually I was sensitive to auras. Drake's, for instance, fiery and worried, pressed around me. "So, you took it?"

"I had to search a long time before I found it. I unearthed it, yes, and took it away to be safe."

"And the dad?" I fixed Drake with my no-nonsense stare. "Was it you?"

"Possibly." Drake shook his head. "Possibly not. But that doesn't matter. What matters is that Bancroft never knows about this egg or gets his hands on it."

Possibly? Oh, Drake. I'd expected him to vehemently deny it, but instead he stunned me with a *possibly.*

Part of my brain started fervently wondering about Drake's relationship with the egg's mom. The other part fixed on the name he'd just thrown out.

"Bancroft?" I asked. "You mean Bancroft of the dragon council, who would love to see me dead, or better still, never having existed? The one who recruited Mick to kill me and then put Mick on trial when Mick decided he liked me, instead? *That* Bancroft?"

"Yes." Drake's quick reply told me he was happy we were on the same page. "He cannot find this egg."

"Why not? Would he kill it?" The sort of mean thing Bancroft would do.

"No. He'd raise him, groom him. Brainwash him."

I knew it was difficult for Drake to admit that Bancroft was so ruthless. Drake had been the dragon council's toady for a long time, believing they could do no wrong, until he'd decided they didn't live up to his exacting standards and quit. Couldn't blame him—the Mighty Three, as Colby called them, were arrogant, spiteful, and dangerous.

"You mean make him the heir apparent," I said. "In Bancroft's image."

"Exactly." Drake seemed relieved I understood. "Bancroft would imprison him and try to mold him, which is the cruelest fate for a dragon. The small ones are quite impressionable. They bond with whomever they see when they hatch. It can't be Bancroft."

"You don't have to convince me of that," I said. *"Hi, I'm Bancroft, your foster dad and complete bastard. Welcome to the dragon compound, where you'll be imprisoned for the rest of your life."* I shuddered. "I'm with you so far. Does Bancroft know about the egg, and is he going to come crashing in here to take it away from me?"

"Bancroft ... suspects ... that this egg exists."

I sat down heavily. "So, he's looking for it."

"Yes. But he has no idea yet that it was taken from Cesnialangus's hoard."

I'd long ago given up trying to figure out the multisyllabic dragon names. They rolled off Drake's tongue—and his name was really *Draconil* ... something—but most of the other dragons shortened them.

"Yet," I repeated. "When is he going to discover that it's gone?"

"I do not know. When he does, he will know I took it."

"Then you're in danger too," I said.

Drake regarded me calmly, as though a powerful and deadly dragon hunting him down was the least of his worries. "It does not matter. As long as he doesn't find the egg."

I drummed my fingers on the desk, my gaze pulled back to the soft sheen of jade. There had to be more behind this tale than Drake not wanting Bancroft to mold the new generation of dragons, but I knew Drake wouldn't tell me unless he thought I needed to know.

"So, you decided bring it to me," I stated.

Drake's eyes darkened. "I came because it will be safe

here. You have wards to warn you of approaching dragons and other evils. Very strong earth magic, and yes, even Beneath magic to stave off attack. Ms. Bryson, your manager, is a powerful earth witch. Your friend the sheriff also possesses strange magics that could help."

"You are not easing my mind," I said. "In fact, you're implying that more people than Bancroft might want this egg."

Drake gave me a reluctant nod. "Dragons are at their most vulnerable when they are young. Creatures who fear them will try to kill them when they are weakest."

"Great." I did some more finger drumming, but the egg's smooth surface kept capturing my attention. "What will you do if I refuse?"

Drake went so silent that I had to look up at him again. "You cannot refuse," he said quietly. "Please, do not."

He didn't have a contingency plan, he meant. It was here or nowhere.

"You're giving me no choice?"

Drake's frown told me I confused him. "Of course you have a choice. This is a dangerous favor. But you have proved that not only are you strong, you are trustworthy."

"What?" My eyes widened. "*Drake* is saying I'm trustworthy?"

"You are." He sounded puzzled. "You have already proved this several times. You have had opportunities to join forces with evil beings in order to do great harm, and to become such an evil being yourself. Yet, you have not."

"My grandmother raised me well," I said lightly. I waved away my tussles with Beneath goddesses, massively powerful mages, and the undead, not to mention dragons themselves. "She'd lecture me if I destroyed the world, and let me tell you, my grandmother can lecture." I shuddered, which was unfeigned. My entire childhood had been me running from the sharp call of *Janet!*

"Your modesty is bewildering and unnecessary." Dragons were never modest. Drake probably couldn't wrap his brain around the concept. "You are the best person to help me. Only for a short while—I will return for it when it is safer. Will you?"

I should have said no. Sent him off, put the entire conversation out of my mind. Returned to my peaceful life of running a hotel full of loud, obnoxious human tourists and magical people who just wanted to lie low.

Agreeing to look after a dragon egg was the height of foolishness—how the hell was I supposed to take care of it? And what did I do if it hatched before Drake came back?

Inside the bowling bag, the egg rocked again. There was a dragon in there, vulnerable, too small and egg-bound to look after itself. Its choice was to be captured by Bancroft or hatch and find itself bonded to Drake.

A bit of warmth touched me, though I couldn't tell if it was the little dragon reaching out to me, my conscience kicking at me, or else the heating coming on to cut the chill of the March night.

No matter what, I found myself resting my hand on top of the bag, meeting Drake's dark dragon eyes, and agreeing.

———

MOST PEOPLE, WHEN THEY LEFT A KID WITH A BABYSITTER, had a list of instructions for the child's care, numbers for who to call when there was a problem, and a sack full of accoutrements like food, toys, and a change of clothes.

Drake simply left the bag on the desk and walked out. When I trotted after him, full of questions, he ignored me. He strode out of the hotel, into the desert to become dragon, and headed home.

Once Drake was gone, I called Mick.

CHAPTER FOUR

Mick didn't answer. He'd gone to Many Farms to spend time with my family, most especially with my father and my grandmother. Dad had moved in with his new wife, Gina, in Farmington, but he made the drive to Many Farms a couple of times a week to check on Grandmother. Not that she didn't have all my aunts and cousins to look after her, but Dad was a worrier. Plus, he loved her.

Mick and I were marrying in June. Mick wanted to make sure that my dad truly accepted him, hence his many visits. Also, Mick didn't want to violate any procedure when we had the wedding, though I tried to assure him that simply going to the courthouse in Hopi County would be fine.

But no, Mick wanted ceremony. Dragons were into that. My grandmother approved—the two of them were working on having us wed in the traditional Diné manner and in our local church. I pretended I wasn't worried about how elaborate their plans would be.

The problem was, I needed to talk to Mick *now*. I knew

Drake fully expected me to tell Mick about the egg—he probably counted on Mick's protection as well.

Mick and Dad might be out in the middle of the desert bonding, leaving phones turned off or behind altogether. I didn't want to call Grandmother and ask where they were, because she'd know something was up and start grilling me.

I highly suspected that Grandmother, who could turn into a crow—or project her consciousness into a crow, I wasn't certain which—already knew about the events of the evening.

By the time I gave up calling Mick and left my office, the Horribles were at last taking themselves out the door to seek dinner. They waved and yelled their goodbyes to me and Cassandra, and we politely waved back. The oldest daughter, Yvonne, turned after the bulk of her family had poured out the door.

"Who was that guy who came in with you?" she shouted across the lobby. "He was soooo good-looking. Is he single? Or do you have your hooks into him?"

I smiled tightly. "He's a friend."

"Is he coming back tonight? You can't have him, you know. You have Mick." Yvonne smirked.

And you're married, I wanted to remind her. "Really, he's just a friend."

"Sure, Janet." Yvonne gave me a broad wink then hurried out to the impatient shouts of her family.

Cassandra sighed in relief once the door had closed. Through the front window, we watched the family cram themselves into two separate cars to head into Magellan and its one diner.

"I will be very glad when this week is over," Cassandra

said. She shivered. "Though I heard them suggest this would be a great place to spend the summer."

I regarded Cassandra in dismay. "Then we need to convince them it's *not*. It will be way too hot here. Right?"

"They haven't come to any conclusions." Cassandra smoothed a strand of hair that had dared unravel itself from her French braid. "With any luck, they'll be halfway home before the argument about whether to stay or go is resolved."

"Let's hope."

Cassandra was usually very professional and impersonal about guests, but the Horribles had gotten under her skin. The youngest daughter, Allie, claimed to be psychic and said she'd come to Magellan to connect with the vortexes.

When Cassandra pointed out that the vortexes were actually quite dangerous—not an exaggeration—Allie had scoffed and said she'd already absorbed vortex magic from the ancients. Allie declared that Cassandra was obviously non-magical and had no idea what she was talking about.

I doubted Allie could do any damage to herself, because her aura was devoid of magic. Cassandra, though, had become angry. Even pretending to touch the vortexes might bring a backlash, and then Cassandra would have to rescue the idiot woman and clean up the mess.

I couldn't disagree with the name Cassandra dubbed the family with, because so far, they were the most demanding and least pleased guests we'd ever had. Even though they spoke of everything with a laugh and told us the hotel was fabulous, they weren't happy with anything— the choice of rooms, the view, the beds, the bathrooms, right down to the hot water, which was plentiful, thanks to Fremont's plumbing and Maya, our talented electrician.

They also dared to complain about the food, sending back many of their meals. They were heading for the diner this evening because Elena, our chef, now refused to cook for them.

Once the lobby was deserted, I told Cassandra in a low voice about Drake's errand. She listened with widening eyes, her hands stilling on her keyboard.

"I'll strengthen the wards," Cassandra said, once I'd finished. "If *any* word of this leaks out … You have no idea how valuable a dragon egg is, do you?"

"You don't just mean because of its gold and emeralds, do you?" I asked then sighed in resignation. "I'll help with the wards. Though my biggest worry is, where am I going to keep him?"

My first thought had been my basement, which held an ancient pool of shamanistic magic that could deter any threat. Elena wielded that magic with the ease of a master.

However, Ansel also lived in the basement. Though he was a good guy at heart, and often spent nights with his girlfriend in Santa Fe, he was a Nightwalker. He sated his bloodlust with cow's blood Elena obtained from a butcher in Flagstaff, but if he woke up in a hungry Nightwalker rage one evening, and an egg with a dragon in it was within his reach …

Ansel fought his urges well, but I couldn't risk it.

My office wasn't the most secure room in the hotel, I thought as I headed back into it, but none of the others would offer any better protection against dragons. My private rooms would be best, but even those had multiple entrances. I relied on our wards to keep evil at bay, but a determined dragon could simply crash through the walls or roof.

I needed Mick's advice. He'd put the problem through his logical dragon brain and spit out an answer. I'd have to risk interrupting his quiet time with Dad to ask him.

I didn't want to use the eavesdropping magic mirror to contact him, though, so I called Gabrielle, my half-sister who shared my crazy-making Beneath magic.

Gabrielle now worked in a glitzy Las Vegas hotel—the *C*—protecting people from wickedness there. She was far more powerful than most supernatural beings that might invade that building. Many guests went to the C for a paranormal experience, and Gabrielle made certain they didn't bring in anything more dangerous than battery-operated votive candles.

However, she'd taken some time off to visit Many Farms this week, and she might know where I could find Mick.

The fact that Gabrielle was visiting Grandmother voluntarily said a lot about how much she'd matured, in her own way.

Gabrielle picked up right away. "I'm a little busy right now, but never too busy for *you*, big sis."

I heard whistles and yells in the background, and what sounded like a crowd alternately cheering or groaning.

"Where are you?" I asked in confusion.

"Your old high school." Her voice receded from the phone. "Oh, come on. That was a foul, ref. Are you blind?"

"Seriously, what are you doing?"

A shrill whistle sounded right in my ear, and I jerked the phone from my face. "Time out!" Gabrielle yelled. "Come on, gather in." She returned to me. "I'm coaching the girls' basketball team."

"You're coaching … What?"

Gabrielle had switched her attention away from me. "Okay, we're doing great out there. Watch out for number 5. She has a long reach, and she can slap the ball out from under you. If you're in possession when she's near, pass as soon as you can. She's a good interceptor, so keep it away from her. And Katie, great shot. All of you are playing some amazing ball."

"You answered the phone in the middle of a game?" I asked in disbelief.

"This is Janet." Gabrielle's voice became muffled. "She used to go to school here. Say hi, everyone."

"Hi, Janet!" a group of adrenaline-spiked girls chorused.

Another whistle signaled the end of the time out. "All right," Gabrielle sang. "Go out there and kick some ass."

"Yes, Coach!" The girls yelled with enthusiasm and pounded away.

"They needed someone," Gabrielle said before I could ask more questions. "The last coach had to leave unexpectedly—family thing. Your aunt Ida recommended that I fill in. I played when I was in high school, so I know a little bit about basketball. The rest I looked up on the internet."

I listened in a daze. "That was nice of you," I said when I could speak again. "You're doing this one game?"

"No, no. I'm hired on for the rest of the season and contracted again for next year."

"But you already have a job," I pointed out.

"I can commute. Especially when I have a dragon standing by to fly me back and forth. Colby's happy to help out."

Gabrielle sounded so excited, so *confident*, that I decided to shut up. She'd been a dangerous mess when I'd first met her, which was no wonder with all the shit she'd been through. If Aunt Ida, who was as much a stickler about good behavior as Grandmother, thought Gabrielle would be a competent coach, then maybe she was a competent coach. Gabrielle could be very persuasive when she wanted something, but I doubted even the most powerful magic would influence stern, no-nonsense Aunt Ida.

"You're only coaching them, right?" I took on a severe tone. "Not helping them win with a little spark of magic?"

Gabrielle laughed. "You'd think that, wouldn't you? But I don't have to use magic to help them win. They're already awesome. Now, what do you want?"

"Do you know where Mick is?" I asked quickly. "I can't reach him."

"He drove out with Pete to watch the moonrise. They go out to the mountain a lot, but they don't *do* anything. They just sit there and look at it."

That sounded like Dad. "Thank you. Good luck with the game."

"It's not luck, Janet," Gabrielle said seriously. "It's training and athletics. Oh, now *that* was a foul. Come *on*, ref!"

The phone went silent. I studied it for a time, letting the idea seep through my brain that my half-insane, Beneath-magic filled, wild little sister was coaching girls' basketball. Well.

Someone would have to explain to her that yelling at the refs might get her kicked out of the game, but otherwise she was busy amazing me.

I'd have to wait to talk to Mick. My dad and I had often driven on fine nights to the flat-topped mountain near our home to watch the moonrise. No phones, no radio, nothing but us, the world, and silence. We hadn't needed to talk.

That Dad was making this journey with Mick meant Dad truly liked him. Trusted him. Wanted to bring him into our family, as chaotic as it was.

I laid down the phone and peered into the open bowling bag on my desk, observing the smooth, pale egg. "I guess you're stuck with me, kid."

Did I imagine that the egg wobbled again? I put my hand on it, but it was still. Warm. As I rested my touch there, it began to vibrate, like a cat purring.

"Poor little one," I said. "Don't worry. I'll look after you."

How I would, I had no idea.

————

I ENDED MY DEBATE BY DECIDING THAT UNTIL MICK AND I came up with a better solution, I'd simply tote the egg around with me. I could best protect it by being next to it all the time. People would wonder at my fondness for the bowling bag, but let them be curious. Everyone thought I was weird anyway.

The hotel was fortunately quiet at the moment, now that the Horribles had gone out. A few of our guests were enjoying Elena's five-star meal in the saloon, but others had dispersed to the eateries in nearby towns. Magellan only had one diner, but Flat Mesa, north of here, had a couple of family places plus a few fast-food joints, and nearby Winslow had a fabulous restaurant at their restored railway hotel.

When I ducked into the saloon, the bowling bag's

sturdy strap draped over my shoulder, the mirror behind the bar came alert. I felt its attention home in on the bag.

"What'cha got there, Janet?"

I glanced quickly around the room because anyone magical could hear the mirror. All the guests were focused on Elena's cooking, however, and not paying attention. Four of the patrons dining together were human, and another table held a Wiccan couple.

I surreptitiously pointed my finger at the mirror. "I'll tell you later, but you keep it quiet. That's an order."

"Oh, girlfriend, you're no fun." The mirror went silent, however, because it did have to obey me. It found plenty of ways to get around that rule, but for now, it shut up.

Headlights flashed through the cracked windows, and Nash's black pickup stopped outside the front door.

Hand on the bag's strap, I moved back into the lobby. A few moments later, Nash stomped in, towing his grandfather, who was still handcuffed. Cassandra rose to watch them intently.

"He needs to stay here," was Nash's greeting to me as he unlocked the cuffs. "I'm too busy to look after him tonight."

Jones Senior sent his grandson a long-suffering stare as he rubbed his wrists in relief. "He means his jail is too shitty for me to sleep in, but he doesn't want me in his house."

"This isn't a detention center," I said to Nash. "I thought you arrested him for stealing a truck and dangerous driving."

"The owner of the pickup says he lent it to him," Nash snapped, displeased. "He'll have to answer to the reckless driving charges, but the defense attorney got him freed."

"Conflict of interest with the arresting officer," Grandad Jones said with a chuckle.

I'd already observed that the older Jones looked much like the younger. Under the soft illumination in the hotel instead of the glare of headlights, the resemblance was even stronger. Both men had square faces, athletic builds, and gray eyes. Grandad's white-gray hair was cut short, similar to Nash's military buzz.

The difference was that Grandad looked as though he enjoyed the hell out of life while Nash had chosen to close himself off from it. Nash had gone through a bucketload of shit when he'd been in a war, with the PTSD to show for it. While I felt sorry for Nash about that, people around Hopi County had told me he'd actually softened since his return from duty.

"There's another motel in town," I pointed out. Emilio Salas's brother owned The Magellan Inn, which filled up with tourists during the high season. "Closer to shops and food."

"It's not secure," Nash said.

"And my hotel is?" I asked in surprise. "Guests come and go as they please. Their key cards open the front door after hours."

"But you can make it so you know when he leaves."

"He means the wards," Cassandra said. "I'm sorry, Sheriff Jones, but those don't work on the non-magical, and Carl is non-magical."

Aha, Grandad's name was Carl. Not that Nash bothered with that information, but Cassandra made it her business to find out everything about everyone.

"You can make an exception," Nash stated.

This was true. We could spell the hotel so we were

alerted when a specific person went through the wards. How Nash knew that I wasn't certain, but Nash was full of surprises.

"You have your own house," I said to Nash. "In Flat Mesa. I've been there, remember? It's nice, and I hear you have several unused bedrooms."

Carl scoffed. "He doesn't want me there messing up his relationship with that pretty young woman. She is *stunning*, Nash. How did you convince her to put up with you?"

I wondered if Maya would be annoyed with Nash for bringing his grandfather home with him, or whether she and Carl would join forces to make Nash's life hell. The second scenario, I was thinking, was probably the real reason Nash had brought him to us.

Everyone wanted me to babysit their strays today.

"Do you mind a room on the ground floor?" Cassandra asked Carl in her professional tones. "We're fully booked upstairs, but this suite will give you more privacy."

The suite was new, opening from the narrow hall between the lobby and my office. It had its own patio and minibar and was our most expensive room. We didn't have many bookings for it yet.

Carl scowled at Cassandra, which made him look even more like his grandson. "Do you think I'm too old to walk upstairs? I still run marathons, you know."

"Five Ks," Nash corrected him. "But yes, he's fit enough for your third floor."

Where we could lock him in. A ground-floor room with a private patio meant Jones Senior could more easily get away.

"The suite will be more suitable," Cassandra said firmly. "Especially if we don't know how long you intend to stay."

"Until my grandchildren treat me with some respect," Carl spat. "Might be a long time."

"I don't want him coming and going without my knowledge," Nash said.

Cassandra gave Nash a sweet smile. She was one of the few in town not intimidated by the sheriff. "I am very good at keeping an eye on my guests. The suite is our most comfortable room and one we don't have need of right now."

Also, the Horribles had taken over upstairs. Cassandra was trying to spare Carl that pain.

"It's settled," I said. "I'll grab the key."

Nash was displeased, but if he wanted to foist his grandfather off on us, he'd have to do this our way.

Carl brightened. "Sounds nice to me. Tell Ada to pack my clothes and send them on." He shot Nash a grin and followed me to the back hall.

Cassandra handed me the key as I passed the reception desk, and I unlocked the door that led to the new, and quiet, guest quarters.

The "suite" was really a large bedroom with a sitting area, a fireplace—gas, fitted with a timer—a minibar with fridge, and a door to a patio. The patio was surrounded by a low stucco wall and gave a nice view of the desert to the east and north. The hotel's kitchen wall on the right screened the patio from the public area and fire pit out back.

Carl whistled appreciatively as he gazed around. "This is a hell of a lot nicer than that crap place in Flagstaff. I'll take it."

"Is that why you ran away?" I asked him. "The crap place?"

His cheeriness dimmed. "A number of reasons. Grand-children are supposed to be a comfort in your old age. Mine are trying to control the world because it pisses them off."

A good description of Nash. I hadn't met his cousin Ada—I wondered if she was the female version of him.

"You like bowling that much?" Carl demanded as he squinted at my bag.

"What? Oh." I flushed and held the bag more tightly against me. "No. It's just something I—"

"Some good lanes in Flag. I prefer the shooting range, myself. That is, when my pesky keepers let me off the leash."

I did *not* want to get into this family squabble, so I kept my tone neutral. "If Ada doesn't send you your things, make a list of what you need. I can have Flora run into town for you."

Carl opened the door to the patio and stepped out. He inhaled the dry, clean night air and let out a long breath. "*This* is more like it. You don't need to run errands for me, sweetie. I'm perfectly capable of shopping for myself, and I have my own money." He hesitated. "I might need a ride, though. Nash impounded my friend's truck."

"Someone really did lend it to you?"

"Larry was my partner in crime for my getaway. We spotted Ada coming, so I hightailed it. I was going to hide out at Dusty's, but I guess someone alerted the cops to look out for me." Carl shrugged. "I figured if I pissed off the bikers, they'd cause a diversion, and I could get away."

Some diversion. He'd brought half the state charging after him into my parking lot.

I sympathized with the guy, but I needed to set rules of my own. If I didn't, Nash would simply drag him back to whatever assisted living center he'd been in, or someplace with tighter security. "If you're going to stay here—"

"What's that?" Carl peered into the darkness, cupping his hands around his eyes to shut out the porch light.

I clutched the bag closer. "What's what?"

"There." He pointed. "I saw a light."

"That's not unusual. People hike at night on the rail-road bed."

Seconds later, I knew Carl hadn't spotted hikers with flashlights.

A bright white light flared out in the hills beyond, but it wasn't lightning from a natural storm. A sudden wash of heat burst over the desert, and the light blasted again, closer this time.

There was a pop and a bang, and the electricity in the hotel shut down, leaving us in dark silence.

CHAPTER FIVE

The bag under my arm jumped. I tried to soothe it, but the dragon inside wasn't stupid.

Something was coming, something bad, with a rush and a roar.

"Get back inside," I yelled at Carl.

"You have a shotgun?" he demanded.

"No, and it wouldn't help. Inside!"

Carl glared at the light that fanned across the sky like a weird white sunrise. Finally, he shrugged and trotted back in. I followed, locking the door behind us. It was a wood-framed glass door, pretty to look at, but no defense at all.

I herded Carl to the lobby. Nash and Cassandra had flashlights out, and Cassandra was at the window nearest the front door, whispering words to strengthen the magics already inside the walls.

I could never find a flashlight whenever the electricity went out—which it did regularly during monsoon season storms—and conjured a small ball of firelight. Mick had taught me this earth magic, but I'd had to practice for years to summon up a small light without destroying anything.

"What is it?" I asked Cassandra.

"I don't know," Cassandra answered. "I've never seen this before."

Didn't sound good. Nash strode past her and opened the door. He didn't exit but remained on the threshold, staring out.

I knew Nash had worried that the door wouldn't open at all. One day a while back, a demon mage had locked him into this hotel with me, Cassandra, Mick, Ansel, and more, and had messed with our powers. We'd nearly died before we'd finally won free. I didn't want to relive that any more than Nash did.

Different problem this time. We were free to go, but did we want to?

Spidery lightning flared to the west side of the hotel, then the east, then the south, surrounding us. Gravel popped where tendrils of light touched down. The flickering snakes wove together and started to close, like a net, over the hotel.

"Ideas?" I asked frantically.

Cassandra continued whispering. The wards *should* keep out whatever it was, I told myself. Anything magical had to get through the spells of a Stormwalker, a dragon, and a powerful Wiccan.

Dust in the parking lot burned in blue-hot fire where the mesh touched it then melted like glass. If whatever that was got inside, would it do the same to us?

Nash said nothing. He squared his shoulders and walked out the front door.

"What the hell is he doing?" Carl demanded.

He tried to rush out after Nash, but I caught him by one arm, yanking him back inside. The older man topped me by almost a foot and a half, but I was determined and held on tight.

"Let him," I said, cradling the bag closer to my body.

"Let him?" The belligerence deserted Carl's voice, and now I heard only fear and concern for his grandson. "He'll get himself killed."

I knew Nash planned to negate whatever this was with the void inside him that cancelled out all magic. I'd watched him suck enormous power into his body and tamp it into neutrality, then wipe a few beads of sweat from his forehead and ask for coffee. Logically, I knew there must be a limit to what he could endure, but so far, he hadn't reached it.

"Get your ass back in here," Carl commanded him. "This isn't something you can bully into submission."

"Oh, he'll try it," I said assuredly. "But give him a chance."

Nash took another step forward. The crackling white mesh of electricity touched the ground about six feet from the front door, enclosing the hotel in its dome. Nash took two more steps and reached a hand toward it.

"Stop, you idiot!" Carl jerked out of my grip and raced forward to tackle Nash at the very moment he pressed his fingers into the web.

I quickly set down the bag and leapt for Carl, grabbing him in the same instant he connected with Nash.

A massive shock went through me. My hair flared out, and my skin heated like I'd walked into a kiln. I heard a scream from my throat, then the sensations died as fast as they'd struck.

My first worry was that the lightning had gotten past me to connect with the egg. I swiftly retrieved the bag and opened it, wilting with relief when I saw the oval snuggly whole in its foam-rubber holder. It wiggled again, but it seemed to be well.

My second thought was for Carl. It couldn't have been good for him to have that much power pumping through him.

"Woo!" Carl let go of Nash and threw both fists in the air. "What a rush. Let's do it again!"

So, he was all right then.

I realized Nash's magic void had sucked in the worst of the jolt, saving Carl's life, mine, and the egg's. The mesh around the hotel, however, was still in place. Whatever this spell was, it was serious. Nash lowered his hand in frustration.

The wall of lightning might be an entity itself. Not long ago, I'd helped Gabrielle battle an earth elemental—maybe this was a fire one? Nothing I wanted to face, and especially not when I was protecting a dragon egg.

Did it want the baby dragon? Or was this Bancroft sending something after it?

"Back off!" I shouted at the web. "If you fry my hotel, I'll take you apart so fast you won't know what hit you."

The curtain of lightning quivered. I watched in incredulity as it blurred, wavered, and then dissipated like mist under a warming sun. The lights flickered once, then came back on all over the hotel.

I stared in bewilderment, but in the next moment, I

realized the lightning hadn't dispersed because of my threat.

A man stood in front of the hotel. He was Native American, though of what tribe, I couldn't say. His long hair that stirred in the wind was an exact mixture of gray and black, as though someone had painted every other strand of it white. He wasn't wearing anything, but for some reason that didn't seem weird. His strong body was male perfection, muscles brushed with gentle moonlight.

He held his hands, palm-outward, in front of his chest. He slowly brought them down and gazed calmly back at us as we gaped at him.

"Who the hell are you?" Nash demanded, always cutting to the heart of the matter.

The man contemplated Nash and Carl in silence then flicked his gaze to me. "You are safe now, Janet Begay," he said in the Diné language.

"Thank you," I answered in the same language. It was courteous to show gratitude to someone who'd just saved your ass. "What was it?"

The man lifted his shoulders in a smooth shrug. "There are many gods and lesser gods permeating the world. This could have been any of them."

A flowery way of saying, *I have no idea.*

"You know my name." I left the statement at that. Nash's demand hadn't produced the man's identity, and I figured asking directly wouldn't do any better.

A smile flickered over his face. "I do. Please greet your grandmother for me."

My brows shot up. "Grandmother …"

The man turned and walked north, toward the empty

desert. His hair floated in the darkness, and that darkness quickly obscured him. Between one step and the next, he was gone, but I swore I heard a flutter of wings in the night.

———

AFTER ZIPPING UP THE BOWLING BAG AGAIN, I SETTLED THE strap over my shoulder and marched into the saloon. The humans were huddled in the middle of the floor, wondering if it was safe to return to their meals. The Wiccan couple had remained seated, staring out the windows in worry.

"Is everyone all right?" I asked.

"None of us is hurt," the Wiccan man answered. He had a square-cut beard and close-cropped hair, with the triple moon symbol of the Goddess tattooed on the insides of his arms. "We didn't have time to help. I'm so sorry."

He was genuinely apologetic, feeling bad he hadn't jumped up and smacked whatever it was back to wherever it had come from. It would have killed him instantly, if what I'd felt had been anything to go by, but it was nice of him to offer.

His partner, a middle-aged woman with a pleasant face and graying red hair, nodded in agreement.

"That's all right," I told them. "It would have happily destroyed you along with the rest of us. This is supposed to be a place of refuge, and *I'm* sorry that it wasn't."

"We will waive the room fee for tonight," Cassandra said to everyone present.

I hid a wince—we needed the money—but better that than the guests fleeing to write horrible reviews about threats from lightning entities. *One star. Could have died. Good food, though.*

The human couples relaxed and drifted back to their seats, appeased by Cassandra's offer. After all, bad storms sometimes happened in the desert.

The Wiccan man nodded in gratitude, but I saw he was ashamed that he and his wife had sat still in panic. I could have told him this was a normal state of things in the Crossroads Hotel.

Carl moved to the bar and hopped up on a stool, patting the countertop. "Give me a whiskey, one of your best," he told my bartender, who'd straightened after hiding himself behind the bar. "My grandson will pay for it."

Carlos glanced at me, and I nodded. I knew Nash would honor the bill and refuse to let me put it on the house.

Nash himself had remained out front to look for traces of whatever had attacked us. I watched him walking back and forth in the parking lot, his flashlight trained on the ground. I doubted he'd find anything. The entity, or whatever it was, had gone. I felt its absence in the night.

Across the lot, Barry's bar was surrounded by motorcycles, some of whose riders had chased Carl here hours earlier. Music thumped inside, and voices poured out the open doorway. No one there seemed to have noticed the lightning.

The mirror above the bar was silent. I'd ask it about the attack, but later, where we wouldn't be overheard.

The bartender, shaken but used to the weirdness here, brought out a bottle of Glenlivet and poured Carl two fingers.

Carl grinned and downed the whiskey in one shot. "Keep 'em coming, son."

I left Carl to enjoy himself and slid into the kitchen to see how Elena had weathered the blackout.

Cassandra was already there, trying to answer questions Elena was barking at her.

"You need to warn me when we're about to be attacked," Elena insisted. "I could have ruined the rest of the dinner." Steam rose from pots on the stove, and everything was as neat and organized as ever. "Who was the man outside? Cassandra says he was Navajo."

"He *spoke* Navajo," I answered. "I didn't get a chance to find out who he was. He disappeared."

"Hmph. You should have brought him to me."

Cassandra broke in. "Nothing for you to worry about, Ms. Williams. We can take care of this." No one called Elena *Ms. Williams* but Cassandra.

"No, you cannot," Elena stated. "You are good with European-style witch magic, but this is my area. Ruby would be even better. Let me call her."

"No!" The last thing I needed was my grandmother stomping in here to tell me what I'd done wrong tonight. I was sure she'd find a way to blame me. "I mean, we shouldn't disturb her. My dad's home, and she's probably busy."

Elena's look told me I didn't fool her.

As I contemplated what to do, I brushed my thumb over Mick's turquoise and onyx ring. The notes of his true name chimed softly in my head before I could stop them.

No one had noticed, but the egg at my side gave a little jump.

Not that Cassandra or Elena—or the little dragon—should be able to hear or sense Mick's name. It was entwined in my psyche, not "heard" at all. However, I didn't need whatever had attacked us tonight dragging it out of my brain.

Magic of any kind was so dangerous.

"Janet."

I jerked my fingers from the ring and snapped my gaze to Elena, who was glaring at me once more.

"Yes?" I asked.

"You haven't eaten anything tonight—how are you supposed to keep up your strength? Go out to the saloon and have a big helping of carnitas."

At her words, I realized how hungry I was. Probably her intent. Elena had plenty of magic herself.

The carnitas, which Elena had slow cooked all day, were the best in the Southwest. I returned to the saloon and the buffet table, scooped a helping from the warming tray onto a plate with a tortilla. Then I perched on a chair, the bowling bag at my feet, as I enjoyed the savory pork.

Carl was still at the bar, regaling the bartender with tales of his youth. The mirror above them remained quiet, which bothered me. It was usually full of opinions and dire predictions.

Nash was still outside when I decided to walk off the carnitas and think, bag at my side. He'd ceased flashing his light around and stood gazing at the moonlit horizon, hands on hips.

"Any trace of the guy who saved us?" I asked him.

"No." Nash's gray eyes glinted as he turned to me. "I mean no trace at all. No footprints, nothing."

I'd heard wings as the man had vanished. I'd wondered briefly if the tall man had been a kachina—a Hopi god—but rejected the idea. A while back, kachinas had followed me around, making sure I didn't turn into the demon goddess who'd, in a roundabout way, given birth to me. I thought I'd proved myself to them, but they still watched me.

But while those gods had plenty of feathers, they were different from the man who'd dispersed the lightning. Kachinas were more ethereal, more benevolent, and yet more frightening at the same time. This man had gazed at me as though I should know him, and his hint of a smile when he'd mentioned Grandmother had been very human.

I had a pretty good idea of who he was, but I needed to check a few things before I drew my conclusions.

"Nothing to say what that lightning was?" I continued.

"Nope."

Man of few words, Nash. "What did you feel when you touched it? I got the worst shock of my life."

Nash shrugged. "Nothing. A little spark, that was all. Is my grandfather all right?"

"He seems to be." I set the bowling bag at my feet and glanced through the wide windows to where Carl rattled on to an appreciative Carlos.

Nash sighed heavily, his usual curtness deserting him. "We don't know what to do with him, Janet. He doesn't need constant care, but he can't live by himself anymore. He fell a few months ago and cut his head halfway open. He lay on the kitchen floor of his apartment for two days before my cousin Ada happened to check on him. She has a demanding job and tiny apartment, and no way to take care of him. Any decent place we can find is fucking expensive. Same with hiring someone to stay with him." He let out an exasperated growl.

"Where did you end up sending him?"

Nash couldn't hide his unhappiness. "To an assisted

care facility in Flag that his insurance would pay for. It's a dump."

"I think I know the place you mean." I'd been in college when I'd lived in Flagstaff, too young and worried about my own problems to notice those at the other end of their lives. I remembered the featureless building near the medical center where people pushed the elderly about in wheelchairs.

I couldn't stop my shudder. Carlos did not belong there.

"We didn't want to use that facility, but after his fall, the doctors told us he needed to be watched twenty-four seven. It was the only choice. Now he's screwed even that up—they won't let him back there, I'm sure."

"Him living here with you is out?" I asked.

Nash made an exasperated noise. "I guess he'll have to. But I'm not home all day, and we're back to paying a home health care service exorbitant fees to look after him. Maya has a heart of gold, but she can't give up her job to stay home with him."

I liked that Nash wasn't the kind of guy who believed his girlfriend or wife should relinquish her career for him and his family. Not that Maya would give him the choice. She was a talented electrician, always in demand.

"Well, he can stay here for now," I said, wanting to help. "There's always someone around."

"Again, expensive," Nash said, though his frown softened somewhat. "I can't expect you to give him your best suite, gratis."

I shrugged. "We'll come to some arrangement. It will be cheaper than a nursing home, and a hell of a lot more pleasant."

Nash looked straight at me, no barriers between him

and his profound love for his grandfather. "Thank you, Janet."

I assumed a modest stance, pretending the simple words didn't touch me. "No problem."

I shut up before I could say anything more sentimental. Nash didn't do mushy stuff. Then again, he'd just told me that Maya had a heart of gold, which was over-the-top emotion for Nash. She'd had a quieting effect on him, believe it or not.

Nash studied the sky again. "I have to get back to Flat Mesa." His reluctance was obvious.

"Carl will be safe here. I promise."

Nash returned to his usual skepticism. "Bullshit. This place is dangerous. But my best option at the moment."

I'd be offended by Nash's lack of confidence if I didn't agree with him. Even with all our wards and protections, this hotel had been bashed, burned, cursed, and invaded by degenerative magic.

"We'll keep an eye on him, no matter what," I said. "Be careful driving back. There are clouds coming in. It's going to be a dark night."

As though they'd been waiting for the weird lightning to vanish, clouds now drifted down from the mountains to obscure the moon and stars.

"I'm not afraid of the dark," Nash assured me.

It was true that Nash wasn't afraid of anything but his own dreams. "It's not the darkness that's the problem. Night can be quiet and restful. It's what's *in* the dark we have to watch out for."

Nash huffed. "No. They have to watch out for *me*."

With that he strode away to his truck, got in, started it up, and glided through the lot, pale dust in his wake. His taillights flashed, and he turned onto the paved road, going the hell home—or possibly back to the sheriff's department. Nash was one for working late.

No sooner had he driven off than I sensed a fiery aura that smelled of cinders and wood smoke. Before I could move, a pair of very strong arms slid around me from behind and held me fast.

CHAPTER SIX

Instead of jumping in shock followed by trying not to kill whoever it was, I leaned back against my assailant and relaxed.

"Why aren't you in Many Farms?" My question was softened by my gladness.

"Gabrielle said you were trying to reach me." Mick's deep voice rumbled through my body, loosening all my tension. "I called, but you didn't answer. I figured I'd come and see what was up."

He'd have covered the hundred or so miles as the crow flew by taking them as a dragon. He'd had time to land, shift, and put on clothes while I was out here talking to Nash.

I melted into Mick, this dragon-man I'd astonishingly agreed to marry. So happy was I to see him that I nearly forgot what I'd been trying to contact him about.

The bag at my feet wobbled, forcibly reminding me.

Mick released me slowly, his attention riveted to the bag.

The dragon tattoos on his arms began to writhe, their black eyes glittering.

"Janet, what are you doing with a dragon egg?"

Mick's voice held a mixture of hard concern laced with rabid curiosity. The world was a fascinating place to Mick, whether he found danger or loveliness.

"Drake gave it to me."

Mick stepped to the other side of the bowling bag and faced me. "Drake," he repeated quietly. "Why?"

"Because I was the most trustworthy person he could think of." I shrugged. "Or the most gullible. I haven't decided yet."

Mick bent down and carefully unfastened the zipper. He regarded the decorated oval, snug in its bed, for some time. The egg went very still under his scrutiny, no more wriggling.

"Cesnia's?" Mick asked.

Drake had used her long, Latin-sounding name—this was the short version, I guessed. "That's what Drake told me."

"Hmm."

There could be a world of meaning in Mick's *Hmms*.

"I hadn't heard of her before. Drake said she lived on a remote island?"

"She does." Sadness filled Mick's eyes. They changed from the deep blue I loved to the blackness of his dragon's. "But if this egg is here, it means she's dead."

I gentled my tone. "Drake said that too."

Mick gazed up at the sky, tears glittering in the corners of his eyes. "She was one of the good ones. Strong but patient, wise but without the total arrogance most dragons have. She tempered her ego, anyway. You would have liked her."

"Why don't know I know anything about her?" If she was so wonderful, why hadn't Mick spoken of her? Or Colby, who was more gossipy?

"Cesnia valued her privacy. She stayed on her island because she got fed up with the dragon council, dragon lords, and all their shit." Mick gave the dark sky one last glare and returned his focus to me. "I hadn't seen her in decades. Maybe a century."

"Drake suspects another dragon killed her."

Mick took on a fearsome scowl. "If that's the case, her killer is a dead dragon flying. Especially since she left offspring."

"How did you know the egg was Cesnia's?" I asked in curiosity.

Mick gestured into the bag. "The decoration on the shell. Each dragon mother uses a different design, different stones, different metals. I think the custom comes from the time when there were many more dragons and nests were closer together. Kept eggs from getting mixed up and also prevented others from stealing them. Everyone would know whose egg was whose."

I pictured a land of volcanoes and vast deserts in between, with dragon nests on top of mountains, packed with glittering gold and gem-studded eggs. Dragons of all colors would fill the sky, dancing on giant wings.

There were far fewer dragons now, according to Mick, and still fewer young ones.

I had a startling thought. "Mick," I said in a small voice. "If we decide to have a kid…will it start as an egg?" I really, really didn't want to think about how big that egg would be.

"What?" Mick's puzzlement was genuine. He stared at me for a long moment, then his eyes became azure once more, and a grin split his face. "Are you asking me if you'll lay an egg?"

I went hot with embarrassment. "Hey, I have no idea how a dragon and a human—or even a half-goddess mess like me—reproduce."

Mick roared with laughter. He pressed his hands across his belly and shook with it. The egg vibrated again, and I sensed amusement instead of fear.

"You can quit laughing at me now, please."

Mick drew a shuddering breath and wiped his eyes. "You are the most amazing woman, my mate."

"Hey, I can't help it if I know next to nothing about dragons, Mr. Cryptic." I was very glad he hadn't confirmed I'd be passing a bowling ball—not that human babies were much smaller—but I was irritated by my ignorance.

Mick shook his head. "Actually, I don't know any dragons who've had offspring with humans."

"No?" My trepidation returned. "Not reassuring me, Mick."

"I meant they exist, but I'm not acquainted with them. They have kids the human way, I'm pretty sure."

"You're *pretty* sure? Are you saying I should bone up on my jewelry-making skills?"

Mick cupped my shoulders with strong hands. "I'm saying it's not something to worry about. We'll have time for all that later. At present, I want to know who killed Cesnia, and why Drake didn't take the egg to its father. Male dragons are sucky parents, but they defend their own offspring."

I remembered Drake's offhand *possibly, possibly not* when

I asked if he was the dad. "It might be Drake's. If so, then he is taking care of it the best he can by having us watch it."

"*Might* be Drake's?" Mick said in surprise.

"He wasn't certain."

"Shit. Cesnia and Drake?" Mick's gaze went remote. "I guess I can see that. They both like solitude. Though since Drake is still alive, it could mean he's not the father."

Mick had once told me that female dragons sometimes turned around and killed their lovers once they were finished with them.

"Maybe she really liked him," I offered.

"Could be." Mick pondered the question. "Cesnia was reasonable, and as I say, not selfish and arrogant. I'll have to investigate further. Meanwhile, we need to keep the egg safe."

"Not easy with the other crap happening." I quickly filled him in on the lightning mesh attack, the man who dispersed it, and our unexpected guest, Carl Jones.

"Interesting," Mick said when I finished. "I can guess where Nash inherited his stubbornness."

"Carl seems more ready to let his guard down than Nash is. Maybe too much so."

"When some humans approach the end of their life, they become reckless." Mick shrugged. "What have they got to lose?"

"Or, he enjoys terrifying Nash," I suggested.

"Could be." Mick slid his arms around me, resting his hands on my hips. "We'll have to guard against more of these weird attacks. Shall we strengthen the wards?"

I knew he didn't mean following Cassandra around chanting as she waved a burning sage stick. Mick had taught me the power that could be found in tantric rites, though we did them privately and didn't join a group.

My entire being tingled in anticipation. Mick knew how to give me an explosion of pleasure that scoured me clean. I'd love to surrender to that right now, blotting out the troubles of the world in mindless joy.

I pressed a kiss to his hard chest through his shirt. "Let me make sure the hotel is secure first. I don't want to be interrupted."

Mick released me to take my hand. "I'll check it out with you."

Carl was still in the saloon when we entered it. He raised his beer to me and went on with a conversation he'd begun with the Wiccan couple. The other guests were talking calmly together, no one worried now that the magic lightning was gone.

Cassandra had returned to the reception desk, taking this quiet time to work on her budgets, which she enjoyed. She was excellent at accounting, and I always let her get on with it.

A motorcycle pulled up in front of the hotel as Mick and I crossed the lobby, and a tall woman in jeans and leather jacket dismounted. She was a wolf-Changer with black hair smoothed into a tight braid, very gray eyes, and a perpetual scowl. Pamela was Cassandra's mate, and never failed to show up if Cassandra didn't leave on the dot of seven in the evening.

Pamela nodded to Mick as she entered the hotel, ignored me, and moved to lean against the reception counter. "Dinner too much trouble for you?" she demanded of Cassandra.

"I just want to finish these projections," Cassandra

answered without concern. "The hotel is doing well—lots of reservations now that the weather's nice."

"It can't project without you?"

Cassandra raised her head and sent Pamela a smile that would melt the stoniest heart. "Not really. I'm almost done, promise."

Pamela softened a little, though only someone who knew her well could tell. She was prickly with anyone she perceived as a threat to Cassandra, which meant most people.

"The weather sucks," Pamela announced. "Lightning everywhere. Are you messing with the storms, Janet?"

"It wasn't a storm," I said. "Magical attack. Don't worry, we got rid of it." I decided not to mention we'd only done so with the help of a stranger. That would raise too many questions I couldn't answer.

"No, you didn't." Pamela swept her leather-jacket clad arm toward the back of the hotel. "The lightning's all over the place out there, especially toward the canyons. I'm hoping I can persuade Cassandra home before we all get struck."

Cassandra looked up in alarm. Mick and I exchanged a startled glance before we headed at a run, bowling bag and all, to the door and out into the night.

CHAPTER SEVEN

The air behind the hotel was cold, but it crackled with charge. Mick and I ran for the railroad bed and scrambled to the top.

For a moment, we stared into blackness that seemed serene. All was quiet except for the wind stirring dried grasses at our feet.

Then I saw it, a flicker of light, like a lightning strike that slammed from the base of low clouds to the ground.

The sky lit up with white for an instant before it flared out, darkness swallowing the land once again. A second flicker shone to the right, then one to the left.

I felt no bite of a storm, no stirring of my storm magic answering its call. The flickers continued far into the darkness, silent and eerie.

"Trying to open the vortexes?" Mick voiced the fear that had sent us both racing out here.

"Would whoever it is be that stupid?"

"Someone trying to grab themselves a vulnerable dragon?" Mick asked. "They'd do anything for that."

Vortexes were swirls of magic that New-Age tourists believed held the secrets of world peace, or something like that. In reality, vortexes were gates to hell worlds beneath this one. Some of those spaces were empty and banal, but most were chaotic and full of pissed-off demons and gods.

One of the vortexes out here, which Mick and I had scaled a while ago, was the entrance to the realm where my mother dwelled. She was a goddess who'd been denied entry into this world by dragons and other gods who didn't really want her up here causing as much destruction as she could.

She'd found a way to partly interact with the human sphere by possessing women who were minding their own business but had strayed too close to her territory. Using these unfortunate women as her vessels, she'd managed to bring two daughters into the world—me and Gabrielle. Our birth mothers hadn't survived the process.

I'd been lucky enough to have a kind father who'd insisted on keeping me and raising me himself. Gabrielle had not been as blessed. That she could now live in my grandmother's house without killing everyone in it, not to mention coach a school basketball team, proved how far she'd come.

As Mick and I watched, the lightning dipped and vanished, then flickered and flared before disappearing again.

Mick rumbled in his throat, and fire streaked his smoky aura. "I'm going to check it out."

I knew nothing I said would stop him, so I made a *go for it* gesture. "Be careful. We don't know what this is, and my storm powers can't do shit right now."

Mick's eyes were blacker than the darkness, his dragon

coming out to play. I sensed his eagerness, which had nothing to do with anger or fear. He liked a challenge.

"I'll find out everything I need to know." Mick stripped off his shirt and handed it to me. I moved the bowling bag on its strap to my side to accept it, holding the warm cloth to my chest.

I wondered if Mick meant he'd learn all about whoever was causing the lightning while his dragon digested the culprit. Dragons tended to chomp first and contemplate things later.

Mick's jeans came off, crumpling at his feet before he kicked them away. He hadn't bothered with underwear, not that I'd let that distract me or anything. Mick had told me he liked to be ready to shift.

He jogged off into the darkness, the prickly grasses and rocks not bothering him at all. In a few moments, a shroud of blackness surrounded him, and from it burst an ebony dragon, its sides streaked with fiery red.

Mick spread his wings, his form silhouetted against the stars, before he whooshed out over the desert and was gone.

I released a sigh. Mick was a beautiful dragon and a beautiful man, and I still wasn't used to the fact that I was going to marry him.

You'll enjoy it, a new voice rumbled beside me.

I yelped, my heart banging as adrenaline spiked. I hated that he could sneak up on me so easily.

Once my breath slid back into my lungs, I turned to the large coyote sitting on its haunches next to me. Wind ruffled his fur, which was touched with a silvery glow.

The mate thing, or marriage, or whatever you want to call it, isn't so bad, he continued.

"You've made up with your wife, then?" I asked when I could find my voice.

Coyote's wife, Bear, was a solemn goddess with terrifying powers. I liked her, though I admitted her relationship with Coyote was too weird for me to understand.

We have our ups and downs. Coyote's tongue lolled from his mouth as he began to pant. *Things are in a good place right now.*

"I'm glad to hear it. What's your take on this?" I gestured to the lights on the horizon, the dragon, tiny now, circling them.

Coyote stared out into the desert, the flashes reflected in his golden eyes. *If you want the truth, I'd call it the tip of the iceberg.*

I regarded him in dismay. "No, no, no. Do *not* tell me there's another big, bad evil coming. I'm tired of big, bad evil. I just want to get through my wedding—which will be stressful enough—and move on with my life."

Coyote's tone held amusement. *You are a child of a goddess who possesses wicked-amazing magic. Your life will always be battling evil. Your massive power attracts those who want it for themselves.*

"Yay?" I said faintly. "This is why I try to surround myself with strong friends, who seem to vanish when I need them most." I glared at him.

We have our own lives. I heard the shrug in his answer. *What you're dealing with is someone who can kill a she-dragon. Only an immensely powerful being could do that. Her offspring was brought to you for safekeeping.* Coyote switched his gaze to the bag at my side. *I wonder why it needs so much protecting?*

The egg moved, though I didn't sense fear from the little dragon inside. Curiosity, yes, and some excitement. It was a dragon, all right.

"Are you talking about another dragon slayer?" Bile rose

in my stomach. "I didn't like the last one." He'd caused serious damage we were still recovering from.

Dragon slayers are out there, yes. Not as many as in the past, but there are still plenty who'd love a stuffed dragon head mounted on their wall. Why, I have no idea. Seems like a weird thing to decorate your living room with. But more beings than slayers want dragons. Dragon power is legendary. What couldn't someone do with a young one?

I rested a protective hand on top of the bag. "Drake said he worried about what Bancroft wants the kid for. To take as his heir apparent, Drake thinks. Train the little dragon to be a dickhead like himself."

Or he'd simply destroy the egg, Coyote said. *A young dragon will be a threat to Bancroft, and he knows it.*

"Because Junior might want to take over the dragon council when he grows up? An improvement, I'd think."

The dragon council had nearly killed Mick and me—multiple times. They weren't the most moral or ethical beings ever. Dragons did what they wanted, figuring no one would stop them. They were mostly correct. Only other dragons could thwart them.

Exactly, Coyote said, as though pleased I was keeping up. *The young overthrow the old, which is how the world works. If you get rid of all the young dragons, or the eggs, then you hold on to your power forever. Dragons live a long time, and they don't like to retire.*

I dragged in a breath of clear, dry air. "You're saying all the dragons are going to come for this egg?"

I don't know. Possibly.

And Drake had decided it would be safest with *me?* "Why does Drake want the egg?" I wondered suddenly. "To use as a bargaining chip? To threaten the other dragons?

Gods, I so don't need to get in the middle of dragon politics."

If Drake is its daddy, maybe he simply doesn't want the others crushing it, Coyote suggested.

Across the desert, Mick was diving at the light, roaring in a way I knew meant he was enjoying himself. The lightning strikes moved farther away, with Mick in pursuit.

"Drake might or might not be its dad," I said. "I can't picture him becoming suddenly warmhearted and loving, even if he is the father. Wouldn't he still try to use the kid to benefit himself?"

We'll have to wait and find out.

Coyote's calm statements were becoming exasperating. "Why don't *you* protect him?" I held the bag out from my side. "You're a god. No one will get past you."

Coyote started, then his panting mouth opened into a grin. *You'd give* me *the bargaining chip, would you? So I could gain control over all dragons everywhere?*

"What? Why would you want to?"

Coyote's eyes narrowed. The intensity of his stare was marred by the lolling tongue, but this expression was somber for Coyote.

Would you *want to, Stormwalker?*

"Have control over dragons?" I asked in perplexity. "What for? They drive me crazy, including the one I'm in love with. I was much happier not knowing they existed."

There is your answer. Coyote swiped his mouth, sending spittle flying.

"Ew." I wiped moisture from my cheek. "You mean the answer to why Drake chose me? Wonderful."

He knew he could trust you to take care of the egg for its own sake. I'd be flattered, if I were you.

"Flattered that I'm such a sap?" I was annoyed with Drake for assuming I'd be willing to defend this egg with my life, and annoyed that he was right.

I supposed I could simply set the bowling bag down and leave it out here in the cooling night, dusting my hands off as I walked away. A wild animal would probably find the egg, tear it open, and eat the little dragon inside. Or the entity Mick was chasing would grab it to use for their unknown purpose. Other dragons might sense the kid was alone and helpless, and waste no time destroying it.

The egg wiggled, as though sensing my worrying thoughts, and I cradled it against my side.

"Drake's right," I said in resignation. "I am a sap."

Aw. I wouldn't like you any other way.

"You don't happen to know how I can defend it?" I demanded in irritation. "Me against a dragon horde? Who want me dead anyway?"

How about you against a dragon hoard? Much easier, right? You'd just take the most portable pieces and go.

"Very funny."

You mean, very punny.

I did want to laugh—Coyote was such a goof sometimes—but I knew he was trying to tease me out of my frustration.

"So, are you going to help me, or not?" I asked.

I never said I wouldn't help. I don't want a dragon training up a young one to take over, under his control. That's asking for trouble. I don't want them killing it either. That's just mean.

"I agree on both points. Thank you."

What bothers me most is that someone took out Cesnia. She was a formidable dragon. Not someone you wanted to tangle with.

I stopped feeling sorry for myself to focus on what

Coyote was trying to tell me. "You mean whoever killed Cesnia is even more formidable than she was? And who we need to look out for?"

Something like that.

"Who did kill her?" I watched Mick skim over the ground, far to the east now, the lightning flickers so tiny they were like fireflies on the distant horizon. "Another dragon? A mage? An entity we don't know about?"

Silence filled the space beside me. I knew even before I turned that Coyote had gone.

Coyote loved to disappear right when the hard questions were being asked. Because he thought I should figure them out on my own? Or because he didn't have the answers?

I vented my spleen at Coyote with a few choice words in the Diné language, English, Spanish ones Maya had taught me, and a couple in dragon.

The egg inside the bag vibrated, bumping against its foam support. I would swear the kid was laughing.

———

MICK RETURNED IN A SOMBER MOOD.

"I chased off whatever it was." Mick stood, hands on hips, his bare body radiating heat. "They weren't expecting me, but I couldn't do much against them. Nothing to get a fix on." By his tone, that bothered him.

"Will they be back?" I didn't like it when Mick was worried.

Mick shrugged. "Probably. They must be after the egg. Will be interesting to see what they choose to do."

Interesting for a dragon was scary and stressful to the rest of us.

Mick reached for his jeans and slid them on. He didn't need to for my sake, and he never felt the cold. But he'd be polite and not shock the people in my hotel.

I handed him back his shirt. Mick took it without donning it and laced his fingers through mine. "We don't need to worry about whoever it was anymore tonight. I gave them something to think about, at least." His voice quieted. "I missed you, Janet."

I'd missed him. Waking up in bed alone was not what I liked.

Mick pulled me close, his strength stirring all kinds of need. The kiss he touched to my lips held his fire plus a longing for me that went beyond anything I understood. That would alarm me if I didn't feel the same profound hunger for him.

Fire, earth, and air wound between us and bound us together.

The bag bumped into my side, the egg jiggling with glee. I broke the kiss.

"We have the kid." I wrapped my arm around the bag, as though reassuring the egg I wasn't about to abandon it.

Mick grinned, his good humor restored somewhat. "It'll be practice for the future."

He took my hand once more and led me back toward the Crossroads at a swift pace.

As I jogged beside him, I realized that before tonight the two of us had never talked about having children of our own. We'd always been so busy fending off enemies that we hadn't had time to speak of anything beyond the wedding.

Tonight was the first we'd even mentioned it.

I'd thought fighting off packs of demons, earth entities, super-mages, and dragon slayers had been scary. I was learning that everyday life might be the most frightening thing of all.

———

We decided to leave the dragon egg in the bathroom, closing the connecting door to my bedroom but not locking it. As I set the bag on a pad of towels, I glanced up at the mirror hanging over the sink.

"Do *not* let anyone but me and Mick in here," I admonished it. "If someone even comes close to the window, you tell us. All right?"

I'd pulled the blinds over the small, locked window that looked across the empty land beyond the hotel, but I didn't trust sneaky entities not to find a way through the cracks.

"Which means I can't watch *you*," the mirror said with its usual pout. "You're no fun, hon."

I pointed to the bag. "Very important. More than your own life. Got it?"

The mirror heaved a sigh. "All right, all right. Drakey had better appreciate my sacrifice."

I hadn't actually told the mirror that Drake had left the bag or what was in it. But the mirror, while annoying, was sharp, and had likely already figured out what was going on. Fortunately, it had said nothing so far, but I needed to make sure it kept quiet.

"Tell *no one*." I pointed my finger at the mirror, something I'd been taught was very rude, but I was taking no chances. "Don't even mention it around anyone but me and Mick."

"Hey, sweetie, I can keep a secret." The mirror sounded offended. "Just watch me."

"I will." I regarded the mirror sternly, though I saw only myself, my hair windblown, my cheeks flushed. "Good night."

"Sleep tight, angel-kins. Don't worry about us, shut away by ourselves in a *bathroom*. No, we'll be fine. We'll be just—"

I fled and shut the door.

Mick was already in bed, his large form dominating it, one light sheet covering his unclothed body. He smiled and reached a lazy arm toward me.

I wasted no time getting myself across the room and into the warm nest he'd made. I heard the mirror start crooning a soft lullaby as I snapped off the light.

———

I WAS IN MUCH BETTER SPIRITS IN THE MORNING. WHEN I entered the bathroom, the bag with the egg lay undisturbed on its pile of towels. The mirror greeted me wearily, then started to snore.

It didn't need to sleep—this was retaliation for making it babysit.

I moved the bag into the bedroom under Mick's watchful eye as I showered and dressed, then I carried the egg out with me to start my day.

Mick remained in bed, saying he was going to catch up on some rest. Life at Many Farms started very early, so I could understand why he welcomed some sleep-in time. Also, he'd been very energetic the night before.

The Horribles were already up, earlier than I'd thought

they would be. They flopped into various chairs in the lobby, sipping coffee and nibbling pastries that Elena baked the night before.

Yvonne was holding forth. "Did you see everyone staring at us at the diner last night? Especially when we were all singing? Oh, and when Allie got up and did her dance?"

Allie laughed. "They so wanted to be part of us. You could tell."

"That's right," one of the husbands said. I peered at him, wondering if he was being sarcastic and realized he wasn't. "Wishing they had a family like ours."

I had a feeling the inhabitants of Magellan were staring for a different reason, but I decided not to enlighten them.

"Oh, hey, Janet," Allie called when she saw me. "That old guy, he took off. He told me to tell you. Or maybe *not* to tell you. I don't remember." She tittered before she turned back to her family. "Let's go to that diner *every* night. We've taken it over anyway."

"What?" I stopped next to Allie, steadying the bowling bag, which was trying to bang against me.

"I said, we should go to the diner every night."

"Before that. The old guy. You mean Carl?"

"Is that his name? Yeah, he left, not too long ago. He took a motorcycle that was parked out back. Oh, maybe he *did* tell us not to tell you." Allie put her hand over her mouth. "Oops."

The only motorcycle parked out back last night had been Mick's—he'd carried it with him when he'd flown here and left it there, too distracted by fighting magical entities and then retiring with me to put it in the shed.

The weather had been dry, and the bike warded against

anything magical, so he didn't worry. Plus, no one in their right mind would steal Mick's Harley.

Except Nash's very stubborn and resourceful grandfather. Mick and I, in the throes of passion and then deeply asleep, hadn't heard it go.

Well, shit.

"Thanks," I babbled to Allie, then I dashed back the way I'd come, charging into the bedroom to give Mick the bad news.

CHAPTER EIGHT

"Where is Carl?" I demanded of the mirror in the bathroom.

For answer, I got more snoring.

Mick had sprung out of bed and dressed when I rushed to tell him that Carl had stolen his bike and was already searching the ground behind the hotel for fresh tire tracks. I wasn't certain why he bothered—there were only so many directions Carl could go on a motorcycle not made for off-roading.

Did Carl even know how to ride a motorcycle? Probably. He knew how to hot-wire one, that was for sure.

Mick's Harley had a piece of the magic mirror ground into one of its side mirrors, as did mine. We used them to communicate when one or both of us were on the road, and to stay in touch with Cassandra at the hotel.

I set the egg back on its towel bed before I half climbed on the freestanding sink and put my face to the mirror. "Wake the hell up and tell me where Mick's motorcycle is."

The mirror snorted and snuffled, as though dragging

itself from deep dreams. I pounded on it with the flat of my hand. "Come on!"

"All right, all right." The mirror's fake grogginess vanished.

It hated being pummeled, though even if I broke this particular mirror, I wouldn't hurt the true one. It was projecting itself from its real form in the saloon and wasn't truly connected with this mirror, any more than it was to the side mirrors on our motorcycles. Even the original getting shot, half melted, repaired, and broken again hadn't destroyed it.

"I see …" The mirror paused as though searching. "Vistas."

"Very helpful. What kind of vistas?"

"Dawn sky, desert highway, thrill of the open road—" It broke off. "Oops, cop."

"Shit." I imagined Carl being taken in by state police. Nash would retrieve him and slap him into a high-security assisted-living facility, and the old guy would never see the light of day again.

"Which highway?" Northern Arizona was crisscrossed by them, all offering desert vistas except the mountain views around Flagstaff. "What does the scenery look like?"

"It's a tribal cop." The mirror let out a wolf whistle. "Well, *he's* cute. I'd say the scenery just improved."

"Show me."

I realized I'd see only the motorcycle's side mirror's field of view, which might not project anything helpful, but I had to try.

Lucky for me, the mirror's angle caught the tribal cop who slid from his SUV and sauntered toward the motorcycle. That Carl had let himself be pulled over was surprising.

The convex mirror elongated the cop in his khaki uniform, long hair pulled neatly into a ponytail. I hoped it was Frank Yellow, a Navajo officer who'd nearly busted me once. He was related to Gina, Dad's wife. Possibly I could use family ties to get Carl out of too much trouble.

As the distortion resolved, I saw that it wasn't Frank. I recognized the broad face, the wise eyes—or wise-ass eyes, whatever mood he was in—and the exaggerated swagger.

"Going a little fast, weren't you?" he asked Carl.

Carl fiddled with the bike's ignition, as though wondering why he couldn't get it to start up and whiz him away from the situation. I could have told him exactly why the motorcycle had suddenly ceased functioning.

"Coyote!" I yelled into the mirror.

Carl, not being magical, couldn't hear me. He continued flicking switches and jiggling the handlebars.

Coyote leaned close so the curve of the mirror would stretch his smile, rendering his human lips into the weird parody of a coyote's muzzle.

"I got this, Janet," Coyote said clearly.

"Janet?" Carl's head snapped up. "You called her? Damn it, I don't need a babysitter."

"Bring him back," I shouted at Coyote. "Before Nash notices he's gone."

"I said, I got this." Coyote brushed his hand in front of the mirror, and the image vanished. I was back to glaring at myself, nothing reflected behind me but my small bathroom.

I kicked at the tile wall, as though that would help. "Nash is going to kill me."

"Sorry, sugar," the mirror said in a small voice. "I lost them."

"Not your fault." Coyote was far more powerful than a mirror, even one that had been made in an earth-magic sink by a witch tampering with stuff far beyond her control. If Coyote didn't want us to see what was going on, we wouldn't.

At least Carl was safe, I told myself with a sigh of relief, not mangled beneath Mick's motorcycle. Coyote had found him and shut down the bike in time. Although whether Coyote brought Carl straight home or not remained to be seen.

I hadn't been able to pinpoint their location. The sky above them had held a few wisps of clouds, but that kind of weather could stretch across the state and into any of the adjacent ones. Coyote had conveniently blocked my view of any landmark mountains, mesas, or valleys.

I patted the mirror to reassure it, did the same with the egg, and went outside to find Mick.

Mick took the news in resignation. "Guess we leave it up to Coyote," he said.

"I wish I could be as calm as you are. If Carl had gone joyriding on my bike, I'd be freaking out." Both for Carl's safety and the motorcycle's.

Mick ran a hand through his unruly black hair. "Running around yelling and stamping my feet won't change anything." He shrugged, but I noticed his eyes were no longer blue. "Let me fly around and check it out."

"Coyote can conceal himself from you too, you know."

"Not as well as he thinks he can." Mick's amusement told me he was recalling his dealings with Coyote in the distant past. Coyote hadn't triumphed in those encounters, but neither he nor Mick had given me any details.

"Just be careful," I said, worry gripping me. Who knew

what Mick had been trying to fight last night, and when they'd be back? "I need Carl home in one piece, preferably before Nash finds out he's gone."

Mick cupped my face in his hands and gave me a firm, hot kiss. "They'll never see me," he promised.

He jogged toward the railroad bed, as he had the night before, waiting until he was on the other side before he started to throw off clothes. I didn't see him shift this time, but after a moment or two, a black speck rose into the morning sky. Anyone looking out from the hotel would believe him to be a large bird, maybe a hawk or a buzzard.

I had to let him go, to trust that both Mick and Coyote would look after Nash's grandfather and return him safely.

The problem was, Coyote and Mick weren't sticklers for anyone else's rules. If they thought Carl was better off far away from Nash, assisted living facilities, and restrictions, they'd help him achieve that. Carl might be happy, but I'd be in deep shit with Nash.

I returned to the hotel's lobby, pleased to see the Horribles piling into their vehicles in search of more food. While Elena couldn't stop them eating her pastries that Cassandra put out for the guests, she'd extended her refusal to cook for them to all meals. If they wanted a full breakfast, they had to look elsewhere.

So busy was I watching the family go—and willing them not to turn back for a forgotten purse, watch, phone, scarf, earrings, hat, or to change into another entire outfit— that I didn't sense the presence of another behind me until a smoky aura tapped me on the shoulder.

I swung around to see a tall man in a gray silk business suit lounging in one of the lobby's armchairs, one pristinely creased pant leg crossed over the other. He had dark red hair, neatly cut, and eyes that at this moment were gray. Or gray-ish. They flickered to tawny even as I gaped at him.

He rose to tower over me, his calm demeanor in place. "Greetings, Janet Begay. Do not be alarmed. Your manager admitted me."

Cassandra, behind her desk, looked up and gave me a minute nod. The wards would have alerted her to his presence while I was outside, but she must have decided he didn't pose a threat, at least not one she couldn't handle.

"Titus." I'd met this dragon that even Drake respected last fall when he'd helped us battle a dragon slayer and other evils. "What brings you here?" Dragons didn't simply drop by to chat.

The egg was still in my bathroom, guarded by the mirror. I'd debated whether to leave it there while Mick was gone, but now I was glad of my decision. I'd never have concealed what it was from Titus.

"You have something of mine," Titus said.

All right, so maybe he already knew the egg was here. Neither Drake nor Mick would have told him, but he could have been following Drake around.

"What's that?" I asked, trying to be casual.

"I'll not be coy and say *you know what it is*." Titus sent me a ghost of a smile, while his eyes turned silver. "It is my son. Or daughter. My offspring, in any case. I know it was placed in your care. May I see it, please?"

I stared at him in incredulity, at the same time I became aware that Cassandra and I were very much alone in this lobby. Elena banged pots in the kitchen, but she'd be oblivious to anything but what she was cooking. No guests were in the saloon, and Carlos's shift didn't start until lunch.

Rooms were being cleaned, so Flora and the other maids were upstairs.

Titus had chosen his moment well. Cassandra and I would be powerful opponents, but we'd have to fight hard to best a dragon. He'd definitely waited until Mick was out of the way to corner us, in his refined way.

"*Your* offspring?" I asked without moving. "You're claiming you're the dad?"

Titus's eyes became very dark gray. I read grief in them. "I was Cesnia's lover, yes."

"I don't want to upset you," I said gently, "but you weren't her only one."

Titus regarded me without surprise. "I know. Cesnia was not one for monogamy. We didn't mind. It was an honor to be with her."

Wow. I was growing more regretful that I'd never met her.

"I thought dragons were possessive of their mates," I said. Mick certainly was.

"We are." Titus's eyes became light green. "Very possessive. Cesnia wasn't my mate. She was no one's mate." His lips quirked into a minute smile. "She was special."

Very special, I was beginning to understand.

"How do you know you're the father?" I asked. "Are there DNA tests for dragons?"

"We don't need them," Titus answered. "All will know without doubt after the dragonling is hatched. It will tell us who is its sire."

Interesting. "Until then, you can't be sure?"

"I still believe it is mine. If I am proved wrong, then I will return the dragonling to its true sire."

My brows went up. "Would you, really?"

Titus had seemed like an honorable guy during our last adventure, helping out against some pretty nasty evil when he hadn't had to be involved at all. On the other hand, he'd been complicit with a dragon slayer in organizing gladiatorial games that had put Mick into grave danger. That had also been about honor, because Titus had been compelled to fulfill a promise.

But I didn't really know him. I'd been around dragons for several years now, and while I could more or less predict what Colby, Drake, and Mick would do in a given situation, I had no idea what Titus was capable of.

More or less predict. Dragons did what they wanted, and very few beings in this world could stop them.

Titus touched his fingertips together, like one businessman patiently waiting for another to agree to his terms. I noted that he didn't answer my question.

"I'm a neutral party," I said. "How about I keep the egg until it hatches, and we know its parentage? That way, there are no mistakes."

Titus's eyes flickered, though they didn't change color again. "But you are not a neutral party. You are Mick's mate."

"Which means I'd give the kid to him?" I asked in astonishment. "Why would I do that?"

"Because a dragon child can bring another dragon much power."

"Wouldn't he bring you power if you're his father? Why would he help Mick, instead?"

Titus heaved a minute sigh. "Such things are difficult to explain."

Dragon-speak for *I don't want to tell you.*

"If you mean the kid can bring a dragon power because

that dragon could threaten him or enslave him, then I'm definitely not giving him to anyone but the true dad."

Not that dragons were known for being fond parents. The dragonling might not be any better off with its father, even straight-up guys like Drake or Titus.

Which took me to another thought. Mick had told me that the mother sang the baby dragon's name to it, while it was still in the shell, the name no one in the world knew but the two of them.

Had Cesnia had time to give her child its true name? And what would be the consequences if not?

Titus opened his hands in resignation. "I will never make you understand. Your best option is to give the egg to me. Trust me on this."

"I'd love to, but I can't." I folded my arms and looked Titus squarely in his eyes, which were now shimmering silver. "The egg stays here."

Titus brushed off the sleeves of his jacket as though they'd grown dusty in my lobby. "You know I could simply take it from you," he said in a mild tone.

"It's protected," I stated. "Try to take the egg through these wards, and it's you who will be scared."

I wasn't sure about that, but I lifted my chin as though dead certain.

I read in Titus's gaze that he didn't believe me, but he didn't argue. "Then you will have to bear the consequences." His tone was somber, even sad. "I tried."

"What consequences?" I demanded. "I hate it when dragons go all cryptic. Explaining would be so much easier on everyone."

"Consequences too awful to contemplate," Titus finished. "If you change your mind …"

Titus reached into his coat. I braced myself, as did Cassandra, the two of us waiting for him to withdraw a weapon of some kind. Instead, he pulled out a small, mauve-colored rectangle. A business card.

He held it out to me. "Give me a call."

I took the card between my first two fingers, careful not to touch him. Titus could fry me into unconsciousness with a small spurt of dragon fire if he chose.

The card held the name *Titus* embossed in silver, and a ten-digit phone number. That was all.

"Sure," I said. "I'll do that."

Titus sent me another of his tiny smiles, made Cassandra a polite bow, then strolled out of the lobby into the sunshine outside the front doors. I followed him, pausing on the doorstep.

Titus continued walking northward across the parking lot, never mind the red dust that must be coating his shoes and the hem of his fine trousers.

The air between him and me shimmered like summer heatwaves, and when they cleared, Titus was gone.

A movement caught my eye. I turned toward it and saw that I hadn't been the only one to watch Titus disappear.

A tall man had stepped out of the Crossroads Bar—which shouldn't have been open yet—and stared at the space where Titus had disappeared. He had long black hair threaded with gray, a strong body, and a firm face.

Last night, he'd been nude, like a Changer who'd just shifted, but today he was dressed in jeans, a sweatshirt, and motorcycle boots.

He regarded the dusty lot from which Titus had vanished, then turned his head to look straight at me.

"Good morning, Janet," he said.

CHAPTER NINE

I started slowly across the lot, as though something drew me to the waiting man. He watched me with the same serenity as he'd done last night when he'd wiped away the lightning mesh with a negligent swipe of his hand.

Was he a god? Or the child of a god, like me? A Changer, in truth? Or simply a powerful entity who'd decided to hang out near my hotel?

I halted a few yards away from him, deciding it prudent not to get too close. "Are you Navajo?" I asked.

He answered me in the Diné language. "Not necessarily."

"Are you here for a reason?"

A smile crinkled the corners of his eyes. "What has happened to hospitality in the young? Or kindness to strangers? You have not learned your grandmother's lessons."

"Strangers too often want to destroy my hotel or hurt my friends," I told him. "Or me. Why were you so handy last night to stop the lightning? Maybe because you caused it yourself?"

The smile reached his mouth. "So very suspicious. It is sad that you cannot look upon the world and revel in its wonders."

"Because those wonders often want to kill me." I took a couple steps closer, still wary. "Sorry if I don't open my arms to every potentially dangerous person who appears out of the blue."

The man gave me a shrug. "I was passing. This place intrigued me. As did you. It is an old crossroads, an intersection between the magical and the ordinary. You built a hotel on it." He apparently found this amusing.

"I didn't build it," I explained. "It's been here for a century or so. I restored it."

"Why did you?"

I often asked myself that question. The derelict pile had called to me, and I'd accepted the challenge.

I knew there had been more to it than that. The vortexes had reached for me, their intense magic coercing me. But even after I'd acknowledged that no coincidence had brought me here, I'd stayed.

This place was a part of me now. It was close enough to my home in Many Farms that I could get there quickly, but far enough that I could live my own life, more or less.

"It was something to do," I said impatiently. "I'd love some answers from you. Why do you find me so interesting?"

"Is that a serious question?" His dark eyes focused sharply on me. "You've brought creatures here who would never dwell together in any other circumstances. Now they dine with one another in your saloon. Dragons, witches,

Changers, goddesses. You've made them your family." His grin spread across his face, rendering him still more handsome. "It's fascinating."

"I didn't have a lot of choice," I said tightly.

"Didn't you? You could leave all this." He swept out a long arm, taking in the hotel, the desert, Barry's bar, and the highway crossroads beyond it. "Return to your small house in Many Farms, or travel the world, as you prefer. You could do anything you wanted to, Stormwalker. Yet, you stay. You protect others, often at the cost to yourself."

"What, I should let them die? Say, too bad, my friends, that monsters are attacking you, but I have other places to be?" I forced myself to calm. "You know a hell of a lot about me, but who are *you*?" I'd had an idea last night, and I was growing more certain of it by the minute.

"Maybe you should get that," he said.

I blinked at the non-sequitur. "What?"

The next instant, my cell phone buzzed in my back pocket. I jumped and pulled it out, then studied the caller's name in dismay.

I swiped to answer. "Good morning," I said as politely as I could.

My grandmother's voice boomed through the speaker. "Janet. I need you back here right away. Bring the egg. And tell that old crow to come with you." *Click.*

The screen went dark. I looked up at the man, who watched me with humor in his dark eyes.

"By *that old crow*, she means you, doesn't she?" I asked.

"Your grandmother is very flattering." He sent me another beatific smile. "Shall we ride? I have a motorcycle here. Much less tiring than flying."

I HAD SO MANY QUESTIONS, BEGINNING WITH HOW MY grandmother knew I had a dragon egg and ending with why the crow-man was really here. His story of happening to pass and becoming interested in the hotel was so much bullshit.

Answers would have to wait. When Grandmother told me to come home, I went. No delay.

I told Cassandra where I was going and then retrieved the egg, still snuggled under the bathroom sink. I grabbed more towels to stuff around the shell so it wouldn't be knocked about in my saddlebag and carried it to my motorcycle.

I settled the egg and wheeled my bike out of the shed. The crow-man pulled up smoothly beside me on his own motorcycle as I started the engine. He'd tied his hair back and donned a helmet and gloves, looking like an ordinary guy out for a ride on his sleek Harley.

"Do you have a name?" I asked him.

"I have many names." A typical answer from the mysteriously magical. "You can call me Nitis."

That was a Diné name, which more or less meant *friend*. Not his real moniker, but entities liked to be enigmatic.

"Whatever," I said. "I can't ride too fast today." I had no intention of wiping out and shattering the egg.

"A wise course." Nitis nodded to the saddle bag. "We will keep it safe."

I gave up trying to figure him out. I'd take him to Grandmother, and she'd pull the truth out of him, if she didn't know it already.

It was a beautiful morning for a ride, I had to admit.

The March air was cool but not cold—the heat that would strike us by mid-April had yet to arrive. The back highway to the 40 was almost empty, and we rode side-by-side, a couple of bikers enjoying the road.

As the crow flew, it was a hundred miles to Many Farms. As the crow rode, it was about a hundred and forty. We sped down the interstate, flying past Holbrook and through the Petrified Forest area to turn north on the 191.

The beauty of the Navajo Nation reached to me as we entered it, valleys in various shades of pink and blue stretching to jagged mountains on the horizon. We slowed for horses that wandered by the side of the road and once had to stop, north of Chinle, while a flock of sheep trotted across the highway.

It was just after noon by the time we rolled through Many Farms, the small community that had been my childhood home. I'd tried to leave it many times, believing my destiny lay in the wider world. Somehow, it always drew me back.

Nitis pulled next to me as we turned up the dirt drive to the small yellow house amid a painfully neat but unadorned yard. I'd hoped my father would be here—my main tug homeward—but didn't see his truck.

The door opened, and Grandmother stepped out onto the small front porch. She didn't call a greeting, only stood waiting as Nitis and I dismounted our motorcycles.

Nitis removed his helmet and hung it behind his seat. He stood in place, the afternoon breeze stirring his variegated hair, and gazed at Grandmother, who stared straight back at him.

I wasn't certain whether to wait until one of them blinked or hurry inside, ignoring them. I opened the saddlebag to find the egg bouncing in its nest, as though the little dragon had enjoyed the ride.

"Humph," Grandmother called to Nitis. "Is that the best you could do?"

Nitis's handsome smile split his face. "How about this?" he asked in Diné.

The man's limbs abruptly shrank, and his features became wizened, his hair thinning until it was a few wisps on his head. His clothes, which didn't change, now sagged on a bent-backed elderly man.

He rested a hand on his bike as though it was the only thing holding him up. "Better?" He cackled.

Grandmother regarded him coldly. "When you are finished playing, we have work to do."

Nitis continued laughing as he morphed back into the tall man who'd ridden here with me. He winked at me and started for the house.

Before I could follow, a tan SUV rattled up the drive, billowing dust in its wake. The vehicle was crammed full of teenaged girls and driven by my sister.

"Hi, Janet," Gabrielle yelled at me. "I'm taking the team to lunch for winning their game last night. Come with us."

I hadn't been aware Gabrielle could drive. I hoped whatever license she had in her pocket was legal, if she'd bothered with a license at all.

"I'm here to see Grandmother," I told her. "She summoned me."

"Go with her, Janet," Grandmother said from the porch. "I must talk with the old crow. Take the bag with you."

I wished Grandmother would enlighten me as to a) how

she knew about the egg and b) why she thought said egg would be safer with Gabrielle and her high school basketball team than in the house.

However, I'd learned at a very young age that it was useless to argue with Grandmother. Maybe by the time I returned, my dad would be there as a buffer against whatever was going on.

Gabrielle grinned at me through the driver's side window. "Come on, Janet. There's room."

I heard a lot of giggling from inside and saw that there was no way I'd squeeze myself into the crowded SUV. Two of the girls in the back were one if my cousin's daughters. They made faces at me through the window, laughing uproariously when I rolled my eyes.

"I'll take my bike," I said to Gabrielle. "Meet you there."

I didn't have to ask where she was going. Our family always went to the Watering Hole in Chinle, which was a large restaurant that served fabulous Navajo tacos and burgers bigger than my two hands. I'd tasted savory cheeseburger the minute Gabrielle mentioned taking her girls to lunch.

"All rightee then," Gabrielle said. "Bye!"

The team shouted their good-byes, a dozen slim hands waving at me, as Gabrielle turned the SUV around and zoomed back to the road.

Grandmother and Nitis, both on the porch now, had resumed staring at each other. The two crows, one of them with white head feathers, had done the same in the juniper tree behind my hotel.

I secured the bag once more, mounted up, and followed

the SUV back down the highway, speeding a little to keep Gabrielle in sight.

The sheep we'd waited for in Chinle had decided to graze on the west side of the highway—it always amazed me how sheep could find the smallest blades of grass to chew on in the vast, seemingly empty desert.

Once past the flock, I turned off toward Canyon de Chelly and the cluster of motels and restaurants that attracted both locals and tourists.

The Watering Hole had known Gabrielle was coming. A long table was ready for the team, and the waitresses greeted them with big smiles and congratulations. The girls trooped around the table, grabbing chairs and plopping into them. Gabrielle had saved a seat for me at one end.

I tucked the bowling bag under my wooden chair and thanked the waitress who set a large glass of water in front of me. The drive had been dry.

"Everyone say hi to my big sister, Janet," Gabrielle sang.

A loud chorus of *Hi, Janet!* rang through the restaurant.

I wasn't certain how to respond, so I just smiled. "Hi, everyone. I heard it was a great game."

"It was a horrible game," Gabrielle contradicted. "We had to fight for every point. But we did it."

"Because of Coach," my cousin Lily called down the table. "They'd have wiped the floor with our asses if not for Coach Massey."

The girls cheered, beaming at Gabrielle with joy. The cheering broke off as menus came around, and the focus went to what food everyone was going to have. I'd already decided and didn't even need to look at what was on offer.

I leaned to Gabrielle while the girls were distracted. "You're loving this."

"I am." Gabrielle snatched tortilla chips from the bowl the waitress had left, propped her elbows on the table, and proceeded to munch. "I've always wanted to be part of something like this, but when I was these girls' age, no one wanted to come near me. That's what I get for being scary as shit, right?" She grinned but I saw the lingering hurt in her eyes.

"Same thing happened to me," I said. "I wasn't welcome on any sports teams or even at the lunch tables. I was too weird." Another reason I'd left home to go to NAU and then hit the road soon after.

One of the team looked up from the intense discussion of what to order. "Hey, Janet, Shirley says you burned down one of the buildings at our high school. Is that true?" Shirley was Lily's sister, two years younger.

My face warmed. On a stormy day, when I hadn't been able to control my newfound powers, I'd directed lightning at a storage shed, which had instantly caught fire.

"Not on purpose," I said uncomfortably.

The team regarded me with awe. "Cool," the girl said. Others shouted "Woo!" or "Nice!" and then they went back to arguing about what to eat.

"They like you," Gabrielle said. "How does it feel?"

I sipped water to cover my embarrassment. "Not bad," I admitted.

Gabrielle smiled in triumph and ate another chip.

I told myself I'd long ago recovered from my adolescent angst, but yes, I'd always wanted to feel more a part of the community. I had a big family, and at the same time, I was an outsider. No one knew who my mother was, and that started me off at a disadvantage. If not for my father, I'd have despaired at an early age and would have probably tried to run away sooner.

I felt a little left out again when the waitress, who knew all the girls by name, took everyone's order but mine. No one seemed to notice.

My self-pity fled when the food arrived, and the waitress set down a large cheeseburger and fries slathered with gravy in front of me. What I always ordered when I came here. Now I felt like an idiot.

Gabrielle smirked as though she read my thoughts. Bratty little sis.

The girls giggled and joked through the meal, but they were in no way rude or arrogant. They were pleased with themselves for winning last night, but as many on the opposing team were friends and relations, they expressed respect for their good playing—though they were happy they'd won.

When I was almost finished with my food the afternoon became even better. The door of the restaurant swung open to admit my dad and Gina.

I was out of my seat and moving toward Pete the moment I spotted him. I wouldn't embarrass him by rushing over and throwing my arms around him, but it was hard to contain my joy.

A warm smile filled Dad's eyes when he saw me. He clasped my hands— demonstrative for him—and gazed fondly at me.

"I did not know you were coming, Janet," my father said. He continued to hold my hands, infusing me with his warmth. Gina, behind him, regarded me with quiet welcome.

"Grandmother called an emergency meeting," I

explained. "Then she told me to go out to lunch with Gabrielle."

Amusement lit Pete's eyes. "Your grandmother's ways are her own," he said.

"A good way of putting it," I agreed.

"Come and sit with us, Janet," Gina said.

I returned to my seat to fetch the bag, murmuring to Gabrielle that I would visit with my dad and Gina at the table in the corner that they'd taken. Dad didn't like to be in the middle of the room.

"Sure thing," Gabrielle said brightly. Before I could turn away, she caught my sleeve and pulled me down so she could whisper into my ear. "Later you'll tell me all about how you got yourself a dragon egg."

CHAPTER TEN

I didn't jump in surprise. Of course, Gabrielle, being the magical person she was, would have sensed the egg's aura, even though she hadn't so much as glanced at the bag. Maybe she'd decided to be discreet and wouldn't ask me point-blank in front of the team, but I never knew with Gabrielle.

"Not a word," I said.

Gabrielle gave me a mock pout. "As if I'd say anything."

I sent her a warning glance, slung the bag over my shoulder, and marched across the restaurant. I heard Gabrielle chuckling behind me.

Gina Tsosie regarded me with her wise, dark eyes as I sat down across from her. Gina was a large woman, about my dad's age, with a sensible outlook on life.

Pete, next to her, rested his arms on the table, his shoulders relaxed, his face holding no tension. My dad was usually uncomfortable in a restaurant—anywhere in public, really—but now he reposed here as though eating in front of people was no big deal. Gina had truly unwound him, and for that I was grateful.

"You have been given a mission," Gina stated to me.

Gods, did everyone on the planet know Drake had entrusted this dragon egg to me? I slid the bag further under my chair with my foot.

"Why do you say that?" I asked in an innocent tone.

"You bear the weight of a burden," Gina said. "I will not ask you what the burden is. But if you need help carrying it, you only need to come to us."

Dad nodded in complete agreement. He wouldn't ask me pesky questions either.

I was struck by how fortunate I was to have these two as my family, and my eyes grew moist.

"Thank you," I said, my voice clogged. "I'll handle it. Don't worry."

They both knew I'd struggle with this but said no more about it.

"I haven't had a chance to ask you about your Hawaii trip," I said to change the subject. "Did you surf?"

Dad and Gina had gone to Hawaii for their honeymoon, and Gina had vowed to take surfing lessons while there. Gina had truly changed my father, because she'd convinced him to actually board an airplane.

"I did." Gina's mouth quirked. "The instructor was a very fit young man, and he had his doubts about me. But he taught these old bones to jump up on the board. After that, it was easy. I have very good balance."

"She does," Dad put in. "Graceful."

The two shared a look only those who have been intimate together can. Weird when it was my own father, but on the other hand, Dad deserved this happiness. He'd been burned by my true mother and then berated by his mom and sisters all his life for his one night of indiscretion. Gina was giving him some peace from all that.

Not that Grandmother would ever stop berating. She enjoyed it too much.

"It was a very nice vacation," Gina concluded. "The island of Maui is a fine one. They have had many troubles, but they are strong. Like us."

Gina was proving to be one of the strongest women I knew. She had a tiny bit of magic in her, nothing compared to what I, Gabrielle, and Grandmother had, but she had a comfortableness with herself and her abilities that my sister and I still sought.

"We're going, Janet," Gabrielle called across the restaurant to me. "Hágoónee'. Did I say that right?" she asked her team. She had been raised Apache and was trying to learn some of the Diné language.

"Close enough," my cousin Shirley said. "Hágoónee', Janet," the rest of the team chorused to me.

I waved back, giving them my farewells. Gina added hers and her congratulations. My father smiled in silence.

I decided I couldn't ask for a better day than this.

———

GINA AND DAD ACCOMPANIED ME HOME. I FOLLOWED DAD'S old pickup along the highway, as he drove sedately to our turnoff. I observed Dad's and Gina's heads, visible through the rear window, one on each side of the bench seat, with lots of space between them. Gina turned often to say something to Dad, but Dad stared rigidly forward, as always when he drove.

I used to be the one in the passenger seat, though I never spoke much as Gina did now. Dad and I would ride in silence for hours, the two of us enjoying the land and sky, and the solace of being away from our sometimes-confining house.

After I'd left home, I'd been sad thinking of my dad driving around by himself in his truck. Now he didn't have to be alone.

It was a wistful feeling, though. I'd left more behind than I'd thought, and now I'd never truly have it back.

On the other hand, I'd never seen Dad so happy. I decided I was nostalgic for the past, but happy for the present.

We reached home to find Nitis sitting at our dining room table, a mug of coffee between his strong hands. He gazed out the wide window to the multihued desert beyond, eyes still. My grandmother was in the kitchen, cooking.

Grandmother cooked whenever she was unhappy. She also did it when she was happy, but the way she went about it told the difference. Right now, she was chopping onions with vigor before slamming them into a pan. Hot oil spattered and popped. She did not look up when I peeped into the kitchen, but she knew we were back.

My father, wise to Grandmother's moods, suggested he and Gina go for a walk.

"Not yet." Grandmother banged out of the kitchen, large metal spoon in hand. "First, the old crow needs to tell Janet something."

"Probably nothing Gina and Dad need to worry about," I suggested quickly.

"I will not keep them in the dark," Grandmother snapped. "They might need to know, eventually."

This made a change from Grandmother being enigmatic about everything my whole life, but I suppose she'd realized that keeping silent about danger didn't help.

Gina solved the argument by seating herself on the comfortable sofa. Pete readily sat next to her. They were very close, unlike in the truck, but not quite touching. I saw protectiveness on Gina's impassive face. If she didn't like what Grandmother said, her expression conveyed, she'd haul my dad out of there.

Grandmother glanced at the spoon in her hand, ducked into the kitchen, and clattered it to the counter. She emerged again, wiping her fingers on a colorful towel. I hoped she'd turned the heat down on the onions, or they'd be little charred bits stuck to the bottom of her favorite frying pan. Guess who'd have to clean that out.

"Janet, please show us the egg."

I hesitated, suddenly uncomfortable with all eyes on me. I'd grown as protective of the little dragon as Gina had become with my dad.

However, no one here was a dragon—Nitis's aura wasn't anything like one—or an evil mage. Nitis's aura absolved him of that too.

Grandmother was not going to rest until I obeyed. Suppressing a sigh, I lifted the bowling bag onto the table and unzipped it. I sent a watchful glance out the window but saw nothing there except the earth stretching to mountains. Even the hawks and other crows were absent.

I lifted out the egg, bringing its foam-rubber nest with it. All attention went from me to the egg as soon as I set it gently on the table. Even Dad leaned forward with Gina to see better.

The egg appeared greener in the sunlight, its jade color

deepening. The gold wire crisscrossing it shimmered, the emeralds winking with intensity.

"How beautiful," Gina murmured. She was the only one to speak.

I laid a hand on top of the egg, and the dragon inside bounced against the shell. I wondered how close he was to hatching—he certainly moved around a lot. Would he know when it was time to break his way out? And then what?

Nitis set down his coffee and rested his hands flat on the table. "There is a legend, ancient and forgotten, about a dragon without sire or dam." His voice was rich and mellow, reminding me of my father's flute.

By contrast, I was hoarse as I asked, "What legend?"

"I do not believe it," Grandmother stated. Her lined face told me differently. She was worried. "I summoned you home because this old crow told me the dragon egg that the Firewalker gave you has a legend attached to it. I brought both of you here so he can explain."

Nitis sent an acknowledging look at Grandmother. She must have wanted to argue with him about it beforehand, which was why she sent me to lunch with Gabrielle.

Nitis continued. "It is said that a dragon born without sire and dam will have immense power. It will rise to become one of the strongest of its kind, and it will slay a dragon lord."

I listened in puzzlement. "That can't refer to Junior, here." I let my fingers glide across the egg's smooth surface. "He had a mother. Cesnia. She was killed. His father is still alive—we just don't know which dragon it is. Could be Drake, could be Titus. Could be one we don't know. Apparently, Cesnia had many boyfriends."

Grandmother scowled at me. "Unless you discover who

sired him, then the legend will stand. The words say *born without parents*. When that egg hatches, he won't have any, unless the Firewalkers decide between them beforehand which one is its father."

So much for Grandmother not believing the legend.

"Who is the dragon lord?" Gina's quiet question cut through the glare Grandmother and I shared.

I switched my gaze out the window, to the east. Santa Fe lay that way, with the dragon compound on its outskirts.

"Farrell is the head of the dragon council," I said. "At least, for now. Bancroft thinks he is, and Drake warned me that Bancroft would try to raise the dragon himself if he didn't destroy the egg entirely." I stroked it again, my fingers catching on the sharp facets of an emerald. "Bancroft is pretty powerful, but Mick and I can keep him at bay, I think. Same with Farrell."

Grandmother said nothing. She studied me in sharp disapproval, as though disappointed in my reasoning.

Nitis, who'd stared at his hands as he spoke, lifted his head. He pinned me with crow-black eyes that held the depths of age.

My caress stilled as a memory swooped at me. Colby, standing in the middle of Death Valley, facing down the dragon council and laughing at them. Mick trying to shut him up. Colby triumphantly proclaiming that the council couldn't sentence Mick to death for his crime of not killing me.

Why couldn't they? Because Mick had long ago won a battle that had saved the lives of many dragons.

Mick was decorated for valor and given the highest status a dragon can achieve, Colby had stated. *Lord and general.*

The vision of Colby, Mick, and the dragons standing in

the dry lakebed, stark mountains rising around us, vanished with a slap. I was back in my small living room, with Grandmother, Nitis, Dad, and Gina, watching me reason it out.

I went cold with dismay, and my heart beat in quivering jerks.

"Oh, shit," I whispered.

CHAPTER ELEVEN

"It doesn't necessarily refer to Mick," I stated when I could breathe again. I felt my Beneath goddess powers rising, as they liked to do when I was distressed. I tried to control my trepidation so I wouldn't hurt anyone, but it wasn't easy. Nitis had just told me I was nurturing the means to destroy the man I loved.

Nitis regarded me without blinking. "Do you know any other dragon lords?"

I scowled at him. "Doesn't mean they aren't out there. Anyway, how do *you* know Mick is one? And how do you know about the legend? You're not a dragon. Where did this story come from?"

"It is old." Nitis smiled. "Like me."

"Winged creatures keep track of each other," Grandmother said with a look of disapprobation at Nitis. "Crows. Hawks. Firewalkers."

She'd never mentioned this before, though it explained how she always knew what was going on at my hotel.

"If it does mean Mick, what will you do, Janet?" Nitis asked quietly.

I sat in silence because I had no idea.

Legends aren't necessarily predictions of the future any more than they are accurate portrayals of the past. For instance, there are all kinds of legends in Northern Arizona that are complete bullshit—made up by white journalists in the early twentieth century to attract tourists to certain destinations. The stories, such as the one about the Apaches massacred at Two Guns, were printed and reprinted, without anyone verifying them or turning up any archeological evidence to support them, until the tales were considered history.

Dragons collected plenty of lore, Mick had told me. Some of it true, some of it invented. Even the dragon council made up things to keep dragons in line.

I had no way of knowing whether Nitis's claim was true, or if he had some ulterior motive for telling me this tale and worrying me. Grandmother trusted him—or he'd not be sitting in her house—but that didn't mean I fully believed him.

However, whether or not Nitis told the truth, did *Drake* believe the legend? Had he given me the egg to guard because he thought he could someday use the kid to take out Mick? Or because he'd truly loved Cesnia and didn't care what legends the little dragon had to deal with?

My thoughts poured forth. "Even if Drake doesn't know the legend or believe it, I'll bet Bancroft does."

"Bancroft is always out for his own power," Nitis informed me. "Whatever his motivation in laying hands on the egg, it will be to benefit himself."

"No kidding." I'd once saved Bancroft's life, but that

had gained me only so many points with him. "The dragon council let Mick out of his death sentence because of Mick's high status. I'm willing to believe Bancroft wants to raise this dragon as a weapon against him. Not Bancroft's fault if a more powerful dragon kills Mick, right?"

I shivered as I said the words. I didn't want anyone killing Mick, or plotting it, or even *thinking* about it.

"You believe the one called Drake does not want to rid himself of Mick?" Grandmother asked. "They have long been rivals, have they not?"

"Drakey wouldn't do that," came an aggrieved voice.

I swung around as Gabrielle, who could move as silently as mist when she wanted to, came toward me through the living room. Dad and Gina didn't look surprised to see her, so she must have used the front door in the conventional way instead of simply appearing.

There was no sign of the basketball team and no sign of the SUV either, by which I concluded it had been returned to the school along with the team.

"How can you be sure?" I demanded of Gabrielle. "Grandmother's right—Drake has never liked Mick."

"Because Drakey has a little thing called integrity." Gabrielle put her hands on her sweatpants-clad hips. She managed to look as svelte and sexy in workout cloths as she did in tight-fitting dresses or low-slung jeans. "If Drake wanted to fight Mick to the death, he'd say so, and do it. He wouldn't come up with weird schemes for raising a dragon to hate Mick and then kill him. Besides, I'm guessing that would take a very long time."

Dragons lived for centuries—years to us was like a week for them. But Gabrielle had a point.

"It is out of character for Drake," I admitted. "And I

don't remember telling you all about Drake, the egg, or the legend, which I'm just now learning of."

Gabrielle sent me a pitying look. "If you want to hide a dragon egg from me, you'll need something more concealing than a bowling bag. I heard about the legend when this guy told you. This house doesn't have very thick windows." She waved at Nitis. "Hi, by the way. I'm Gabrielle, Janet's obnoxious little sister."

"So I have heard." Nitis gave her a nod. "Not about the obnoxious part, but that you are very powerful."

"Ooh." Gabrielle shot Grandmother a wink. "I like him. Where did you find him?"

Grandmother's never-ceasing frown deepened. "Do not be rude, Gabrielle. I believe the trash has been piling up in the kitchen bin since you have been out with your basketball team."

Gabrielle's sunny expression deserted her. She scowled, then heaved a long sigh of resignation. "She means *Gabrielle, stop butting in.* I'll take care of it." She trudged to the kitchen, where I heard bags rattling and the trash can lid banging.

It was amazing and a bit unnerving to watch Gabrielle —who'd first introduced herself to me by trying to kill me —obediently scuttle out the kitchen door with the trash bags and empty them into the outside receptacle.

The old Gabrielle might have blown up the trash, or the kitchen, or the entire house. But her derision for ordinary life and family had retreated. She'd had a shitty upbringing, so learning to handle the mundane reality of everyday living was a big step for her.

Grandmother focused on me again. "Regardless of the

Firewalkers' motives, the question is: What will you do, Janet?"

They all studied me—Grandmother, Nitis, Dad, Gina. I was spared only the scrutiny of Gabrielle, who'd started singing loudly as she dumped the trash.

I again laid my hand on top of the egg. I was already fond of the little one, who jumped and danced inside his shell at my touch.

Who the hell was going to take care of him when he hatched? Drake? *Me?* How much tending did a baby dragon need? Lizards came out of their shells ready to run around and eat bugs, but birds had to be nurtured and fed.

Which would a dragon more resemble—lizard or bird —or would it be completely different from either of those? I desperately needed a *How to Care for Your Baby Dragon* manual.

"I'm not giving the egg to Bancroft," I said resolutely. "Or to any of the other dragons. Maybe not even Drake." I'd have to discover Drake's motives before I trusted him. He was honorable yes, but he wasn't always clear about his intentions.

My dad spoke from the sofa, his voice quiet. "Will you tell Mick?"

"Yes," I said immediately.

I was sure Mick wouldn't crush this egg when he heard a maybe-true, maybe-not-true legend. He was one of the most caring guys I'd ever met.

A little voice in the back of my mind reminded me that Mick was also an efficient killing machine. The council had chosen him to find me and take me out because Mick was ruthless and got the job done. That Mick had become fascinated with me and stopped himself was simply my good luck.

Since then, Mick had been protecting me from all comers, including the dragons who'd set him against me in the first place.

Mick also never, ever gave in to fear. He sometimes felt afraid, he'd once told me, but he hid it well and never let it drive him. I didn't really think his first reaction on learning about the legend would be to slay Junior without giving him a chance.

The others in the room, I could see, weren't so certain.

"I trust Mick," I said resolutely. "He's earned that. Proved himself many times over."

"Well, that's good." Gabrielle was back, trash done, hands clean. Again, I hadn't heard her come in, and again, I was the only one not startled. My family must be used to her now, and I didn't think anything could surprise Nitis.

"Thank you," I said to Gabrielle, then my eyes narrowed. "Do you mean you agree with me?"

"I mean, it's good, because he's *here*." Gabrielle pointed out the window.

Mick was approaching us, fully dressed, sauntering in from the east as though he strolled across the high desert every day. He must have landed and morphed somewhere beyond the hills, though where he'd stashed his clothes, I didn't know. Dragons kept caches of personal belongings all over, apparently, so who knew what niche in the rocks near my house held his extra jeans and T-shirts?

I opened the door for Mick as he reached the porch. He gave me his hot, bad-boy smile and brushed a kiss to my lips before he entered the house.

Mick's smile died as he ran into the force of everyone's stares.

"What?" he asked.

Gabrielle spoke first. "The dragon in this egg is going to grow up to kill you, Mick. Unless you know another dragon lord. Then it might kill him instead." She shrugged under Grandmother's glare. "Better to tell him straight out than beat around the bush. Right?" She wrinkled her nose. "*Beat around the bush.* Where does that saying even come from? Some British hunting thing?"

"Yes," Mick rumbled. "Refers to the beaters flushing out ground birds so the hunters could catch them. In later centuries, to shoot them."

"Poor birdies," Gabrielle said.

"In medieval times, they had to eat." Mick studied our expressions. "Did you all expect me to flame the egg as soon as I knew?" He raised a hand, as though ready to let fire stream from his palm.

Since his eyes were brilliant blue, and the dragon tatts on his arms were calm—almost amused—I knew he wasn't about to flame anything.

"It would be the quickest way to end a potential problem," I said. I had my arms tightly crossed over my chest, but I'd blast Mick with Beneath magic if I was wrong and he *did* try to flame it.

Mick moved to the egg and gazed down at it. My father, trusting me and my faith in Mick, relaxed back into the sofa. The others remained tense, though Nitis sat calmly.

"I would never do that to Cesnia." Mick's voice went soft. "She'd not have let herself die if she'd thought Drake couldn't keep the egg safe. She also had to know that Drake would seek help, and the most powerful help was you, Janet.

I'm guessing Cesnia knew the legend, but she trusted I wouldn't be cruel in order to protect myself."

"Wait a minute," I said, perplexed. "She *chose* to die? I thought someone killed her."

"They did. But if Cesnia had believed her offspring would perish without her, she'd have hung on with all her strength until the egg was safe. She knew it was all right to let go."

I stared at Mick. "I'm very confused."

"It's a dragon thing." Mick said this as though it explained everything. "I don't know exactly what happened to Cesnia, so I can only guess. She obviously wasn't worried I'd kill her child, or else she'd have put some sort of ward on him to keep me from coming near." He gently touched the top of the egg.

I felt no fear from the little dragon inside. In fact, the egg wobbled slightly, as it did for me, as though happy for my touch.

Grandmother's scowl lessened, and Gina exhaled in relief. Nitis's expression didn't change at all.

"Looks like you were right about him, Janet," Gabrielle said brightly. "Everyone else thought you'd kill it immediately, Mick."

Mick nodded, unoffended. "A natural assumption, but no."

I was still trying to follow Mick's logic regarding Cesnia letting herself be killed.

"Cesnia couldn't have known about her kid being part of a prophecy to bring down a dragon lord," I said. "The legend says that a dragon born *without sire or dam* will slay you. Cesnia didn't know her child would be born without father or mother, did she? She'd assume she'd be there when it hatched, and that Drake or Titus would be around too."

Mick raised his brows. "Titus?"

Mick had been gone before Titus arrived. "Apparently, he was one of Cesnia's favorites, too," I said. "My point is, Cesnia wouldn't have warded the egg against you, because she wouldn't have known there'd be a reason to."

Mick listened with his usual intense interest. "*Wouldn't* she have known?"

I pressed my hands to the sides of my skull. "Please, don't mess with my head, Mick. How could she have known her egg would be the one the legend was about? That she'd die before it hatched? She wouldn't have until the moment she realized her life was in danger, and even then, she might not have remembered this legend."

Mick's slow shrug reminded me why dragons drove me crazy. "We can't know what Cesnia foretold. Dragons are canny. She might very well have predicted her own death, or knew she was in danger of dying. She'd have alerted Drake to be ready to rescue the egg before she even went into battle." Mick finally bothered to look troubled. "I wish I understood better what happened."

I made a noise of exasperation. "Dragons are so—"

"Cool," Gabrielle said quickly.

"Focused," I finished.

"That too," Gabrielle said. "And infuriating. And fun. And hot."

I pretended to ignore her, but I had to concede that her adjectives were apt.

Mick interrupted us. "I don't expect anyone but dragons to understand. I am not trying to insult you, but—"

"It's a dragon thing," I filled in for him. "We puny humans can't grasp it."

"He's right." Nitis spoke up for the first time since Mick's arrival. "We can't truly understand. Mick has to figure this out."

Mick pinned his unnerving stare on Nitis. "Ruby, who the hell is this?" he asked Grandmother in a conversational tone. "*What* is he?" He cocked his head as though trying to understand the man.

"He's an interfering old coot." Grandmother tapped her walking stick to the floor. The cane was a plain one from the drugstore, not her formal one decorated with turquoise and silver. "Following me around, telling us prophecies about our family."

"Not a prophecy," Nitis corrected her, while I tried not to let my jaw drop that Grandmother described Mick as family. "A legend. A tale passed down among the winged creatures. Not a prediction. I only seek to warn you."

"What does his aura tell you, Janet?" Mick asked me without looking away from Nitis.

I tried to tamp down my worry about the egg, Mick, the legend—all things that would prevent me from seeing clearly—and focused on Nitis.

I sensed darkness in the man, but not the shadowy, evil kind. I felt the soft blackness of cool nights that bring peace and starlight. Also, the sable featheriness of a crow, who shook out its plumes and cocked an eye as you went by, as though laughing about the ridiculousness of the world.

"He's …" I hesitated. "Fine."

Nitis flashed me a brief smile. "You flatter me."

"How did you defeat the lightning?" I demanded. Though I didn't sense evil from him, that didn't mean he wasn't powerful and dangerous. "Something attacked our hotel," I told the others when they looked puzzled. Well, everyone but Grandmother. She'd known.

"That was easy." Nitis shrugged. "It wasn't really there."

I blinked. "You mean it was an illusion?"

"Not quite. It could have been deadly, but it was more of a warning. Simple to send off."

"Mick chased it away," I said.

"Mick chased away the dregs," Nitis said. "The source of it would have killed him."

Now I had to worry about what *that* meant.

"One problem at a time," Mick rumbled. "For me, the most pressing question is: What actually happened to Cesnia? It's bothering me enough that I want to visit her lair and see what I can find." He turned to me, his mischievous smile lighting his eyes. "Are you up for a road trip?"

CHAPTER TWELVE

"Can I come?" Gabrielle asked immediately.

"No," Grandmother and I said at the same time.

"Aw, Janet gets to have all the fun." Gabrielle feigned sulking, but I could tell she wasn't truly upset.

"You have a team to coach," Grandmother reminded her. "You don't get to rush off on your responsibilities because something more interesting comes along."

Gabrielle's petulance abruptly vanished. "There's nothing more interesting than my girls. I'd never desert them, don't worry. Besides, flying to a remote island to poke around a cave isn't my idea of a good time. No yummy restaurants."

"You should not take the egg." Grandmother switched her commanding tone to me. "It will not be safe in the deceased Firewalker's lair. Leave it with me."

I widened my eyes. "Will it be safe *here*?" I glanced at the windows that could be broken in a high wind. The entire house always rocked in a storm. Though Mick and I had warded the walls, and Grandmother had woven her ancient magic into them, they'd never withstand a dragon attack. And I still didn't know whether to trust Nitis.

"As safe as anywhere," Grandmother said. "Your hotel would be less safe without you in it."

I hesitated. Mick was ready to go—when he thought of something, he acted on it. No stepping back and waiting for him.

"Can I speak with you outside, Grandmother?" I asked.

Nitis, who knew I wanted to talk about him, sent me a smile.

Grandmother, mouth in a sour pinch, stalked out the front door. Mick followed, but he went to my motorcycle, checking it over, leaving me alone with Grandmother. I wasn't certain which mode of transport Mick would ultimately use to reach Cesnia's lair, but we'd have to be away from our neighbors' prying eyes before he went dragon.

I led Grandmother off the porch and a little way from the house. She exaggerated her limp as she came after me, exuding annoyance, her cane thumping.

"What do you want to talk about?" Grandmother asked when I finally halted. "This is hard on my old bones." She'd been complaining about her old bones since my birth, and very likely before that.

"I can't leave the egg with you when I don't know anything about Nitis," I said. "Is it safe from *him*?"

Grandmother made another of her *humphs*. "Nitis. Is that what he told you his name was? I call him Old Crow. Because he is one."

"I've seen him behind my hotel. With you."

Grandmother shrugged. "I can't help it if he follows me about."

I knew she could prevent him, if she wanted to. No one approached Ruby Begay with anything but the utmost respect, and sometimes fear. Nitis wouldn't have stayed if she hadn't accepted him.

It occurred to me that Grandmother hadn't driven away Nitis because she was lonely. My grandfather had died before I'd been born, and Grandmother had never remarried. She'd never, since I'd known her, given the slightest hint that she wanted another relationship. My grandfather, from all accounts, had been an amazing man, a hard act to best.

But now my father had moved to Gina's house in Farmington. Grandmother's daughters were grown with families of their own, and I was busy with Mick and my hotel. Maybe she simply wanted someone to be with.

I liked the idea of Grandmother having a significant other, but Nitis wasn't a sheep rancher from Chinle. He was a magical being and might be anything from a crow-shaped demon to a god.

"What do you know about him?" I persisted. "Had you met him before, or did he just show up out of the blue?"

Grandmother lifted her cane and tapped me on the chest with its wooden handle. "The young are so certain they have the answers to life, bright, snappy ones. They think we old women are too slow to understand. But remember that the old have seen everything. Trends come and trends go, and the answers to life change, sometimes so much that no one knows the questions anymore. When I was young, people were trying to erase our language, our culture, our very names. But we endured, and here we are, with all this knowledge inside us. The young know nothing about that."

"Yes, Grandmother," I said obediently. "You're right. And I know you always lecture me like this when you want to evade a question."

Grandmother scowled and lowered her cane. "I am trying to say that you should take my word that the Old Crow in there is harmless. At least to me, you, Mick, and the dragon egg."

"Why won't you tell me who he is? Is it because you don't know?"

Grandmother stuck out her lower lip. "I know exactly who and what he is. It is his business, not yours."

Without waiting for my reaction, she turned on her thick heel and stamped back to the house. Her limp seemed to have disappeared.

While I did trust Grandmother, who was able to dominate everyone around her, including Gabrielle, I still wasn't easy about Nitis. He'd told me the lightning he'd brushed away hadn't really existed, and that it had, at the same time. He knew much about me, Mick, and dragons. Nitis had said that "winged kind" communicated, but this was the first I'd heard about it.

I approached Mick, my body heating as always when he turned his amazing smile on me.

"Coyote has your motorcycle," I said. "I think. The mirror showed me he picked up Carl, anyway."

"I know." Mick nodded. "I saw. Coyote won't let anything happen to it." Mostly because Coyote had discovered the wisdom of not pissing Mick off.

"What do you think about Nitis?" I asked. "And leaving the egg here?"

Mick smoothed back a lock of my hair and gave me a lingering kiss. I wished for a moment that Drake had never sought me out, so I could hole up with Mick in oblivion and let the world go on without us.

Mick scanned the horizon, always alert for danger. "Ruby is right that it will not be safe if we take the egg to Cesnia's lair. An enemy might have set a trap there, in case someone brings it back. We could be ambushed or maybe distracted by an attack while an associate steals it away."

Mick thought like a military man—tactics, contingencies. Though he would take off at a moment's notice to check something out, these kinds of thoughts continuously ran through his head.

"Even so, I don't need dragons or whoever to bombard this house with Dad and Gina in it," I said.

"Nitis is powerful. No, I don't know what or who he is, but I can see that much. *I* wouldn't fight him without knowing what I was getting into. Plus, Gabrielle is staying here a few days, isn't she?"

"She has another game tomorrow night." Gabrielle and the team had told me so at lunch.

Mick chuckled. "We're going to have to trust someone with our offspring someday. Think of this as practice for choosing a babysitter."

I grimaced. "Not making me feel better."

Mick patted the motorcycle seat. "Drive or ride?"

Driving meant compensating for Mick's weight behind me, but while I loved riding behind him, he could be wild, especially when he was in a hurry to get somewhere. Mick could heal himself, and me, if we wiped out, but I'd rather skip the pain.

Mick lifted his hand from the seat and rested on the handlebar. "You drive. Be in control."

I shot him a dark look. "Right, because you'd let anyone control you."

Mick caught me as I moved to the bike and pulled me close. "Only those who are the most special to me."

Though everyone in the family must be watching out the front window, Mick slid his hands beneath my hair and drew me up for a spectacular kiss.

I staggered when he released me, catching my balance with the bike. I quickly swung onto the seat, grabbed my helmet and jammed it over my head as though my heart-beat wasn't rocketing.

Mick waved at those in the house and settled himself behind me. He was too large for my bike, but I suspected we wouldn't be riding far.

I warmed as he slid his arms around me. I started up and leaned into the turn to take us down the drive back to the highway.

―――――

MICK DIRECTED ME NORTH, TOWARD THE UTAH BORDER. The Navajo Nation flows past state lines, its large swath encompassing New Mexico, Utah, Arizona, and Colorado. Though Arizona as a state never changes to Daylight Saving Time, the Navajo Nation, to have a consistency within its borders, does. That meant from March to November, my hotel was an hour behind my family at Many Farms, a point Grandmother was certain indicated my bad choice of a place to live.

We rode along the 191, the desert around us vast, empty, and dry. After a time, Mick indicated I should turn west on the 160, heading toward Kayenta and Monument

Valley. Before the monolith buttes came into sight, he directed me onto a small dirt road that led into the folds of Chinle Wash.

Mick showed me where I could park my bike well out of sight of the road. Though I'd ridden this area with Dad all my life, I marveled that Mick knew how to find hidden places better than I did. How he planned to go dragon and fly off into the wide-open spaces with no one seeing him, I didn't know, but Mick could pull off amazing feats.

I wondered, as I helped him conceal the bike behind thick brush near the wash's edge, if he'd been flying this land for centuries. He'd have seen my ancestors living without restrictions, then the coming of European conquerors and the vast changes they'd wrought. Had Mick helped my people survive? Or had he simply observed, as dragons liked to do? I'd have to ask him one day and hope he gave me a straight answer.

"This way," Mick said as he led me along the wash.

A line of water about a foot wide flowed through the bottom of the arroyo. Rains in January and early spring brought relief to this dry land, though it would be arid again soon. Trees adhered to the steep sides of the cut, and grasses and plants burst with brilliant green, a sharp contrast to the red-brown desert above.

Mick moved around a bend to a deep crevice in the little canyon, which was shielded by an overhang, the shadows cool.

Though the land seemed empty, people lived here. Small houses clung to the top of the wash, near the water to utilize it, yet far enough from it not to be swept away by flash floods. It was a guarantee that most of those who dwelled here would know my grandmother, hence Mick's need to stay out of sight.

I didn't comment when he reached into a niche in some rocks and drew out a backpack. Without inhibition, he stripped off his clothes, neatly folding each garment to tuck them into the pack. His motorcycle boots went on top of it all then he zipped up the bag and handed it to me.

I watched him undress with pleasure. Mick was a beautiful man, his movements a joy to observe. He had another tatt across the small of his back, flames that could sometimes glow red hot.

Mick's eyes glittered as he lifted his gaze, enjoying my scrutiny. He shot me a grin then turned and sprinted down the wash, his feet splashing into the water before a shroud of darkness enclosed him.

From that darkness sprang a dragon. Black as night, streaked through with iridescent red, he whirled along the canyon wall and zipped back toward me.

Mick was flying low and fast, keeping below the desert floor, which was a hundred feet above us. How he flattened himself so well, I didn't know, but he arrowed to me, one talon reaching out.

I groaned, clutching the backpack. "Oh, I hate this part."

The dragon's claw wrapped around me and, surprisingly gently, lifted me off my feet. I closed my eyes as we rose, my stomach lurching.

I made the mistake of peeking when Mick launched himself from the canyon and climbed into the empty sky. The ground rushed away faster than I really wanted it to, and I squished my eyes closed again.

Just before I did, I saw a flash of light below, as though someone had bounced a beam through a mirror. It glanced past Mick's wing and faded into the blue.

CHAPTER THIRTEEN

"Mick," I said in alarm. Mick couldn't answer in words while he was dragon, but his growl rumbled back to me. He'd seen the light streaking past.

Had it been the same kind of lightning that had attacked the hotel? Or a chance beam from something else? Or the piece of magic mirror on my motorcycle, pissed off that we'd left it behind?

We hadn't entirely deserted the mirror—I had a shard in my pocket and Mick would have brought one, which would now be in the backpack.

I hunkered down in Mick's talon as the air grew colder. I wore a leather jacket, as we'd been riding across the desert on a cool day, but it wasn't enough for the high altitudes Mick was reaching.

He'd never climb so high that I couldn't breathe. Mick had to breathe as well, so he stayed far below the heights that aircraft was able to reach.

I saw no more streaks of light as we flew. It might have

been a chance flash of a car's mirror or some such, but I didn't truly believe that.

Once Mick leveled out, doing smooth glides instead of climbing, I could peer down between his claws and discover where we were.

To my surprise, we traveled east. I saw the tall mountain that bordered Albuquerque, and beyond that, more desert, which segued into green circles of irrigated fields.

I'd expected us to go west, out over the Pacific, where Mick's lair lay. I'd been to his home a couple of times now. It was a remote island of tropical beauty, though not so remote we couldn't go to Honolulu for a fine dinner or walk beautiful beaches on Kaua'i.

Mick sped along, the farm fields giving way to oil wells pumping at the ends of dirt tracks in west Texas. Next came the greener areas of the Hill Country and east Texas, and the bayous of Louisiana. From there, Mick dove out over water, heading south across the Gulf of Mexico toward the Caribbean beyond.

Dragons liked remote islands—these were dotted all over the world, some inhabited, many not. I hoped Mick wasn't going all the way to Africa—I'd need a break before that—but soon he slowed and began to circle.

An island lay below us, compact and green. A mountain rose from the middle of it, its peak shrouded with rain-clouds, while the rest of the land folded down to pristine, bright beaches. When I'd been younger, I'd thought all Caribbean islands were flat, but I realized that came from watching movies, filmed on cays or in sets. When Mick had taken me on a vacation to St. Lucia, I'd learned that my preconceived notions were wrong.

This island was isolated enough that I couldn't see any

other land from here, nor did I see any hotels or houses dotting it. It likely had escaped development because it was too remote and rugged. There was barely any level land between mountain and sea, which would make any kind of building difficult. There was also the question of what nation had claimed it.

Or possibly it had simply gone unnoticed. If Cesnia had spent centuries here, she might have shrouded it from the world. Dragon magic could do that.

Mick had found it without a problem, but if he'd been friends with Cesnia, she might have shared the secret with him. However Mick knew, we'd arrived.

As he circled the lone mountain once more, I spied a place in the dense forest that had been charred, as though dragon fire had burned it. I didn't have time to observe more before Mick abruptly dove through the dense clouds. I yelped as freezing dew enveloped me.

We came out of the thick fog to a green valley tucked between the sharp sides of vegetation-covered cliffs. Mick glided over this valley a few more times before he landed on a pruned and curiously neat meadow.

Mick opened his talon, steadying me as I staggered onto the lawn. He moved away to morph into his human form.

I was astonished to behold a long, low house made of pale stucco that hugged the edge of the meadow. The abode had wide windows that must give a fabulous view of the mountain on one side, sea on the other. Tall trees and borders of bright flowers framed this lovely home.

"Cesnia lived *here*?" I blurted out.

Mick chuckled, his body warm behind mine. "You think all dragons dwell in caves? Caves are great for storage and keeping others out of your business, but they get a little uncomfortable."

Mick was building a house on his island, which was going to be luxurious when finished, but I'd assumed he was doing this because he was mating with a human. I was grateful to him for providing me a place to sleep, though I'd told him it didn't have to be much.

Now I wondered if he was constructing it to replace whatever home he'd destroyed in one of our adventures a few years back. I didn't want to bring up bad memories, so I didn't comment.

"What exactly are we looking for?" I asked.

Mick gently pried the backpack from me and withdrew his clothes. He didn't have to dress himself on my account, but a thin rain was falling, soaking us thoroughly. The temperature now that we were out of the clouds was warm, but I kept my jacket on to stay dry.

"Any indication of what dragon killed Cesnia," Mick answered. "Also, a hint of what she intended for her egg. I'm hoping she already sang it its name, or that might be up to us."

"Up to us?" I regarded him in alarm while he leisurely pulled on his jeans. "How would I know how to name a dragon? And how to sing those notes?"

"If we need to adopt him as our own—there's a ritual for that—then we'll be able to give him a name. The dragon in the shell already knows it, and sort of tells us what it is. That's the theory anyway."

My alarm didn't ease. "Sounds very mystical and dragon-y."

"I don't understand how it works, myself. Apparently, it's a two-way song between mother and baby dragon."

Whatever happened, it sounded both scary and nice. I remembered my cousins when they were pregnant, talking to their babies before they were born. A similar thing?

"I'm not a dragon," I pointed out.

"And I'm not a mom." Mick's eyes twinkled. "Let's hope she already named him."

"How will we know?" I thought about the prettily decorated egg that I was already worried about. I should call home and make sure everything was all right. I pulled out my cell phone, which remarkably was still in my pocket, intact.

"There will be residuals of the name lingering inside the egg." Mick scanned the clearing and the cliffs above us, always on the lookout for trouble. "Not the name itself, but a note here and there. I might be able to hear it, since I'm a dragon, but you might not. Then again, you possibly could." He studied me in that *what-a-curious-specimen* way he sometimes had.

"Why? Because I know *your* true name?"

Mick shrugged. "You've been exposed to my name and know what it sounds like. You could recognize notes that other humans wouldn't. Also, you have more magic than anyone I've ever met."

"Gabrielle's pretty powerful," I reminded him. "She's nearly kicked my ass several times."

"Not the same." Mick reached for my cell phone and slid it back into my pocket before catching my hands to tug me close.

I became aware that we were entirely alone in this place, and that Mick hadn't bothered to finish dressing. Warmth penetrated my bones, and not just because of the subtropical breezes.

Mick drew me to him, arms holding me steady. I rose on tiptoe to meet his kiss, which heated parts of me that were not already steaming.

I hadn't had much time to be with Mick, between my hotel being consistently full and him flying off to ingratiate himself with my family. It was nice to stand here and kiss without hurry, surrounded by scented yellow and orange flowers. The sound of a hidden waterfall among the cliffs was soothing in the quiet.

Mick's hands went to my hips, his strength fanning excitement through me. He was always gentle—then again, we could get into things that only a dragon and a Stormwalker could handle. We had safety words, but to date had never used them.

Before I could become too hopeful, Mick eased the kiss to a close and rested his forehead against mine. "When we're finished," he whispered.

"Oh, yeah," I said. "It will be great."

I looked forward to Mick and I shutting ourselves into his new house on his island, where we could keep out the world and all the terrifying things trying to kill us. We'd bask in each other there, reveling in our aloneness.

Mick touched my cheek. "You're an amazing woman, Janet."

I wished we weren't on a dire quest and that I wasn't so worried about those I'd left at home. When we had time to celebrate, it would be incandescent.

"You're not so bad, yourself," I said. "So, do we explore the house?"

Mick's eyes flicked to dragon black before resuming their deep blue. "That would be a good place to start. I think her cave is up there." Mick pointed to the top of the cliff. "We'll have to fly."

Oh, goodie. I hoped we found all the information we needed inside the house, so I could keep my feet on the ground for a while.

Mick led the way up the flower-lined walk. I let him, because if there were booby traps to stop intruders, he'd find and disarm them. *I'd* flail over the wire that sent sharp stakes springing out from a concealed crevice, but Mick never would.

We made it to the house without mishap. No traps, Mick told me, which troubled him, I perceived.

The front door wasn't locked, but why would it be? We were on a remote island that didn't have a place to land a boat. Cesnia wouldn't fear any intruder except the dragon kind, only admitting those she'd invited.

We entered the house to find a wide, tile-floored foyer and airy rooms that led one into another. The entire back of the home was open to a terrace, which was like an outdoor room. A round dining table suggested Cesnia could eat a meal out there while enjoying the view down the cliff to the ocean crashing below.

"What happens during a hurricane?" I asked. No windows or doors blocked the way from the outer terrace to the living room. "The rain and wind just come on in?"

"This island is pretty far south and west in the Caribbean Sea," Mick said as he studied paintings that hung on one wall. "Hurricanes mostly sweep from the Atlantic up the eastern islands and north. Also, there's this."

He lifted a remote from the long table under the paintings and clicked a button. I jumped back inside the living room as thick glass walls slid from recessed panels across the terrace's opening. The strong breeze died, as did the bird-song and whisper of wind-stirred plants.

Mick set down the remote. "That will keep out any weather." He moved to study the panels. "Looks like multi-layered glass with air cushions in between. Nice."

I knew he was contemplating installing this kind of sliding door system in our new house.

"Why did Cesnia leave it open?" I asked. "If she'd gone out to fight whoever attacked her, wouldn't she have shut the windows? Even if she didn't worry about burglars, a rainstorm could have come up."

"I don't know." Mick's uneasiness returned. "She must have meant to leave for only a short time. Or else someone came in here and took her away with them. He didn't bother closing anything behind them as he hustled her out."

"I have a hard time believing dragons could be hustled anywhere," I said. "You told me lady dragons are seriously fierce. She'd have put up a struggle, but I see no sign of that here."

I wandered from the living room to a kitchen with long counters, multiple cabinets, and a vast kitchen island with a granite top. Up-to-date appliances as well. I could imagine Elena salivating over this setup.

Beyond the kitchen was another sitting area that contained a large sofa positioned to look out tall windows toward the mountain. Past that was a bedroom that had *me* salivating—huge, comfy bed, massive walk-in closet, and a bathroom with a circular tub in the middle of its tiled floor.

Cesnia hadn't kept many clothes, I saw as I entered the closet, but what hung there were beautiful sleek gowns plus chic casual clothes. Colorful sarongs were folded neatly on a shelf, and even her tatty shorts and T-shirts were enviably pretty. Cesnia had also collected kick-ass shoes to go with the gowns. A dragon who knew how to dress.

"Did she go to many formal dinners?" I asked Mick as I emerged from the closet. "There are no labels in her dresses, which means they were made for her. By famous designers, no doubt."

"Cesnia had many friends in the human world." Mick rested hands on hips as he turned in a slow circle in the middle of the room. "She went out on the town—whatever town—as often as she wanted."

"I'm starting to wish I was a dragon," I said.

The corners of Mick's eyes crinkled. "It's not a bad existence, but I like you the way you are."

"Yes, why have a dragon, when you can have the daughter of a crazed hell goddess who's seriously unstable whenever a storm happens?"

"Exactly."

I flushed as I wandered past him into the bathroom, which was like paradise in marble. A lot of bamboo as well, in benches, towel racks, and little boxes for accessories. A stand of bamboo grew outside the window, which would shade the room from the intense sun when it was out.

I compared this marvel to my tiny bathroom with its white tile and old-fashioned fixtures. Dragons knew how to live.

"No signs of a struggle at all," I told Mick when I came out. "I'd say Cesnia left the house voluntarily and thought she'd be back soon. I'm guessing she went out to meet someone."

"Agreed." Mick had focused his intense gaze on the wall beside the bed. It was an interior wall, opposite the long windows and the perfect view. "But friend or foe? Her killer? Or someone she thought would help her?"

I closed my eyes. I'd solved puzzles in the past for people who'd come to me looking for missing persons or wanting to know why their apartment was haunted. I could see auras both of people and of events. Ghosts are really the taint of a terrible act clinging to a place, not the shade of a deceased person. Some humans are sensitive to such things without realizing it, and they interpret the feelings as a haunting.

I searched for the auras in this room and quickly found a few. Cesnia's was most prevalent, of course—gold, shot through with sable, blue, and flecks of white. Beautiful, matching the colors present in her house.

The darkness of Drake lingered here, and I felt a frisson of their passion. Drake kept himself in tight control at all times, but that didn't mean he didn't have emotions, only that he didn't like to share them.

Drake had shared his emotions in this room, that was for certain. I didn't find any lingering fear, only desire and happiness.

I perceived the residual of Titus's aura as well, his more multi-hued and changing, like his eyes. His presence wasn't as prevalent. Drake had been here more often.

I then sensed the aura of the egg, gold and greeny-white like the jade of its shell. I experienced Cesnia's joy as she tended it, and then the tiny dragon's bewilderment at Cesnia's sudden absence.

Tears welled in my eyes. I sensed Drake's dark aura again, sliding in, and then he and the egg were gone.

I opened my eyes to find Mick watching me in worry. "You all right?" he asked softly.

"Yeah." I wiped my cheeks. "Nothing violent happened here. Cesnia was thrilled with the kid." I balled my hand. "I really want a talk with whoever ended that elation."

"Me too." Mick's tone was grim. "I found something I want to explore. Come with me? There's a bigger rainstorm on its way, so if you don't want to risk it, I'll go myself."

Now that he'd mentioned it, I felt the light rain intensify. The long-leafed trees outside the window bent with growing wind, and the clouds we'd flown through thickened, blotting out all light. Not a hurricane or even a thunderstorm was on its way, but a good, heavy tropical deluge.

"You want me to stand here playing with the rain while you disappear who knows where?" I asked in mock incredulity. "Waiting and worrying about you in the middle of a storm? That will not go well."

Mick sent me a smile. "I wanted to give you the choice."

"I choose to come with you. Where are we going?"

Mick opened a drawer in one of the nightstands. He fished inside it then made a noise of satisfaction when he pulled out another remote.

He clicked it, and the entire wall behind the bed dissolved. No sliding glass this time. It simply vanished.

"We're going there." Mick gestured to the darkness behind the bed. Without waiting for me to respond, he strode inside and was instantly lost in the shadows.

CHAPTER FOURTEEN

I hesitated for about three seconds before I plunged after Mick, locating him by bumping into his back.

Mick slowed, and I caught hold of his waistband and let him tow me along. Who knew how large the passageway would be, or when the floor would drop out from under us? Mick could react to those dangers more quickly than I could.

I did not like underground spaces, but I seemed to find myself constantly inside them. In the same adventure when Mick's lair had been destroyed, I'd been dropped into a sinkhole that had nearly swallowed me. I'd had to fight a battle with Mick himself at the bottom of that sinkhole. That was a few months after some gods had sealed me into a mountain so they could have a talk with me.

Nope, underground and me did not get along.

"Any chance of a light?" I asked into the inky darkness.

"Don't want to risk it yet. I can see fine."

Good for him. He meant that he didn't want to perform any magic that might awaken, or upset, whatever was possibly lurking in the darkness. The small amount of magic I could do to make a light was also out. I'd have to keep it tiny, and now that I sensed heavy rains begin outside, I might not be able to contain it. I was glad we'd shut the terrace door so the beautiful living room wouldn't be ruined.

"What happens to the lair, now that Cesnia's gone?" I asked in a murmur as we inched our way forward. "The kid inherits it?"

"If he wants to. He might obliterate it, to guard his mother's secrets."

It would be a shame to destroy this lovely house, but dragons valued privacy more than they did material objects.

"And if he decides to never come back here?" I asked.

"Then we, or Drake, will have to destroy it for her. Dragons who raid another's lair can amass too much power. Also, it's a desecration for another dragon who isn't the heir to move in."

"Too bad. It's a sweet house."

"Junior might want it, when he grows up. It would save him the trouble of building a new lair from scratch. Of course, many kids want the exact opposite of what their parents had."

"Like me," I said. "What about you? Did you take over your parents' lair, or decide to go your own way?"

Mick was silent for a couple of heartbeats before he answered. "My parents were dead before I hatched. I was raised by three other dragons, who are likewise gone now."

I stopped in my tracks. Mick, pulled back by my hold on his jeans, turned to me.

"A dragon born without sire or dam," I said, stunned.

"Like in the legend Nitis told us about. That means *you*. Have you slayed a dragon lord?"

Mick was quiet for so long, I almost brought up a ball of white magic so I could see his expression. Only my caution, born of horrific experiences, made me wait in the dark.

"Yes," he answered.

"Shit, Mick." I thought the ground rocked, but no, it was still solid.

"It was a long time ago."

"More of your past you don't feel like revealing?" I demanded. "When you know every iota of mine?"

The unevenness in our knowledge of each other had always bugged me, though I'd come to understand that a dragon telling you casually how he was doing on any particular day was a huge expression of trust for them.

"A *very* long time ago," Mick said. "When I first came of age. I was arrogant, selfish, and sure I was right about everything."

A chill wove around me. "You were a teenaged boy, in other words."

"The equivalent of a human adolescent stepping out into the world before he's ready." Mick shifted his stance, as though he didn't relish the tale. "The dragon lord at the time was a cold-hearted shit who was wreaking havoc on innocents, simply because he could. He was in danger of exposing us all when we preferred humans to be ignorant of us. I decided to save the dragon world, and incidentally the humans he was hurting."

I relaxed slightly. "Okay, I don't blame you for going after him. But you thought you could best a dragon lord?

Wait, *you* were made one because you won this huge battle. Is this the one you're talking about?"

"No, that came much later. Dragon lords aren't pushovers, which is why the other dragons hadn't stopped him. I decided they were all wimps and that I could do better." He breathed a short laugh, deriding the conceited youth he'd been.

"But you were able to kill him."

"Barely. I didn't realize what I was up against until we were well into the fight. None of the other dragons would help me—they figured that if the dragon lord won, they'd be toast if he knew they'd assisted. Plus, I'd be one pesky young dragon they no longer had to deal with. Natural selection, if you will. The dragon lord very nearly killed me. You are looking at one lucky, stupid-ass dragon. Or you would be if it wasn't pitch dark."

My throat went dry as I tried not to picture the immense violence the battle would have entailed, not to mention how close I'd come to never meeting Mick.

"I'd say it was more than luck," I told him shakily. "You must have been a better fighter than you realized."

"Maybe." Mick was always modest about how badass he was, apparently very different from the youth he'd been. "I didn't tell you before, because it's embarrassing. I was a complete idiot to go up against him, though I learned a lot during that fight. However, the other dragons didn't pat me on the back and hand me a coronet for ridding us of a dangerous dragon. They backed off and gave me space. Waiting to see if I'd become drunk with power and decide to take out more dragons for the hell of it. If I had, they'd have ganged up to stop me."

"Did you become drunk with power?" I asked, keeping my question light.

"Shit, no. I could barely move. Took me decades to recover. The dragon lord had been a truly bad guy, and that battle beat the stuffing out of me. I was very polite to other dragons for a long time. I didn't want another fight until I got over the terror of that one."

I had a hard time envisioning Mick cowering in fear, barely speaking to anyone, but I imagine the battle had given him the first taste of his own mortality.

"Did you know about the legend?" I asked. "Is that why you thought you could best the dragon lord?"

"No, I'd never heard of it." Mick's regret for the past fled, and his present curiosity returned. "Nitis telling you is the first time I've become aware of it. Keep in mind he might be making it up for reasons of his own."

"Well, it came true, didn't it? A dragon born without sire or dam slayed a dragon lord. I'm really sorry about that, by the way. Losing your parents." While I'd had a weird upbringing, my dad had always been a pillar of strength beside me. My heart went out to Mick, a child on his own, never knowing who was on his side.

"Thank you." Warmth infused his answer. "It was difficult for me to understand what I'd lost at the time, though I grew to realize it later." Mick paused. "It is interesting that the legend seems to have come true in the past."

"Interesting, he says." I sighed in exasperation. "A revelation that could kill him in the future, and he finds it *interesting*."

Mick chuckled. "Not everyone clutches their face and screams when something unnerving is revealed. I'd have rubbed my skin off years ago if I did."

I couldn't laugh. I'd had too many crazy revelations for one lifetime. "Like you said, Nitis could be making it up."

"He could be. Why he would, is the mystery."

Mick turned around again, done with the conversation and ready to move on. I grabbed his waistband as before. I did *not* want to get lost in here.

Mick kept his pace slow, probably for my sake. As frustrating as he could be, I had to acknowledge that he always looked out for me.

After a while of silence, Mick stopped again. "I don't sense anything in here but us. Shield your eyes. I'm making a light."

I turned my back and closed my eyes tightly, knowing a sudden illumination after a long time of darkness would be painful. A flare reddened my lids as a ball of dragon fire went up.

I waited until the glow softened before I blinked open my eyes. I let them adjust and then I looked around.

And gasped.

Mick's fireball illuminated a place of stunning beauty. A cavern soared above us to a ceiling dripping with stalagmites, which appeared tiny in the distance. The walls of the massive cave glittered red, green, blue, amber, pink, and purple, as though every kind of gem in the world had been embedded in its stone.

Not far ahead of us lay a flat pool of water that shimmered under the dragon fire. Its clear surface revealed more jewel-like rocks on its bottom.

"Are these real?" I asked. "The gemstones? Or are they just different colors of quartz?"

Quartz could manifest in a rainbow of hues. Granite also glittered with multiple shades, because it was made up of quartz and feldspar, sometimes with mica thrown in. I'd learned this from my friend Jamison, who was a sculptor and knew much about the bones of the earth he dug out to make his art. He always thanked the earth for letting him borrow a bit of it.

"Some are quartz," Mick confirmed. "But also diamonds, amber, sapphires, emeralds."

"Diamonds?" My eyes widened as I caught their sparkle. "And no one has blasted their way in here to mine them all away?"

Mick scanned the cave in reverence. "These probably didn't occur naturally here. Dragons collect, remember? Cesnia created this place."

"So, *this* is her lair? I thought you said it was high in the cliffs."

"There's a cave there, yes. That's the lair she'd have let other dragons see. Drake, for instance. Titus. Any of her lovers. This one was special. Private."

"If it's so private, how did you know it was here?" I was as curious as Mick about all of this, but I also felt awe, worry, and confusion.

"I didn't. When I looked around her bedroom, I realized the wall behind her bed was there and not there at the same time. She created that illusion. Since Cesnia is gone, her magic is weakening and the illusion fading, just enough for me to sense it. The remote control was a nice touch," he finished in appreciation.

"Her personal space," I said. "Her woman-cave."

Mick grinned. "I think it's called a she-shed."

"Hey, women can have caves too." Not that I had much personal space of my own—Grandmother had raised me to believe that sharing space was more important than isolating yourself.

"I suppose," Mick conceded. "And men can have he-sheds."

I wanted to laugh. "We're getting ridiculous."

Mick slid his arm around my waist. "I like being ridiculous with you."

He melted me in the best way, I thought as I sank into his side. If we continued to find nothing more ominous on this island than Cesnia's beautiful treasures, perhaps we could take a little time for ourselves before we went back home.

Almost as soon as the thought formed, Mick's pocket vibrated. Not from his phone. I suppressed a groan of annoyance as a small voice issued from the region of Mick's hip.

"Hey, let me see what's out there. I'm sensing something *bad*, sugars."

Mick immediately pulled a chamois bag from his pocket and loosened its drawstring. He drew out his shard of magic mirror and flashed it around the cave. "What's up?" he asked it.

The mirror was a shit, but it was also canny and perceptive. If it said there was a problem, then there was.

"Wow," it sang. "This place is awesome. But there's something on the other side of the pool. Something seriously dangerous. How about you leave me here to look at the pretty rocks while you go check it out?"

"Not a chance," Mick said, and headed at once for the silvery sheet of water.

CHAPTER FIFTEEN

I felt the intensity of the rainstorm outside increase as I followed Mick around the clear pool to the far side of the cavern. Moisture beaded on my forehead, and water began to drip from my fingers.

The walls beyond the pool were even more loaded with gems, facets glittering under Mick's small fireball. I wondered if Cesnia had taken some of the jewels from these walls to decorate the egg, singing softly to it as she worked.

As the thought went through my head, I swore I heard a whisper of music, a clear note echoing from the emeralds around me.

"Mick," I called.

His name resounded through the room, but he didn't turn.

Mick had focused on an outcropping of rock beyond the pool, one that jutted raggedly from the cavern floor. I heard the thin wail of the mirror as Mick neared it.

"Don't take me any closer, pleeeeze!"

Mick moved relentlessly onward. His lack of fear of most things meant he marched right in where others, me included, dared not tread.

When Mick reached the outcropping, I swore it moved. The sound of pebble clicking on pebble reached me, dying into silence.

Mick halted to study the rock, but did he run away, like a sensible dragon? No, he calmly observed as the outcrop elongated upward, its sides squeezing to compensate for its changing mass.

The column of rock soon towered over Mick, becoming a six-inch diameter stalagmite growing from the floor. It began to arch down toward him, the top of it opening like a maw.

Mick tilted his head back to watch, the dragon tatts on his arms writhing in anticipation. He had fire to fight with, and he could turn dragon and whack the rock to bits, but I had a very, very bad feeling about this.

Did I run away, like a sensible Stormwalker? No, I hurtled forward, my hands bunched into fists that filled with water at every step.

The rainstorm hit the island with a slap. I couldn't see it or hear it deep inside the earth, but I felt it with clarity. Outside, the vegetation bent, the earth turned to black mud, and rain struck Cesnia's windows like grains of sand. The storm found me, rendering my body a living column of water.

The rock dove for Mick. He raised his hands, throwing a barrier of fire between him and it …

Which the entity plowed right through. I screamed as the column of rock went for Mick, that mouthlike point ready to devour him.

Mick ducked just before the mouth would have hit him, tossing out more fire as he scrambled out of its way. The entity, with no sound but the grating of rock on rock, gathered itself for another strike.

I reached Mick as he finally spun to run. "No, Janet," he shouted as I raced past him.

The rock thing was far more frightening up close. It didn't bother taking on any kind of human form—why should it? It raised itself again, mouth open as it fixed on Mick, ignoring me completely.

The boulders that composed the entity were huge, even when compressed. I saw sandstone entwined with basalt and granite. I didn't know the geologic composition of Caribbean islands—I assumed they were volcanic, like Mick's place in the Pacific. Dragons like volcanoes. The rock thing, though, looked as though it had clumped itself together from various sources.

Mick was shedding his jeans, ready to go dragon. He'd dropped the mirror, which was keening somewhere in the dark.

The rock creature struck before Mick could change to his super-strong beast.

I lunged between the entity and Mick, a very scary place to be. I lifted my dripping fingers.

"Rain," I whispered.

Water gushed forth from my hands, my mouth, my arms. It rocketed to the entity like the most forceful fire-hose, striking the being across its middle. I directed my hands to its maw, narrowing the stream of water to a hard jet, right into the opening.

The entity didn't scream. That would take lungs and

vocal cords, and this thing was nothing but an animated pile of stone.

It shuddered and shivered under my onslaught, bits of rock splintering off to fall to the cave floor.

Cathedrals are cleaned by blasting them with water, which grinds away the dirt but also layers of the stone if it isn't done carefully. I didn't take any care with the being trying to eat Mick. I would erode it to nothing and walk away.

The magic flowing through me lifted me a few feet from the floor. My hair and clothes were soaked, and water poured from my boots.

Rainstorms are the worst to recover from. Thunderstorms fill me with crackling lightning, dust storms let me dance on the spiraling drafts, but rainstorms waterlog me until I can't move, and ruin my clothes too.

Because rain is relentless. I beat on the stones with it, gleefully watching the entity shudder and crumble under my onslaught.

My burst of storm magic stirred the Beneath powers inside me as well. I'd promised not to use them to kill, but I couldn't believe Coyote would hold me to that against a supernatural rock creature that tried to creak toward Mick, even while I battered it.

Mick took advantage of the distraction to change to dragon. The cavern was plenty big enough for him, having been fashioned by a dragon as her retreat. He didn't have the space to launch a massive attack from above, but he barreled at the entity, fire spewing.

His fire bounced off the rock creature as though it had coated itself with flame retardant. Dragon fire hit the water jets that poured out of me and filled the cavern with steam.

Mick flapped past, amazement in his large dragon eye. He whirled to come at the rock again, intending to simply knock it apart with his impact.

The creature flowed abruptly downward the instant before Mick hit it. It spread itself across the cavern floor, reforming as Mick hurtled onward. The dragon roared in frustration.

I didn't wait for the rock being to reform. I floated above the floor and blasted its boulders with water laced with Beneath magic.

At the same time, I reached down to lift the shard of mirror in my watery grip. The mirror howled in protest, but I directed my combined magic into it, reflecting a double dose of power into the spreading rocks.

There was a sound like masonry imploding. A thousand shards of rock flew upward then angled down at me as though intending to go through me like bullets.

The rainstorm in me slapped the shards away. I skewered the individual pieces with the white hot Beneath magic, magnified by the mirror.

Now I did hear a scream, a psychic one, as the pebbles the entity had been disintegrated to dust. I kept burning and flooding even the dust, not wanting one speck to adhere to another and reform the creature.

The thing gave one last screech in my head and then vanished altogether.

Dust stirred at my feet. I held myself ready, but the particles shimmered and then disappeared. Whether the creature had died completely or had been pulled back to wherever it had come from, I couldn't say.

I found myself doubling over, hands on my knees as I gasped for breath on the drenched cavern floor. Mick circled above me, the hot gust from his wings barely warming me. The cave's walls glowed with the inner fire of the gems, the mirror catching the light and throwing spangled facets over my face.

Mick landed, his form shrouded in darkness before he emerged from it, tall and strong.

Water continued to pour from me, the rain above the cavern not abating. I could barely move in my soaked clothes, my hair a sopping mess down my back.

I yanked off my clothes, letting them land in a wet thunk on the ground. I turned, spread my arms, and dove into the gleaming pool.

I was water. I glided across the pond, the liquid within me and without combining into one. No need to hold my breath—I existed without oxygen. The currents I created brushed my skin, and I floated with them.

More rain pounded down outside, and I embraced it.

A crash sounded beside me, a heavy weight pushing aside water. Hard hands grabbed me, and I shouted in fury. I was dragged upward, painfully, out of the beautiful water and back to the cold, hard surface of the cavern floor.

I struggled, but Mick held me down, his face set. I drew a breath to berate him for taking me out of my beautiful haven, and choked.

I coughed and coughed, my need for air kicking me in the gut. Water poured from my mouth and nose, making me panic.

Mick laid me facedown, hard hands on my back to squash all the water out of me. I belched it up, which hurt like hell, but finally I drew a blissful, if grating, breath.

"I'm okay," I croaked when Mick kept pressing. "I'm okay."

I wasn't, but I needed Mick to stop crushing me. He was strong.

Mick lifted away and gathered me to him on his lap. We were both naked, which was fine with me. His skin was warm, while mine was brutally cold.

Mick cradled me close. Fire laced his fingers but didn't burn. He was drawing off the extra energy of my storm magic before it shattered me.

He'd done a similar thing the first night I'd met him, a sign that he was the only one for me. Took my brain a little while longer to figure that out, but an instinctive part of me had bonded with him that night.

Little by little, under his touch, I calmed. The rain outside continued, but it no longer consumed me.

"Thank you," I whispered.

For answer Mick kissed me. I could breathe now, thank the gods, and I kissed him back with deep pleasure.

Our combined magics were a powerful aphrodisiac. Mick laid me down, and we entwined in a more physical way. He'd somehow managed to land me on a pile of his clothes, cushioning my back from the hard rock.

For a time, we gloried in each other, thankful we'd survived another dangerous encounter. Thankful we were together.

"Aw, Mick, honey, why'd you drop me face-down?" the mirror asked fretfully. "I can't see *anything*."

I knew Mick had done *that* deliberately too.

————

"What was it?" I asked a long time later. I lay on my

side against Mick, tracing gentle designs on his chest. "That rock thing? Did I kill it?"

"I don't know, and I don't know." Mick smoothed my still-damp hair. "It didn't give a shit about anything *I* threw at it, that's for sure. I am happy you were with me."

I gazed into his eyes, which were so very blue. "Has the big, bad dragon finally found something to be afraid of?"

Mick sent me a puzzled glance. "I'm afraid of a lot of things. Pissing off your grandmother, upsetting your dad. You getting hurt. But yeah, when it shrugged off my fire, that unnerved me. I hit it full blast because I feared it would turn on you."

He had no idea how much his answers made me want to kiss and hold him. "So, we've figured out it's impervious to dragon fire. Also good at evading you barging into it." I drummed my fingers on his chest. "But Stormwalker and Beneath magic bested it or drove it away. I don't know which one did the trick—I probably needed the combination."

Mick's voice rumbled in his chest. "You were amazing."

His admiration scared me all over again. Mick believing in me was why I was still alive, and why I was able to better balance the roiling magics inside me. If I'd tried what I had today a few years ago, I'd have blown up the cave, the house, or maybe the whole island.

"Do you think that thing killed Cesnia?" I asked, growing somber.

"Again, no idea." Mick didn't like not having answers. "Drake found her, you say?"

I replayed my conversation with Drake in my head. "He didn't say that specifically, only that she was dead. I wonder if Titus found her instead. He was certainly upset. For Titus, I mean."

"We will have to ask them if they encountered this thing, plus find out what it was. A manifestation from a powerful mage? Or was it a creature with its own volition?"

I shivered. Something that could kill dragons with impunity put the egg in great peril. I hoped Grandmother, Nitis, and Gabrielle would be able to withstand something like that, and that Mick and I coming here had drawn attention away from Grandmother's house.

"Either way, not good," I said. "It was very different from the lightning mesh that attacked my hotel. Do we have one enemy using various methods? Or many different enemies?" Neither answer appealed to me.

"Mmm." Mick rested one hand behind his head, as comfortable as if he lay in the super-soft bed in Cesnia's house. "Only one would be easier to fight."

So far, nothing had been easy. "Nitis told me he didn't have much trouble driving off the lightning at the hotel because it was an like an illusion. But I felt it. Nash sucked away some of the shock, but it struck his grandfather and me. If Nash hadn't been there, I'm pretty sure we wouldn't be alive to talk about it."

"Which means I'm grateful to Jones for existing." Mick caught my hand and squeezed it. "I chased that lightning off, but I couldn't affect it. It left because it wanted to."

I snuggled down on Mick's shoulder, stealing a moment of stillness. "I prefer dealing with one enemy at a time."

"So do I. All of this bugs me. Nothing made of earth magic should be able to withstand a dragon. We are the most powerful earth-magic creatures alive."

I pressed a kiss to his neck. "Who don't have huge egos, or anything."

Mick didn't smile. "It has nothing to do with ego. It's a simple fact."

"Of course." I touched another light kiss to his damp skin. "You're right that whatever is causing this is an earth-magic entity. I didn't have any sense of Beneath from the lightning or from the rock. Or god magic, either."

"What about the rock thing's aura?" Mick asked. "Any hint of someone else controlling it?"

"I didn't have time for a precise read. Too busy being terrified." I forced my thoughts back over the fight, my pulse fluttering with vestiges of fear. "I didn't sense anyone else. When a creature is made or controlled, there's another aura superimposed on it. I didn't feel that."

"Great. An earth-magic creature I've never encountered who can best dragons, acting on its own volition." Mick let out a growl. "Much as I hate to say it, I need to call a meeting of the dragon council."

I groaned and slumped against him, my arm over my face. "Just when I thought this day couldn't get any worse …"

———

MICK AT LEAST CONCEDED TO LET ME SLEEP IN CESNIA'S comfortable abode overnight.

When we returned to the house, we sealed up the wall behind her bed to keep anyone else from stumbling across her secret lair. I then seeped Beneath magic into the wall in case any other earth-magic creatures were in there ready to come out after Mick. That bit of magic would also alert me to any dragons trying to break in.

Mick had scraped up the ash from where I'd burned the rock creature and put it into a little vial he happened to have with him. My dragon biker boyfriend was nerdy about science things.

I called Grandmother as soon as we were done, to make sure all was well. She told me everything was quiet, grumpily, as though annoyed I didn't trust her to guard the egg. I could hear the others conversing in the room behind her before I hung up, the camaraderie pulling at me. I needed a long visit home. But at least the egg was fine for now.

We didn't feel right sleeping in Cesnia's bed, but we found a guest room that turned out to be very comfy. I imagined Titus stretching out on the mattress in here and making himself at home. Drake had probably sat up all night analyzing why he'd come and how he felt about it.

I pictured them in the guest room, because from Mick's descriptions of lady dragons, they weren't ones for sleeping with their lovers. Cesnia might have been different, but she would have been cautious about letting down her guard.

All the rooms in the house were clean and pristine. This made me wonder who did the housework. At the dragon compound, the head dragons had a host of human lackeys devoted to them. Did Cesnia? And where were all these people?

Despite the thoughts spinning in my head, I fell asleep quickly and slept hard. The rainstorm had abated, becoming a soothing patter of rain outside the windows. Mick passed out with me for a time, but I woke alone.

I wasn't alarmed when I didn't find Mick beside me in

the morning light, because I heard him clanking pots and pans in the kitchen. The appealing aroma of coffee and sizzling bacon floated to me.

"Can the house on your island be like this?" I asked as I wandered into the massive kitchen, dressed but my hair still a mess.

Mick glanced at me from the stove. What's hotter than a gorgeous man cooking you breakfast?

"If that's what you want, sure."

"What do *you* want?" I pushed tangles from my eyes. I needed a shower, but my willingness to drown myself yesterday in the cave made me wary of jumping into the tub.

Mick considered my question with all the seriousness of a debate on world peace. "I want us to be content, wherever we are, whatever house we live in. I want you to be happy. And me to be happy right alongside you."

He said this in a warm rumble, without much force, but I heard the sincerity in his answer. Also, the simplicity. Dragons lived complicated lives, as much as they protested they didn't.

Mick wanted happiness, for both of us together. That was all.

"You constantly remind me why I'm in love with you," I said.

His brows rose. "Just answering you honestly."

"And there too." I went to him and slid my arms around him from behind. "You did it again."

Mick's body vibrated with his laughter. "I'm glad it's so easy."

"I'd drag you back to bed and show you how much I

love you, but I'm really hungry. Storm hangover does that to me."

Mick removed the hot pan from the burner and shut off the stove before he turned and lifted me into his strong arms. "I always remember why I'm in love with *you*," he said.

———

THE BREAKFAST HAD GROWN COLD BY THE TIME WE GOT back to it. Mick rewarmed the eggs and bacon, and I devoured everything on my plate, doubly hungry after our quick session on a kitchen chair.

As I enjoyed the delicious repast, Mick told me he'd contacted Bancroft at the dragon compound and filled him in on what happened. The council would be waiting for us, Mick said, which curbed my appetite a little.

After I finished breakfast, I made myself shower— alone, or we'd never get out of there. I worried that my residual Stormwalker magic would make me try to become one with the water again, but apparently, I'd returned to my normal self. I washed up as I always did, with no urge to meld with the water.

Afterward, I tidied up the soap I'd dripped on the glass shower walls and put the used towels in a hamper.

I wondered if anyone would come now to look after the place. I'd have to find that out, so I could keep it nice for Junior. Cesnia would want that, I'd think.

We shut up the house, Mick making sure all was secure against the next storm. I put on my jacket, though it was warm here, and closed my eyes, bracing for the chilly and motion sickness-inducing flight to New Mexico.

Mick carried me as gently as he could and flew without too much bobbing around. There's only so much a dragon can do, though, when he has to flap massive wings plus stay out of sight of passing planes and ground control.

That meant a lot of flying inside clouds. Clouds look beautiful and puffy when you see them up in the blue sky, but they are soggy and cold on the inside. After my session on the island, I was thoroughly tired of being coated with water.

In midafternoon, Mick circled over Santa Fe before coming to rest outside a large house built on a high cliff. Once Mick morphed to human outside the large Spanish-style front door, he quickly put on the clothes I'd carried for him in the backpack and donned his motorcycle boots.

The dragons inside must know we were here, but they wouldn't come out and greet us like friends or welcome visitors. We were neither.

Once he'd finished dressing, Mick smoothed his unsmoothable hair, stepped closer to the intricately carved wooden door, and pushed the doorbell.

The door opened almost instantly, but the dragon who appeared on the doorstep took me by surprise. Why *he* was answering, instead of one of the many servants I had no idea.

"Micky!" Colby roared. "How are you, my friend? Janet!" He grabbed me and spun me off my feet in a hug. I'd seen Colby a month ago, when I'd gone to Las Vegas to visit Gabrielle, but he always acted like we hadn't been in touch in years.

Colby set me down and turned to Mick. "You're late," he stated. "Bancroft is about to shit a brick. Something I really don't want to see. So, let's get to the meeting, shall we?"

CHAPTER SIXTEEN

The dragon compound was as I remembered it—a lush stucco and brick house built around a central courtyard that held thick trees and a riot of spring flowers. A tiled corridor ran alongside a row of French windows that led to the garden.

Side passages turned here and there off the main corridor, with niches holding narrow staircases that twisted intriguingly out of sight.

The dragon compound was beautiful and quietly opulent, but I was never easy inside it. The house held too many secrets and too many rooms where a person could be confined. I'd learned both facts the hard way.

There was no sign of the human lackeys who offered a variety of services to guests of dragons as Colby led us through empty halls to a large room in the rear of the house.

This chamber was built right above the cliff, giving a beautiful view of the canyon below and the city of Santa Fe on the other side. Dragons knew how to pick stunning locations.

Equally stunning was the long, polished cedar table, around which the dragons had gathered. The chairs were exquisitely carved, with seats embroidered in colorful geometric designs reminiscent of the art of local Pueblo peoples.

All three of the dragon council occupied the head of the table. Farrell sat in the middle, with Aine, a female dragon with snow-white hair, on his right, and Bancroft, his hair buzzed short, his eyes black-dark, on his left. I could feel Bancroft, who lived in this compound by himself, bristling at being shunted to third place. But Farrell was head of the Council, and Aine outranked Bancroft.

The two men, Farrell with threads of gray in his dark hair, wore impeccably tailored suits, while Aine sported a flowing white garment embroidered with silver curlicued designs. When I'd first seen Aine—at Mick's trial—she'd been naked, with tattoos of the same delicate patterns on her ice-white skin.

Also present were Drake, his face carefully expression-less, and Titus, nattily dressed, as usual.

The five dragons looked up sharply as Mick and I entered, me windblown and exhausted, Mick cool and casual.

Colby gestured at us with a wave of his arm, his intri-cate tattoos flashing in the sunlight. "They're here," he announced. "Finally."

"Had to avoid a lot of air traffic around Houston," Mick said in apology. "Thank you all for coming."

Farrell opened his mouth, probably to admonish Mick

and me for anything he could think of, but Bancroft cut him off.

"We know why you want to consult us," Bancroft announced.

"Well, yeah," Colby said. He plopped into a chair at the foot of the table and stretched out his legs, crossing one motorcycle boot over the other. "Mick called *you* and told you what happened."

"I meant that we know what caused the phenomenon he encountered," Bancroft said stiffly.

Drake had seated himself near the middle of the table, equidistant from Colby and the Council members. He'd quit working for the Council, but he wasn't quite the rebel Colby was … yet.

Titus, across from Drake, appeared the least concerned of all. He watched us coolly, his eyes, at the moment, a golden-yellow.

"Fill me in." Mick moved easily to a place two up from Drake, scraped out the chair and sat down. He rested his arms on the table and stared at the Council without blinking.

I slid in next to Colby. "Thanks for being here," I whispered.

"Hey, this sort of shit scares the daylights out of me," Colby murmured back. "I need to know how to fight this, too."

Aine eyed him coldly. Dragons had great hearing. "They are referred to as Phantomwalkers," she said in answer to Mick.

"Phantoms like ghosts?" Colby scoffed. "Those aren't real. Right, Janet?" He fixed me with brown eyes that pleaded for me to back him up.

"Not the way humans think of them," I confirmed. "Auras, yes. Actual haunting spirits, no."

"I said they are *referred* to as that," Aine informed us in her chilly way. "Phantomwalker is shorthand for a complex set of beings who were born at the same time as dragons were created. Their goal for millennia has been the elimination of all dragons."

The room was silent as all those not on the council absorbed this.

"Well, shit," Colby said with feeling. "And here I *liked* thinking I was invincible."

"I've heard of them," Mick said without surprise. "Stories to scare children. Aren't they supposed to be dragons who were incomplete?"

"Incomplete?" I asked in bewilderment. "Incomplete, how?"

"I have heard rumor of them myself," Drake broke in. "Dragons were created from magma, when volcanoes were active in most parts of the world. According to the tales, our gods formed several different sorts of creatures, but decided dragons were the best of them. But some of these creatures were only half-formed. Either the magma ceased flowing, or cooled too fast, or the beings weren't molded correctly. No one knows for certain."

"They didn't die," Aine said. "They still exist, have for millennia, and they have developed a hatred for dragons. Envious of our power, they decided to band together and end us."

I shivered as I listened, but things didn't add up. If they'd been working together to eradicate dragons, why were we just hearing about this? Why didn't Colby know about them, and why had Mick and Drake only heard children's tales?

"That rock creature that attacked Mick was one of them?" I asked.

"From what Micalerianicum told us on the phone, yes," Aine answered. "It was a weaker example."

Weaker? Shit.

Mick produced his vial of ash. "I brought its remains, if you want to study them. Don't worry," he added as the dragons around the table drew back. "It's quite dead. Janet saw to that."

I saw Bancroft, Aine, and Farrell flinch at Mick's reminder of how powerful my magic could be.

"What good will studying a bunch of ash do?" Colby demanded. His face held a sheen of perspiration.

"Might give us some idea of its composition," Mick said. "Besides magma, I mean. A clue about how to defeat its kind."

"Why are they here now?" Colby asked, echoing my thoughts. "I've never heard of these guys until today, but suddenly they're attacking Micky and following him and Janet around."

"Did they kill Cesnia?" Titus asked before anyone could answer Colby. His voice held a cold and deep rage.

"It's possible," Mick said, his reply gentle.

Drake and Titus exchanged a determined glance, two rivals who could unite in their grief at Cesnia's death. I felt sorry for the Phantomwalker who got in their way.

However, I thought knew exactly why these things had suddenly shown up. I caught Drake's eye. He'd told me Bancroft would want Cesnia's egg. I didn't want to blurt out my theory if the dragon council was still in the dark about that.

Drake gave me a sad nod. "Go ahead and say it, Janet. They know."

The three dragons at the head of the table rested their cold gazes on me, mouths set in dislike. Colby, Drake, and Mick stared at me too. Titus, on the other hand, gazed out the window, as though he didn't want to be here anymore.

"The Phantomwalkers want Cesnia's egg," I said.

The dragon council was silent while I stated the obvious, but Colby regarded me in shock. "Cesnia's *egg*? Holeeee shit."

Bancroft gave Colby a slow nod. "Cesnialangus decided to breed," he said with cool disapproval. "Dragon hatchlings are few and far between. The Phantomwalkers must want to stop us from having any more young."

"I think there's more to it than that," I said. "There's also a legend that an orphan dragon will grow up to slay a dragon lord. The only dragon lord I'm aware of is Mick, who doesn't seem worried about it." I paused to shoot a glare at my boyfriend, who regarded me stolidly. "I think they'd more want to control a dragon with that kind of power than kill it. Sounds like Junior will be pretty powerful. Use a dragon to destroy dragons?"

While Bancroft and Farrell watched me in disdain, Aine nodded. "A plausible theory. A Phantomwalker must have killed Cesnialangus to get at the egg, but Draconilingius managed to take it away in time."

The fact that Aine the ice queen agreed with me was an amazing occurrence I'd have to think about later.

Farrell bathed me in a freezing stare. "Draconilingius took the egg to *you*. He should not have."

Drake sat in stubborn silence, not leaping to defend himself. His aura showed his anger as white-hot streaks on sable black.

When I'd last seen Farrell, the oldest of the three council members, he'd been sentencing Mick to a nasty punishment for the crime of letting me live. I saw no reason to answer him, either.

"You must bring the egg to us," Bancroft said to me. "We have ways of protecting it."

Sure, I'd hurry to obey *that* order. Their idea of protecting it would probably be locking it away in some vault in this compound. I imagined an isolated cell, with Bancroft's armed lackeys observing the lone egg through a slit in the door.

I thought of Junior and his vibrant bouncing, reacting to my touch, my voice, the events around him. Locking him in a cell would be incredibly cruel, but then dragons could be.

"Nope," I said.

Bancroft lost his composure. He rocketed to his feet, eyes blazing. "You have *no* idea how important Cesnialangus's offspring is. She was one of the highest born of us. I'll not leave her get in *your* clutches."

"I have clutches, do I?" I gazed straight back at Bancroft, no longer intimidated by him. The fact that he called the baby dragon Cesnia's *get* was infuriating. "The only way Mick survived the attack in Cesnia's lair was because of my Stormwalker and Beneath magics, which you all are so terrified of. You couldn't keep one of these Phantomwalkers away from the egg no matter how deep under this compound you hid it. But *I* can. I don't know if

Drake was aware of all this when he brought Junior to me, but he made a wise decision."

"I did know," Drake said. He was not one to modestly deny his canny perception.

"Where is the egg now?" Farrell demanded.

"Safe," I said. "I certainly wasn't going to bring him *here*."

"Good choice," Colby said. "Suck it up, Mighty Three. If Phantomwalkers can't be harmed by dragons but Janet can kick their asses, I say leave Junior with her."

"And cease calling it *Junior*," Bancroft said in disgust.

"Better than *it*," I countered.

"I did not say Phantomwalkers could not be harmed by dragons," Aine said indignantly. "Only that it is very hard to fight them and that they are determined to kill us. But we can best them if we band together."

Mick had been listening to this exchange with a look of vast amusement. "But can dragons band together?" he asked quietly.

"It has been done before," Aine answered.

I recalled Colby's story of Mick leading a phalanx of dragons against demons, saving Aine's and Farrell's lives, and thus winning him the title of dragon lord. Mick had never given me many details, but then, unlike other dragons in this room, he was self-effacing about his achievements.

"In very dire circumstances, yes," Mick said. "There aren't as many dragons left in the world now. The Phantomwalkers are winning a war of attrition."

"Are there many of *them*?" I asked in trepidation.

"No one knows," Aine said.

The expressions of unhappiness on the faces of the dragon council members told me this was true.

I realized the dragon council didn't care much about what harm the Phantomwalkers could cause the rest of the world. Dragons cared about their own power, their individual might. They rarely lived near each other, Mick had told me, because they didn't get along. The fact that Farrell, Aine, and Bancroft sometimes worked together was remarkable. Colby was friendlier than most, but even he gave the other dragons their space.

"How can we find out more about the Phantomwalkers?" I asked. I directed my question at Mick, who knew how to research better than the best human academics, but Aine answered.

"*We* can find out," she said coldly. "The information about dragon enemies is protected from all but the most—"

My cell phone rang, the shrill peal of an old-time telephone splitting the air and making every dragon jump. A spurt of fire flared in Bancroft's hand.

I set my ringtones to be loud and obnoxious because I was usually on the other end of the hotel from the phone when someone decided to call, and I never could remember where I put the damn thing. I pulled out the device to silence it but saw the name *Gabrielle* blazoned across my screen.

"Sorry, I have to take this."

The air in the room froze as the council, Titus, and Drake fixed their aggrieved gazes on me. Mick said nothing, and Colby grinned.

"Tell her, *hi, Babe,* for me," Colby said.

"Sure thing." I hastily exited the room.

The fact that Gabrielle was calling me and not using the shard of magic mirror I'd persuaded her to keep with her meant it wasn't a dire emergency. She'd have contacted me through the mirror if the egg was in danger, or Grand-mother, my dad, or Gina.

I jogged a long way down the hall and around a corner before I answered. I didn't want to be overheard, though I knew the dragons would still catch some of the conversation. I found a niche with a carved wooden bench in it and plopped down to swipe on the phone.

"Gabrielle," I said breathlessly.

"Have you been running, Janet? That's bad for your health, I've heard. Anyway, I'm calling to remind you that the game is in a few hours. You *will* be there, won't you?"

CHAPTER SEVENTEEN

I closed my eyes as Gabrielle's excitement came to me. This was important to her, so important she'd risk calling me when she knew I was trying to figure out what new danger I had to deal with.

"I'm so sorry, Gabrielle. I might not have time for this one—"

My words faded as my grandmother's voice sounded loudly over Gabrielle's. "You will make time, Janet. If her team wins this game, they win all of the finals."

"No, if we win, we'll *be* in the finals," Gabrielle corrected her. "I explained—"

"The team will need you there, as will your sister," Grandmother continued. "Where are you now?"

"Santa Fe," I said weakly.

"Good, then you are close to home. Tell Mick to bring you here within the hour."

"Say you will, Janet!" Gabrielle sang. "Wait, I'm not finish—"

Her voice cut off abruptly, and the phone went dark.

I knew I'd have to go. No choice. The fate of all dragons and possibly the world would have to wait until Gabrielle's basketball team made it through the semifinals.

I pocketed the phone and returned to the meeting room. I heard raised voices as I reached it and paused to listen before I entered.

"The egg stays where it is," Drake was saying in a hard voice.

"At that hotel?" Farrell scoffed. "The one that can be crumpled like paper in a light rain? If the Phantomwalkers don't already know about the Crossroads Hotel, they will find it. They will take the egg without the Stormwalker being able to do a thing about it."

I jerked open the door. "First of all," I proclaimed loudly. All the dragons but Mick started—Mick always knew where I was. "I never said the egg was at the hotel. Second, there's plenty more magic guarding that place than you understand. Now that I know what I'm up against, I'll add to it. We gotta go, Mick."

Mick rose immediately without question. I wondered if he'd heard my grandmother's command ringing down the passageway, or whether even Grandmother's voice had been drowned out by arguing dragons.

"Did you give Gabrielle my message?" Colby asked.

"No, sorry. Didn't get the chance."

Colby looked hurt, but he shrugged. "It's okay. I'll tell her myself." His good spirits returned as he anticipated that.

Mick paused to issue a command. "Drake, Titus, please do some research on the Phantomwalkers. We need to know their weaknesses, and exactly how to eliminate them. This is bad, my friends."

Though the dragon council members scowled their fury, Drake and Titus nodded without arguing.

"What do you want me to do, Micky?" Colby asked.

"Help me guard our secret weapons." Mick sent me his fond smile. "We'll need them."

Colby jumped to his feet. "Now, that I can do. Let's go, Janet. I know where you're headed, and I'll be there too. If I miss it, my hide might get burned off, and I like my hide. Laters, Drakey. Tites."

Both he and Mick pointedly said no farewells to the dragon council. Colby's wicked grin when he turned to follow us made me want to laugh.

———

WITH THE RAPID WAY MICK FLEW, WE REACHED MY motorcycle and then home in plenty of time to make it to the school where the basketball game was being played. Colby had landed in the darkness near Many Farms and was waiting for us at the gym's door.

The three of us entered the warm building to find bleachers full of the girls' families and friends, plus the teachers who'd come out to support the team.

Gabrielle, in her black sweats striped with the team's colors, chatted with a woman holding a clipboard. My little sister looked so adult and responsible discussing whatever it was they were talking about that I had to stop and watch her in admiration.

Also with fondness, I realized. Gabrielle and I had been through a lot, both apart and together. To see her so enthusiastic about something as real-life as coaching basketball was gratifying.

I heard my name being called from the crowd. Scanning the bleachers, I saw my family, and I mean my *entire* family. Not only Dad, Gina, and Grandmother, but my three aunts, my grown cousins, and their kids. They'd come to cheer the Begays on the team.

Gina hefted the bowling bag, which I assumed still carried the egg, so I'd see they hadn't left it behind. I nodded at her in thanks and lifted a hand to wave at my dad. He smiled a little, as undemonstrative as ever, but the smile warmed me all the way through.

Nitis wasn't there, as far as I could tell. I wondered whether he saw no need to attend a basketball game or had something else to do. I'd like to know what, if so.

The woman with the clipboard hurried into the locker room, and Gabrielle spotted us.

"Janet! Colby! Mick! You made it!"

Girls from both teams were already bouncing balls around the court and taking practice shots. Gabrielle skirted them with easy grace and bounded toward us. She moved past me and launched herself at Colby, who caught her in a tight embrace.

"No hot stuff, here," Gabrielle admonished good-naturedly when Colby tried to kiss her. She eased his arms from around her. "I have to set a good example." She winked at Colby, who let her go, not offended.

"So glad you made it," Gabrielle said to me, and I could tell she meant it. "Sit down here with me, okay? Everyone's all right with that because you're my sister. Sorry, babe," she added to Colby.

Colby laughed as though Gabrielle had made the best joke ever. "Not a problem. Micky and I will be cheering you in the stands. Right, Micky?"

Mick, who hadn't said much since we landed, shook his head. "I'm going to scout around a little."

"Have a good time," Colby told him. "I love these games, and I love watching my lady doing her stuff. Yell if you need me."

Colby gave Gabrielle's shoulders a squeeze, gave mine one too, and headed for the bleachers. "Pete," he called up to my dad. "Good to see you."

My father nodded at him without worry. His life had changed drastically in the last couple of years, including becoming friends with dragons. Dad took it all in his calm stride.

Mick sent me an understanding smile before he faded through the watchers still trickling into the gym and departed. While I'd have preferred his comforting warmth next to me, I liked knowing he'd be on guard outside.

Gabrielle led me with enthusiasm toward the folding chairs that constituted the coach's area. As I took my seat, I recalled my own days in this school. I hadn't been on any teams, because my burgeoning magic had either made me fumble everything or cause small explosions. Or I'd miss the try-outs because I'd be walking the land, attempting to forget my troubles. I hadn't been the best student, needless to say.

Some of the teachers I'd driven nuts were here tonight. I hoped they didn't recognize me or were too excited by the game to be in a condemning mood.

The gym was nearly full as starting time ticked nearer. Most of the girls were out on the court, their anticipation rising to a fever pitch.

"You know what the best thing about this job is?" Gabrielle raised her voice to be heard over the growing noise. She stood and pulled a gleaming silver object from under her jacket. "They let me have a whistle."

Smiling gleefully, she put it into her mouth and gave three shrill blasts.

Immediately, her girls stopped dribbling balls and gathered around her like ducklings to their mom.

Strong, agile ducklings, I amended my assessment. Young women growing up. A few of the girls were already quite tall, though my second cousins were not. No one in our family had any real height.

Gabrielle drew them in close for a last-minute pep talk. "Like I say every time, remember it's just a game." The girls nodded, eyes fixed on her. "And like I say every time, it's *not* just a game. Everyone's counting on us. So, give it all you've got."

The team absorbed this confusing advice without a blink.

Gabrielle then gave them pointers like watching for openings, or to remember their formation but not be afraid to break it if necessary. To make sure their best long thrower got the ball if she had a chance at a shot—same for their good inside shooters.

Then they got in a huddle, arms around each other.

Gabrielle counted down. "Three, two, one ... Go, Lobos!"

The team erupted in screams so bloodcurdling, that two hundred years ago, they'd have sent any colonizing Europeans racing for the hills. Maybe they should have let the girls be in charge back then.

Gabrielle gave more blasts on her whistle, for no reason I could tell. The refs gathered the players for the tip-off, a horn blew, and the game was on.

I settled in to watch. Gabrielle was on her feet, yelling and gesturing. The opposing team's coach watched her in sour disapproval.

I wasn't familiar with all the moves of girls' basketball, but Gabrielle obviously was. She'd played when she'd been younger, she'd said. I'd never heard her mention that until a few days ago, but obviously she knew her way around the court. She kept a sharp eye on her team, calling for time-outs when she knew they needed a break or to regroup.

The crowd yelled and cheered for the home team, and I found myself jumping from my chair, shouting my encouragement. The girls played with focus, taking shots only when they were certain of making them. They were especially good at interception. I saw Gabrielle's hand in that because they were sneaky yet well within the rules.

Not until after half time did I sense anything amiss.

I assumed a wind had rushed up outside, as it often did in spring in northern Arizona, because the gym roof started rattling. However, my storm magic didn't tingle in anticipation of a coming tempest.

Mick was out there patrolling, I reminded myself. He'd alert me if anything was wrong.

The moment that thought formed, the mirror shard in my pocket started to keen. I heard an identical noise at the court's edge, and realized Gabrielle carried her shard as well.

Gabrielle jerked around to glare at me. "What the hell?" she bellowed, as though the mirror's warning was my fault.

The roof shivered again, and I looked up in time to see it dissolve. No beams or shards of steel or fiberglass—or whatever the roof was made of—fell on us. The ceiling simply ceased to be.

It resolidified in the next instant, but not before a dozen beings I'd never seen in my entire weird life descended to hover beneath it. The ghostly apparitions had elongated skulls with empty eye sockets, and long bony bodies covered with ragged gray cloth.

A player on the other team missed a shot. She grunted in frustration, then she looked up, her arms sagging to her sides when she saw the floating wraiths. The ball bounced away, tap-tap-tapping into the abrupt silence.

CHAPTER EIGHTEEN

"Holy fuck!" Colby's voice sounded across the floor. In the next instant, about half of the spectators screamed. The other half swiveled heads in bewilderment, wondering what the others were reacting to.

Not everyone could see magical beings. There was now no doubt who in this gym came from shaman clans.

Phantomwalkers, Aine of the dragon council had called them. These things were much different from the rock formation, which had been creepy, but not ghostlike. The skull creatures hung noiselessly above us, ragged robes floating. An icy chill emanated from them, making my breath fog.

My first panicked thought was for Mick, who didn't burst inside the gym to fight. Had they hurt him? Or had he been the one to send the warning through the mirror?

If they'd harmed Mick, I'd know, I told myself. The bite of his magic in my ring would alert me. But how they got past him worried the hell out of me.

I found myself gripping the ring, willing it to tell me

what had happened, while my feet were frozen to the floor.
Literally. Ice welled up around my boots and adhered me to
the wood.

Gabrielle was similarly shackled. Ice crept up the legs of
her sweatpants, imprisoning her in place.

Before it could trap her entirely, she whipped the whistle
into her mouth and blasted it over and over. White fire
came out of her hands and streaked toward the phantoms.
They ducked out of the way, spun, and reformed in a line.

Gabrielle spit out the whistle. "No!" she roared. "You
get out of here, right now! No way am I letting you fuck up
my game. It's the *semifinals.*"

Her shouts distracted the Phantomwalkers long enough
for me to call up a burst of Beneath magic to crack away
the ice that bound me.

The phantoms watched Gabrielle with their black-holed
eyes as though they didn't know what to make of her. They
were focused on dragons and hadn't expected the crazy that
was Gabrielle, I thought gleefully. I'd make sure they didn't
see my brand of crazy coming, either.

I grabbed whatever wind I'd heard outside and found a
thunderstorm building, though many miles to the west, nearer
the Crossroads. I let that storm ground me, weak as it was from
here, while I called a hot ball of Beneath magic to my hand.

Without a sound, I threw it at the Phantomwalkers, my
feet coming off the floor with the effort.

The phantoms sprang apart in alarm, and my magic
tore through one of the roof beams. I swore one of my old
teachers sent me a scowl.

Gabrielle had the whistle in her mouth again, the ice
that had held her down now in melting shards around her

sneakers. She shot herself into the air the moment she was free, Beneath magic dancing in her hands.

I added my power to hers as Gabrielle torpedoed the Phantomwalkers, letting out a long trill on the whistle as she charged them.

Gabrielle passed right through the line of wraiths as though they were insubstantial and smacked hard into the wall beyond. Her whistle fell from her mouth, bouncing on its cord around her neck.

I feared Gabrielle would tumble to the ground and prepared a cushion of magic to catch her, but she rallied. She spun, pushing off the wall to take another run at her target.

"Colby," Gabrielle yelled. "Warm it up a little!"

Colby had been sensibly herding people out of the gym. My father and Gina were also guiding them while leaving themselves, thank the gods. Gina had the bowling bag looped over her shoulder, and my father hovered protectively near her.

Colby broke from the crowd and directed a blast of dragon fire at the phantoms.

The beings shrugged it off, as the rock creature had, but Gabrielle dove right into the stream of flame. She shrieked as it seared her, but I realized what she was doing. The Phantomwalkers had frozen her when she'd tumbled through them, and she was trying to counteract their icy magic with Colby's fire.

Half her team, including my cousins, remained on the gym floor, in spite of the other coach shouting at them to flee. The girls raised fists and voices, yelling their encouragement.

"Get 'em, Coach!" "Send 'em back to hell, Ms. Massey!" "Teach 'em not to mess with us!"

I pulled out my shard of magic mirror. "Where is the storm?" I bellowed.

"I don't know," it screeched back at me. "I'm so scared I have my eyes closed."

It didn't have eyes, but I didn't have time to debate that right now. "Can you channel some of whatever storm is going on near Magellan to me here?"

"I don't know." The answer was more thoughtful and less panicked. "Let me try."

Gabrielle battled above me, smacking the phantoms again and again with white streaks of Beneath magic. A few of the Phantomwalkers dispersed into tatters of cloth, but too many remained. They were oblivious to Colby's dragon fire, but he stood stolidly below them, unwilling to leave Gabrielle.

I was torn, desperate to find out what had happened to Mick, and also to make sure the egg was safe. But Gabrielle needed my help, and her girls were still here … and so was my grandmother.

Grandmother stood at the foot of the bleachers, hands on her cane, glaring up at the phantoms as though ready to scold them. Gabrielle, above her, destroyed another. Its ashes rained over Grandmother, dusting her gray-black hair, but she didn't flinch.

My young cousins started throwing basketballs at the phantoms, and their teammates soon caught on. Grabbing all the balls stacked up in racks, they hurled them upward, granny-style, smacking the ghouls right in their skulls. Their aims were perfect—no wonder they won so many games.

The balls didn't damage the phantoms but at least

diverted their attention. Gabrielle used the opportunity to strike and double-strike, clearing out more of them.

"Got it." The mirror's voice was unexpectedly chirpy. "One thunderstorm, coming your way."

The mirror's surface crackled like a glowing spider web. The glass went dark immediately, and then blasted bright again. I heard a faint rumble, as if the sound came through a weak radio signal.

My body tingled as the magic buried inside me flared to life. I stood taller, the confidence that my storm powers brought me wrapping me in assurance.

I grabbed the lightning on its next flash, married it to my Beneath magic, and shot it at the Phantomwalkers.

A flying basketball exploded midair. The girls below shrieked and ducked out of the way of the falling rubber shards.

Gabrielle's laughter was maniacal. She dove for the phantoms, wrapped her magic around mine, and streamed the lot into the ghouls.

They keened. I gathered power from another lightning strike and whacked them with it.

Grandmother, as if waiting for a cue, raised her walking stick and sang long notes in Navajo—at least, I thought it was the Diné language. Maybe not. I couldn't understand a word.

Her wailing voice tangled in the mix of magic from me and Gabrielle, and our combined powers formed a whirling mass of white and black. Streams of magic shot from this seething ball into each of the phantoms, shattering them into fragments.

Three of the Phantomwalkers remained intact. They flowed together, merging into one giant creature with three skull heads. Instead of turning and attacking me, Gabrielle, or Grandmother, they sought a high window and streamed out into the night.

"Janet, you must go after them," Grandmother commanded me.

I was racing for the exit before Grandmother finished the sentence. Gabrielle landed with a thump next to me as I flung open the double doors.

I shot out into the dark parking lot, Gabrielle right behind me. The team followed her with an energy I envied.

Many of the spectators—families and friends of the girls or those from the local community—were still there. It warmed my heart that they'd stayed to make sure we all got out safely, but on the other hand, there were now more people in danger.

"Mick!" I yelled into the crowd.

I didn't see him, but I did spy Dad and Gina with a clump of my aunts and cousins. Gina, thank all the gods, still held the bowling bag.

The three-headed phantom swooped at those gathered in the parking lot. People screamed when the wraith neared them—its icy coldness burned me as it swept by.

My aunts were trying to shoo my dad into his truck, admonishing him to get away. Dad stood stubbornly, ignoring them, Gina as resolutely next to him.

I reached my senses into the mirror, looking for another round of lighting, but I found nothing. Either the storm had dispersed, or the mirror had lost its ability to direct it.

Gabrielle shot more Beneath magic at the combined phantom, and I joined mine with hers. The huge Phantomwalker evaded most of the stream, but I saw it flinch when stung by the blast's tail. Though the Phantomwalkers were learning to avoid our strikes, they couldn't brush off our magic as they could dragon fire.

The phantom bundle turned and swooped at Gabrielle and me, determination burning in their black eyes.

Grandmother stepped out from the gym and raised her cane once more. Again, she chanted the words—ancient ones, I decided, which was why I knew they were Diné but couldn't comprehend them.

Her voice rose to meet the stars and the faint wisps of clouds that floated among the blackness. The phantom-being arrested its strike at me and Gabrielle and dove for her.

"No, you don't!" I yelled. I leapt in front of Grand-mother, Gabrielle right beside me. I turned toward the creatures, staring right into their leering skull faces.

The sound of wings broke the night. Not dragon ones. These wings had feathers, and spread themselves in a black wave, blotting out the stars.

I gaped upward, and Gabrielle clutched my arm. A giant crow flapped its wings, hot wind stirring my hair and sending dust across the parking lot. Its head, huge now, held white feathers mixed with dark, and its eyes were pools of blackness.

Only Grandmother didn't react to the crow's sudden appearance. She continued to chant, her voice rising and falling in beautiful notes.

The phantoms ignored her to meet the new threat. The crow cocked its head to fix them with one glittering eye as it watched them approach.

The Phantomwalker split from its clump back into three separate entities and tried to attack. The crow wheeled aside, coming around to strike them with his huge claws.

He ripped into one phantom, which screamed as it fell to pieces, disintegrating before it hit the ground.

The crow wheeled on his large wing, fixating on the remaining two. They backed away, then suddenly turned and fled, streaking across the sky until they disappeared in a flash of light. A bang, like a sonic boom, followed.

The crow gave a croaking caw, almost like a laugh, before it flapped into the sky. It looked back at Grandmother, and I swore I saw it wink before it skimmed away toward the dark horizon.

Grandmother lowered her cane, and her song ceased.

Those gathered in the parking lot were silent for a moment, then they began to excitedly chatter, as humans do when suddenly released from fear.

Colby headed for us. "Damn," he said, gazing in the direction the crow had disappeared. "Good thing it didn't do a dump before it left. That would have been ginormous."

Gabrielle laughed and flowed to him, wrapping her arms around him. "I was thinking the same thing."

The opposing team's coach, who'd rounded up her players, started for the gym. "We'll schedule a rematch," she announced to Gabrielle as she passed. "Come on, girls. Let's get your things."

Her team enthusiastically agreed as they trotted after her.

"Sure," Gabrielle muttered at the other coach's back. "A rematch. Because *we* were winning."

The teams' families and friends, breathing sighs of relief, began to pile into cars and trucks for the ride home. Those who lived closer walked out of the parking lot, heading for nearby houses. Supernatural shit didn't get anyone down for long.

The only one missing was Mick.

I shouted for him again as I scoured the dispersing crowd. I expected him to come strolling out of the darkness, saying he'd followed the beings to get more info on them or was keeping others safe, or something.

But he didn't appear.

"Dad." I jogged to him. "What happened to Mick?"

Pete met my gaze with one equally as worried. "I don't know, Daughter. I haven't seen him." Gina, still protectively holding the bag, also shook her head.

My panic rose. I lifted the shard of mirror I'd been holding so tightly it creased my palm. "Where is Mick?" I demanded of it.

"Don't know, sugar," the mirror said in a small voice. "He must have dropped me. Out in the desert somewhere."

The mirror didn't always know directions unless it could see exactly where it was. If Mick's shard lay in dead grasses pointing at the ground, or up at the dark sky, it couldn't guide me.

I let out a few choice words about mirrors, Phantomwalkers, and dragons foolish enough to follow them.

Nitis came out of the desert beyond the parking lot, clad in sweatpants and a jacket, as though he'd raided a men's locker room for them. His hair was sleek and straight, the white threads almost glowing among the dark.

He shot Colby a glance as he passed him on the way to Grandmother's side. "Next time, I *will* bless you with some droppings."

Colby tried to assume an innocent expression, but

Gabrielle laughed. Her laughter was tinged with hysteria, fear, and relief. She held Colby tighter.

"You took your time, Old Crow," Grandmother snapped at Nitis.

"I was following Mick." Nitis turned to me, his dark eyes serious. "They have him, Janet. He fought but was captured. I was trying to find out where they were taking him when I was called back."

"We needed you," Grandmother said defensively.

Nitis nodded. "It is why I answered. You and your granddaughters bested many, but they would have overcome your defenses and stolen the egg."

I barely noted their exchange, or the fact that Nitis included Gabrielle as a member of Grandmother's true family.

"Where did they take him?" I nearly screamed at Nitis. "Which way?"

Nitis pointed north, in the direction we'd gone yesterday to hide my motorcycle. The desert out there was vast and empty.

I ran to the edge of the parking lot, holding the mirror in front of me, as though I expected it to penetrate the gloom and pinpoint Mick.

"Mick," I whispered. The wind took my words and wafted them into the darkness, the name floating into the night.

CHAPTER NINETEEN

Mick had been taken from me before. On one occasion, a witch had imprisoned his mind, though Mick had been physically free to do what he liked. He'd also let himself be locked up a couple of times to complete a dragon-y ritual. In those instances, he could have escaped his prison if he'd wished, but he'd felt honor-bound to remain. He'd even been annoyed whenever I'd tried to rescue him.

This time was different—Mick had been captured by beings he couldn't fight. I knew by the sharp sting in my ring finger that he wasn't dead, at least not yet. But he could be anywhere, in this world or in some weird dimension inhabited by the Phantomwalkers.

"We will find him, Janet."

My father's gentle voice brought me back to myself. I stood in the sand a few steps beyond the parking lot, wind chilling me, the darkness dense. Most of the spectators had gone by now, and so had the bus driving the other team back to their town.

My aunts and cousins remained. I vaguely heard my young cousins babbling excitedly about how they'd whacked the skeletal demons with their basketballs. Hadn't that been so cool?

With them were Dad and Gina, Grandmother and Nitis, Gabrielle and Colby. I should have been one of a pair as well. My heart felt hollow.

Dad had drifted away from them to speak to me, and we stood relatively alone.

"He's in deep shi— in danger, Dad." I barely had the breath to speak.

My father laid a warm hand on my shoulder. "I know. But you and he have many friends. We will find him and bring him home."

I wanted to cling to him and weep. My dad didn't do wild embraces, so I controlled myself. His hand on my shoulder was enough.

Dad was right. Everyone in my circle liked Mick, and Titus and Drake at least respected him. I knew people. I had resources.

I swallowed. "I just don't know what to do. Where to start."

"Start with your grandmother. She always found *you*, didn't she?"

I choked out a laugh and swiped tears from my cheeks. Dad's wry smile held understanding. True, Grandmother had usually known where I was and always when I was getting into trouble.

We turned together and made our way back across the lot to where the knot of our family waited.

My young cousins were bouncing with excitement

around Gabrielle. "I didn't know you were a shaman, Coach," Shirley said.

Gabrielle didn't correct Shirley about what type of magic she wielded. She managed a mysterious expression. "I try to keep it under wraps."

Colby, who knew exactly how much Gabrielle didn't bother to conceal her magic, chuckled.

"You were really badass," her sister Lily put in. "You can make sure we win *all* the games. We could go to nationals!"

Gabrielle sent them both an indulgent smile. "I won't use magic to cheat. You ladies are good—no need to enhance that except with training."

The girls looked a bit disappointed, but I felt a swell of pride in Gabrielle. It would have been a bigger surge if I hadn't been so concerned about Mick.

"Don't worry, Janet," Gabrielle said with confidence. "We'll find him. Mick is amazingly strong. He'll be all right until we do."

Colby didn't appear as optimistic. He'd seen firsthand how impervious the Phantomwalkers were to dragon magic.

"I appreciate it," I managed to say. I could barely speak —breathing was like lifting a heavy weight.

They'd taken Mick north, Nitis had said, but that was a fairly vague direction. Many things were north. The rest of the Navajo Nation. Utah. Montana and Wyoming. Canada. Alaska. The fucking North Pole.

Plus, they could have turned aside anywhere, heading a different way entirely.

I needed to think. I also needed a witch who could locate people.

"I'm going back to the hotel." I wheezed the words. "Can anyone give me a ride? I don't think I can drive myself."

"I can lend you a wing," Colby offered.

"And I'll ride your motorcycle back for you," Gabrielle said brightly.

Grandmother broke in firmly. "No, you will not. The Firewalker will carry Janet to the Crossroads because she needs to go swiftly. You will follow with Pete, Gina, and me in the truck, and the Old Crow will take Janet's motorcycle."

Gabrielle's dismay at the prospect of being squashed for several hours in Dad's pickup with Grandmother was palpable, but she bravely lifted her chin.

"Sure thing," she said in resignation. "Don't drop Janet, Colby. I've only just started liking her."

Colby pressed a hand to his chest in feigned offence. "I'd never do that. I'm a careful flyer."

I'd had Colby fly me places before. No, he was not.

I had no choice now, however. I needed to reach Cassandra and start hunting for Mick.

I lifted Mick's backpack from my motorcycle and hugged it to my chest. After a moment's inner debate, I decided to leave the egg in Gina's capable hands. If the Phantomwalkers attacked Colby en route, he wouldn't be able to defend himself, and I might drop the egg trying to save him. Gabrielle had proved she could fend off the Phantomwalkers, and so the egg would be safer with her. Nitis had proved this as well, though I still wasn't certain I could trust him. I trusted Grandmother, though.

I swallowed as I patted the bowling bag in farewell, hoping all of us made it to the hotel in one piece.

Colby, once dragon, took off in the way he always did
—arrowing up into the sky and doing a near somersault to
straighten himself out. I bit back a scream, willing my
stomach to stay in place. It did no good to yell at him—he
wouldn't listen even if he could hear me.

Thankfully, we reached the hotel in only about twenty
minutes. Colby set me down beyond the railroad bed before
flapping off into the darkness to become human.

I left his clothes in a pile for him and trudged to the
hotel. Setting Mick's backpack in my bedroom, which was
cold without him, I made my way down the short hall to
the front rooms.

A party was going strong in the lobby. I stood in the
doorway, taking in people everywhere, drinks in hands,
music booming. Carlos ran from the saloon with a tray to
replenish empties. Flora helped him, chattering and smiling
at everyone as she liked to do.

"Oh, hey, Janet." Fremont Hansen saluted me with a
beer bottle as he sauntered toward me. "What's up?"

"I was about to ask you that." At least I could talk once
more. My breathing was almost normal again, though I
had a stitch in my side as though I'd been running.

"Carl Jones's idea. He's celebrating not being taken to
jail."

I recalled the image of Coyote picking up Jones's grandfather on the side of a highway yesterday, after Carl had
taken off with Mick's bike. Coyote might have threatened
to lock Carl up then pretended to go easy on him and
brought him back here. The threat would have been empty,
because Coyote wasn't a real cop, but Carl wouldn't know
that.

"Great," I said wearily. "Where is Cassandra?"

Fremont waved his bottle in a vague direction. "Some-where. Those girls are wild, aren't they?"

The Horribles were in full swing. The daughters danced from male to male, which included their own husbands, Carlos, Grandfather Jones, and a Native American man dressed in a tribal cop uniform.

"Coyote!" I yelled.

He either didn't hear me or was having too much fun shimmying his hips in time with Allie's.

With renewed strength I marched over and laid a firm hand on Coyote's shoulder.

"Hey!" Allie shouted with a glare. "He's dancing with *me*."

Coyote started to make kissing noises at both of us, but then he saw my face. His grin deserted him.

"Sorry, babe," he told Allie. "I gotta take this."

Allie pouted, but then she caught sight of Colby, who'd come in through the patio, and brightened considerably.

"Hey, who started the party without me?" Colby asked the room.

Allie squealed in excitement and made a beeline for him. No one answered Colby, but Allie grabbed his hands and pulled him into the dance. Since Colby could worry about dire danger *and* enjoy himself at the same time, he put his hands in the air and started waving his butt in rhythm to the beat.

"What's going on?" Coyote asked in a serious tone as I ushered him into my office. "You okay, hon? You look beat."

I slumped into the chair behind my desk and buried my face in my hands. "Mick is gone."

Before Coyote could ask me startled questions, I told

him the tale, from Mick and I seeking Cesnia's island, to heading for the dragon compound, to the battle in the school gym.

"Phantomwalkers," Coyote repeated when I'd finished. "Is that what they're calling themselves? Holy shit. I thought they were long gone."

"You know what they are?"

"Mistakes." Coyote's expression was grim. He settled into the visitor's chair and rested his arms on his thighs. "They were dragons *almost* created. Not quite finished. Like pottery that melts or breaks in the kiln instead of hardening. The gods who created dragons threw them out—as one would with ruined pots. They kept on until they'd perfected the dragons we now know and love."

His explanation was similar to Farrell's. If true, it was no wonder the Phantomwalkers hated and wanted to kill all dragons. Gabrielle had loathed me for a similar reason—our mother had caused Gabrielle to be born and then rejected her in favor of me, because I had a mix of Beneath and earth magic, instead of only Beneath. Gabrielle had nursed a resentment that had nearly killed me. The perils of bad parenting.

"They don't look anything like dragons," I said. "One was made of rock. The others were like dead humans."

"Because they didn't fully form, they can swap out their appearance," Coyote explained. "They're inspired by nightmares, or what people—or dragons—fear most. In any form, they can kill, and as you said, dragon fire doesn't harm them."

"Dragon fire harms other dragons," I pointed out. "They just have thick hides and are good at getting out of the way. Why wouldn't it harm these phantom things?"

Coyote shrugged. "I don't know all the laws of physics for dragonkind. Or what their gods were capable of creating. Let's take it as given that dragons have no defense against Phantomwalkers. What are we going to do?"

"I was hoping you would know," I said, frustrated anger rising.

Coyote left the chair and moved around the desk to gather me into his arms. I resisted at first, because I feared I'd fall apart if I surrendered, but his warm comfort overcame me.

I sometimes forgot Coyote was a powerful god, ancient, wise beyond any understanding of the word. He held me in a kind embrace, which soothed rather than bound.

I sobbed, ugly crying that had wanted to emerge since Mick had disappeared. The memory of us in Cesnia's guest room last night, making love on the soft mattress, welled in my head. And the wild time in the cave, after we'd defeated the rock creature, Mick's wicked eyes and loving smile making me come apart.

The tightness in my side loosened while I cried, as did the final heaviness in my chest. I blubbered like a baby on Coyote's shoulder, and he patted my back and held me like a friend.

Coyote smelled of desert things: wind, dust, grasses. For a moment I thought I saw a coyote superimposed on his large human body, the two beings one. At the same time, I caught a glimpse of something unfathomable, a light that would blind any mortal who gazed at it too closely. Coyote kept himself in a form we'd understand, I realized, so we'd survive an encounter with him.

I blinked, and the image vanished. I was resting on a

man's muscular shoulder, his khaki police uniform now
damp with my tears.

I raised my head, drying my eyes. "Sorry."

Coyote shrugged. Here was the affable man who hung
out in the middle of town, telling stories to tourists, and
making kids laugh. I hadn't imagined the amazingly
powerful being I'd witnessed in him, but he did his best to
pretend I'd seen nothing remarkable.

"You needed to get that out of your system," Coyote
said as he sat down again. "Now, what are your plans for
getting Mick back?"

The whirling thoughts in my head were nothing like
plans, but I had some ideas.

"Cassandra might be able to get a fix on Mick's position," I said, drawing a shaking breath. "I need to alert
Drake and Titus. Once I know where Mick is, even more or
less, I'll take Gabrielle and the dragons with me to rescue
him. Nash could be useful too, if he understands the
danger. His null magic worked against the lightning mesh
the Phantomwalkers threw at us, so maybe he can counteract them. Also, Nitis. He seems to be the only one
besides me and Gabrielle who can harm these creatures."

"Nitis?" Coyote frowned. "Who's Nitis?"

"He's been hanging around here for some time,
watching the hotel." I wondered if Nitis had known what
was about to happen with the egg and everything else, or if
he'd only been following Grandmother. "Grandmother calls
him the Old Crow."

Coyote drew back. "Seriously?"

I blinked at his reaction. "Yes, why? I don't know
anything about this guy, except he can become a huge crow,
and he's saved our butts a couple of times."

Coyote glanced out the window, as though checking to make sure Nitis wasn't out back. "He's an ancient being," he said surreptitiously. "Like me."

"Don't tell me." I drew a breath, relieved my lungs were functioning normally again. "You and he have tangled in the past?"

"Maybe. You know how Coyote the Trickster goes after the ladies."

I rolled my eyes. "You went after his lady? That's just great, Coyote. Since I've never seen her around, can I take it she rebuffed you and stayed with Nitis?"

"No, she ditched us both. She decided to go to Norway and hang out with Norse gods instead. I guess she likes the cold. The Old Crow wasn't too happy with me."

I gave him a narrow-eyed stare. "This was before you married Bear—right?"

"Right. Right. Of course," Coyote spluttered, but I couldn't tell if he lied or was simply nervous talking about his formidable wife.

"Well, patch things up with Nitis," I said. "I need him, and I need you. These things could kill Mick, not to mention Cesnia's kid and all the other dragons too."

Coyote recovered his self-assurance. "Dragons have done a lot of bad things to you, Janet, if you recall. I understand why you want to save Mick, and I'll help you with that, but your life would be much easier if the other dragons were gone."

I huffed in irritation that rose to outrage. "Colby is a friend. Drake and Titus are decent guys, and I'm certainly not going to let anything happen to Cesnia's egg. The other dragons are pains in my ass, yes, but they don't deserve to be slaughtered. It's not their fault their makers couldn't get things right during the formation of the Earth."

Coyote nodded along as I burst out with this speech, his approval rising. "I'm glad you think that way. That's my girl."

"And I wish everyone would *stop* expecting me to turn into my evil goddess mom," I snapped. "I'm saving Mick and the rest of the dragons. End of story."

Coyote lifted his hands. "I'm just saying I love you."

"You have the most aggravating way of showing affection, I swear—"

A male voice raised in fury in the lobby cut me off. "What in the hell is going on in here?"

"Oops," Coyote said. "We maybe forgot to tell him Carl was safe. Or that he took off at all."

"Forgot?" I was up and around my desk in a heartbeat. "Thanks a lot, Coyote. You know who he's going to blame for *everything*, right?"

"You know, both of you need to cut Carl some slack," Coyote answered with a frown. "He's allowed to live his life even if it inconveniences you."

"I'm happy to let him do whatever the hell he wants, as long as I don't have to answer to his grandson."

I marched out of the room to find Nash, furious, his gray eyes glinting as he glared at Carl, who danced happily with one of the Horrible sisters.

Nash saw me. *"Begay."*

I raised my hands in surrender. "He's fine," I yelled over the music.

"Not the point."

Maya Medina tripped in behind Nash. She appeared as

annoyed as he was, until she surveyed the room and the dancers.

"Why didn't you tell me you were having a party?" she yelled to me. "I would have dressed up."

Maya looked gorgeous, as always, in dark blue jeans, clingy sweater, and a short jacket. Even in sensible sneakers, she managed to be sexy.

Allie waved her arms over her head. "Join us."

"I will." Maya pushed past Nash and was dancing before she reached Allie and Colby. Carl and Yvonne joined them.

Nash curled his lip at me and pointed at the relatively empty saloon. I sighed heavily and followed him in.

The music was not as loud in here. Cassandra had taken refuge at a corner table, her face pinched as she tried to work on her laptop. Pamela, who must have come to pick her up, had planted herself in the chair across from Cassandra, arms folded in impatience.

"Why didn't you tell me my grandfather had gone for another joyride?" Nash demanded as soon as we could hear ourselves. "Fremont's cousin happened to mention it to me while Maya and I were grabbing some dinner." Of course, Fremont would have spread the tale through his gossipy family. "You promised me you'd take care of him."

"First of all, I can't handcuff him and lock him in a cell." I was sorry as soon as the words left my mouth, because I saw Nash thinking that was a good idea. "Second, Coyote found him quickly and brought him home safely. Third, I've been a little *busy*." My voice broke, concern for Mick gripping me anew.

"Damn it," Nash growled. "I'll have to find a high-security assisted-living place, which I can't afford, because no one can keep him out of trouble." His fury abruptly abated. "He's my only family."

I decided not to point out his brother in New Mexico and his cousin Ada in Flag. I realized he meant the only family he worried deeply about.

I opened my mouth to argue that Carl was obviously fine and currently enjoying himself, when the mirror shrieked.

"Stop! Oh, nooo! Jaaa-*neeettt*." Its screech cut off as darkness filled the mirror. The inky blackness blotted out the reflected saloon, me, Nash, Cassandra and Pamela, and the dancers in the lobby.

Cassandra jerked her head up, and Pamela rose like the predator she was, her wolf's snarl in her throat. Nash, who couldn't hear the mirror or detect when magical things were happening, stared at me in exasperated bafflement.

Cassandra gasped as the empty skull faces of five Phantomwalkers filled the mirror's surface. Five voices, nearly identical and overlapping each other, floated out in a guttural whisper.

"Give us the egg. We give you Micalerianicum."

CHAPTER TWENTY

"Where is he?" I yelled at the hovering skulls. "Where did you take Mick?"

Pamela advanced, her eyes wolf gray, her fingertips changing to claws. "Show us Mick. Proof of life."

Nash started at her words—he couldn't hear the Phantomwalkers. Cassandra murmured under her breath, hopefully working a really useful spell.

"The egg," the voices said. They didn't speak in unison, which caused a weird echo effect. "Show *us*."

I couldn't, because Gina was holding it as she rattled to Magellan in my dad's pickup. Their demand relieved me in one respect—they hadn't pinpointed the egg on the highway. Gabrielle must be shielding them, either consciously or automatically.

"Nope," I said in a hard voice. "Mick first."

A sliver of dragon face abruptly filled the mirror. Only that slice, because Mick must be peering through the piece of magic mirror he'd dropped and the Phantomwalkers had no doubt picked up. I saw Mick's fiery eye, full of rage, and a fragment of his dragon face which contained a glimpse of massive teeth.

Just eat them, Mick, I willed him.

It was very possible he couldn't. If his dragon fire didn't harm these phantoms, he probably couldn't chomp them either.

Mick didn't speak in words in his dragon form, but a spark jumped on my ring, and I heard his snarl in my head. *Don't even think about doing what they want.*

I quickly touched the ring. *Where are you?*

Mick only growled and disappeared, the Phantomwalkers replacing his image. Either Mick hadn't heard me, he couldn't tell me for some reason, or he didn't know.

I lifted my chin. "Where do I bring the egg?"

Nash put himself next to me. He couldn't hear the Phantomwalkers or see Mick, but he was canny enough to figure out what was going on. "No, Janet. You never negotiate with kidnappers."

I had no intention of negotiating with them or of giving them Junior, but I needed somewhere to start.

"Come to the place you call Canyon Diablo," they said.

Canyon Diablo was one of many crevices that crisscrossed the land between here and Flagstaff, through which water ran down from the mountains during torrential rains. It had once held a notoriously violent town while a railroad bridge had been constructed—the town was gone but the railroad bridge was still in use.

It was also in the middle of nowhere in a precarious desert and had the reputation for being haunted.

I thought rapidly, wanting to name a place I could control. Several ideas came and went, but then one occurred to me that they wouldn't expect.

"I will take the egg to the bowling alley on Route 66 in Flagstaff," I announced. "You have Mick there, in human form, before I arrive. I'll leave the egg, and Mick walks out with me. It will take me a couple hours to get there. Mirror—break the connection."

Instantly the glass went dark. The reflection of the saloon, distorted from the cracks radiating from the center of the mirror, returned.

"How did you shut them down like that?" Pamela asked. Her face had elongated into wolf form, but not so much that she couldn't speak. She looked bizarre but also ferocious.

"The mirror is compelled to obey me," I said. "Mick understands why I shut it off."

No one exclaimed something like, *Janet, you can't take that poor helpless baby dragon to them!* They knew I never would—at least Cassandra and Nash did. Pamela believed the worst of me, but she also understood I'd try something underhanded.

"Nash, will you come with me?" I asked.

Nash scowled. "If you'll tell me exactly what happened."

I filled him in—and Cassandra and Pamela—on the attack at the basketball game and Mick's disappearance. Nash gave me a grim nod when I finished.

"You should bring more people than me," Nash said. "I saw Colby here."

"He'd be in more danger than we will," I said. "Gabrielle is already on protection duty, so it will be you and me. Cassandra, were you doing a locator spell? Any luck?" I hadn't yet had the chance to ask her to help me

pinpoint Mick, but she would have done her best to deter-
mine where the Phantomwalkers were contacting us from.

Cassandra shook her neatly coiffed head. "I couldn't
find them. Fissures in the earth, was all I got."

"Volcanic?" I pictured geysers or mud vents like those
in Wyoming or Iceland.

Cassandra considered. "Possibly. Nothing active,
though."

Well, that was a bonus. I could fight better if I wasn't
breathing sulfur or being boiled in lava.

"What are those things?" Pamela demanded. Her face
had eased back into its human form, but her eyes still held the
yellow glint of wolf. "Why do they want Mick, or this egg?"

I briefly explained what Coyote and the dragon council
had told me about the Phantomwalkers. "I don't know if
either of you can fight them," I said to Cassandra and
Pamela. "I'd rather have you here as defenders anyway."

"Won't they be suspicious if you don't bring more
muscle?" Pamela asked.

"Nash is the best muscle I can think of," I said. Nash
looked annoyed at being called muscle, but he nodded his
agreement. "Oh, Cassandra, do you know if anyone here
has a spare bowling bag?"

———

I'D TOLD THE PHANTOMWALKERS I NEEDED A FEW HOURS,
even though the bowling alley was only about fifty minutes
away. I wanted to wait for my family to show up before we
went.

I didn't expect the Phantomwalkers to actually release

Mick, and they'd tumble to the fact that I'd duped them pretty quickly. Whether they expected me to or not, I wasn't certain. How perceptive were they about human wiliness?

Regardless, I'd use the encounter as a starting place. From there, I'd either follow the Phantomwalkers or bully them into revealing where they held Mick. There were plenty of former volcanoes around Flagstaff, one a tall cinder cone.

New Mexico had old volcanoes as well, and then there were dragon lairs like Cesnia's all over the world. The Phantomwalkers might be holding Mick in his own lair in the Pacific. He'd certainly been pissed off, wherever they were keeping him.

If they killed Mick, I'd take them apart, molecule by molecule.

About twenty minutes later, I was happy to see my father's pickup make its slow way in from the road and roll past the Crossroads Bar, which was hopping. My dad was safe, along with Gina, my grandmother, and Gabrielle. Nitis rolled up behind them with my motorcycle.

"Nice ride," he said to me as he dismounted. I was too worried to warm at the compliment.

As the family moved to the hotel, Grandmother regarding the noise inside in disapproval, I noticed Nitis hadn't followed them. I scanned the lot, but he'd disappeared.

"I don't keep account of him," Grandmother said sourly when I asked her where Nitis had gone. "The Old Crow comes and goes as he pleases."

Of course, he'd vanish just when I needed someone who could destroy Phantomwalkers. "Ask him to join us at the bowling alley," I said, after I'd explained the situation. "Any help he can give will be welcome."

"I can try," Grandmother said doubtfully. "Your plan, it sounds risky."

I couldn't argue with her.

"We will keep this little one safe," Gina promised, cradling the bag. "You go get Mick."

When I'd first met Gina, I'd tried not to like her. After all, she'd come to take my dad away from me. I'd realized within five minutes of speaking to her, that it would be impossible not to respect and love this woman. I was very glad she'd joined our family.

I gave her a nod of gratitude, and Gina sent me a slow nod in return.

Gabrielle joined us, the desert wind stirring her long hair. "Anyone gets near this egg, they're toast," she promised. "But why don't they just come and take it from you? Why kidnap Mick and do a whole cliche exchange thing?"

Exactly what I'd wondered. Were the Phantomwalkers trying to draw me away from the Crossroads, or did they really believe I'd bring the egg to them? Maybe Mick, who had a canny dragon mind, had convinced them I would.

"The hotel has a lot more defenses," Nash said. "Not that they prevented one old man from stealing a bike to go joyriding." He glared at me.

Gabrielle laughed. "I heard about your grandfather. I have *got* to meet him." She sailed into the hotel to be swallowed by the thumping music.

I took Dad and Gina in through the party and unlocked the door to my private suite.

"I'll make sure Gabrielle and Cassandra are two steps away," I told them, handing Gina the keys. "Colby too, though I think he'll need as much protecting as the egg."

"We will be fine here," Gina assured me. "You go fetch Mick home."

I reached into the bag and patted the egg, hoping it understood we'd take care of it. Junior jumped against my hand in enthusiasm, as though happy to see me.

Once he was hatched, he'd be able to fly all over the place. Keeping track of him would be fun then, I imagined. I patted the egg again, enjoying the smooth jade against my hand, and reluctantly departed the suite.

Colby was not happy that I wanted to leave him behind, but I persuaded him he was needed to look after my dad and Gina, the egg, and Gabrielle. He knew I was bullshitting him—I wanted him here with Gabrielle's magic to keep him safe—but he agreed.

In the lobby, Gabrielle danced enthusiastically with Carl, her hips and hair swinging. Colby joined them after I spoke to him, already having made friends with Nash's grandfather.

Grandmother humphed at the goings-on and stalked into the kitchen to seek Elena, who was cooking for the crowd.

My request for a bowling bag—and ball—was fulfilled by Fremont. He had a custom-made ball in his truck, which he used for his league games. Magellan didn't actually have a bowling alley, but there was a nice one in Flat Mesa, ten miles away.

Not that I ever went there. Me and bowling did not mix. I tended to land a lot of gutter balls, even using those lane bumpers meant for little kids—my balls would go right over them.

Once, when Maya had convinced me to go bowling with her, I'd tried a little magic to keep from humiliating myself. I'd ended up exploding the pins and frying the end of the lane. I was asked not to come back to the Flat Mesa alley.

"I'll buy it from you," I told Fremont when he handed me the bag with the fifteen-pound ball inside. "I'll have to leave it, with no guarantee I can get it back."

Fremont shrugged. "That's okay. I have a couple. Besides, I don't mind the sacrifice to save Mick. Sure you don't want me to come with you?"

"No," I said quickly. Fremont had some magic in him, but nothing that could counter the dangerous beings I'd face. "I need you here to help guard."

Unlike Colby, who'd scowled as I'd placated him, Fremont brightened. "I'm your man. And Flora is your gal. Our magics are seriously compatible, if you know what I mean." He winked.

I held up my hand. "TMI, Fremont. TMI."

Fremont chuckled. "I didn't mean it like that. She's moved in with me, you know."

I'd heard that from several sources of town gossip. I was happy for Fremont, whose luck with relationships up until now had bordered on disastrous. Flora was nothing like the vibrant and evil beauties into whose clutches Fremont usually fell, thankfully. She was kindhearted, wise, and had a lovely voice I enjoyed listening to.

"I'm glad," I said sincerely. I wished I hadn't been so distracted with saving Mick, protecting Cesnia's egg, and defeating evil beings, because I'd take them both to dinner.

Fremont grinned and patted me on the shoulder. "Go get 'em, Janet."

"Thanks." I wasn't sure if I was about to kick the bad guys' asses or run headlong into their trap.

Didn't matter. I'd spring the trap, kick ass anyway, and bring Mick home.

———

I RODE MY MOTORCYCLE BEHIND NASH'S TRUCK AS WE headed for Flagstaff. He'd tried to insist I go with him in his shiny F250, but I wanted the magic mirror that had been ground into my sideview to reinforce the shard wrapped in my pocket.

Maya admonished me before we left not to get Nash killed. She told me, in detail, exactly what she'd do to me if I did. I hugged her, startling her—neither of us were huggers—and promised to keep him safe.

Nash carried Drake's bowling bag in his truck. I'd switched out the egg for Fremont's ball, gently settling the egg into Fremont's newer, more sturdy bag, designed for several balls and accessories. Junior got an upgrade.

I'd exchanged them in case any of the Phantomwalkers had noted the color and shape of the bag Drake had brought to me. I needed them to believe, if only for a few minutes, that I was doing what they asked.

Normally, I loved riding in the cool darkness on the I-40. The weather was great, the stars brilliant, the traffic calm. It was a beautiful night for a ride, but I hardly noticed in my anxious state.

I kept Nash's taillights in view as we gained elevation,

the outline of the large peaks on the night sky drawing ever nearer. Nash drove the exact speed limit, which meant it took us longer to reach Flagstaff than Mick and I usually did.

After what seemed like forever, we passed the Walnut Canyon turnoff and then the cluster of hotels at Country Club Drive, where we left the freeway for the historic Route 66 that snaked through town.

The bowling alley was located East Flagstaff, not far from our turnoff. I'd chosen a place here because the downtown area could be cramped and crowded. From the bowling alley we could zip off for a quick getaway and endanger fewer people. I didn't intend to have a showdown in the bowling lanes but planned to lead the Phantomwalkers out of town to empty wilderness, or up into the mountains, whichever proved more expedient.

Mount Elden loomed large on the north side of the road, its nine-thousand-foot height a shield of darkness. Behind it were the higher peaks of Agassiz and Humphreys —at least those were the white names for them. The Native American ones were more musical. They were sacred mountains, and once upon a time, I'd been trapped under them by gods who'd been annoyed with me.

The parking lot at the lanes was full, as leagues often bowled on Friday night, plus the club next door had a live band playing. Mick and I had gone to that club several times, both when we'd first dated and more recently. Set back from the road, the club had a log facade and a wide parking lot full of cars and people.

Nash took his time parking—he didn't want to be too close to any other vehicles in case they dinged his precious truck. I put my bike with others nearer the bowling alley's front door.

Carefully lifting the bag from his truck, Nash carried it to the building, appearing as any other bowler out to find a lane on a Friday night.

I'd brought Nash because he'd been able to suck down the lightning that had enclosed the hotel and not feel a thing. I was convinced now that the attack had been the Phantomwalkers after the egg, though I think at that point they'd been testing my defenses. I hoped Grandmother found Nitis and gave him the message to meet us here, because we'd need him too.

I heard a few harsh caws in the trees behind the lot, but that was not unusual in Flagstaff, even this late at night. I'd had a pair of ravens nesting above me when I'd lived in an apartment here as a student. Others thought I should chase them off, but I figured they needed somewhere to live, and they were good company.

Crows were rarer, not liking people as much, but they were still around. I glanced in the direction of the noise, wondering if one of the cawers was Nitis, but I couldn't see much beyond the glare of the parking lot's lights.

Nash and I walked into the bowling alley together. People stared as we went by, but I doubt their attention was caught because I was Navajo. Plenty of Native Americans lived in and around Flagstaff, which lay on the edge of two Indian nations. They stared because Nash bore down on them with a determined stride, while I, still a mess from my previous fight, struggled to keep up with him.

Bowlers parted to let Nash through. I darted quickly in his wake before the sea of bodies could close again.

As I'd suspected, a few leagues were here tonight, clustered around lanes on the far end of the alley. Nearer the entrance were groups of friends or parents and kids, out for a night of fun.

Nash ignored them all. He planted himself in the middle of the long building and scanned the crowd.

"Mick isn't here," he announced.

CHAPTER TWENTY-ONE

I did not crumple to the ground in shock when Nash announced Mick wasn't sitting in a corner, waiting for us. I'd already known he wasn't here—I hadn't felt his aura or any tingle through my ring.

I did feel a pain in my heart beneath my worry. Some part of me had hoped against hope that I'd see his blue eyes or hear his sexy voice asking me if I missed him.

"I didn't think he would be." I kept my voice steady. "They're evil beings. Probably not big on keeping their word."

"If they were supposed to have been dragons, then they would keep their words," Nash said sternly. "Your boyfriend has told me a number of times that dragons are all about honor."

"Maybe it's one reason the Phantomwalkers' creators gave up on them." I folded my arms and shivered. It was hot in here, but my terror for Mick was building anew.

Nash held out the bag. "Where do you want me to put this?"

"The deal was, I leave the egg when I see Mick. I don't see him."

The only auras I sensed were human. Some of the people in the alley were enjoying themselves, while others were anxious about their game or something else in their life. I sensed the focus of the league bowlers, the boredom of kids with their parents, the giddy excitement of girls on a night out together.

As I scanned the crowd, fighting despair, a stain on this normality began to seep in like a cold touch. Alert, I scoured the room but saw nothing that should alarm me.

The evil was outside, behind the building.

"This way," I told Nash, and headed back out the way we'd come in.

———

REVELERS SPILLED OUT OF THE CLUB NEXT DOOR AMONG raucous shouting, thumping music, and exuberant laughter. The fetid aura I sensed came from behind the club and a little to the west, where trees towered in the darkness.

There was a park in that direction, in the middle of a residential neighborhood. What I felt might come from beyond it, but it would be a good place to reconnoiter.

"Follow me," I told Nash as I headed for my motorcycle.

He wanted to argue, because he was Nash. I ignored him and thrust on my helmet, starting my bike. Nash, clutching the bowling bag, had to run for his truck so he wouldn't lose me.

To reach the park, I ducked out to the 66 and then took side roads that wound uphill through houses and trees,

Nash's headlights behind me. I slid into the park's lot, which was empty—too late now for evening picnics or tennis. Even the skateboarders had gone to bed.

Clouds piled up over the mountains, blotting out the stars The frigid air of the high peaks grabbed the moisture swirling around them and spit it back as rain. Or at this time of year, snow. Skiers were still enjoying deep powder on the summit.

Nash parked next to me, his window down. "What are we doing here?"

I couldn't answer. I only knew that something waited for me. Did it think me stupid enough to bring the actual egg? Possibly.

I shut off my motorcycle, removed and stowed my helmet, and then jogged under the tall pines that made this place a shady haven in the summer. Patches from the last snowfall lingered, pale smudges in the darkness.

"Where is Mick?" I called into the night.

Wind moved the pine boughs in a soft sigh. The breeze was sharp, carrying cold from the higher elevations. The sky grew darker still.

If the beings thought a storm would send me into hiding, they were wrong. I stretched my senses to the gathering clouds, the icy wind, the bite of snow. Not a very volatile storm, but it was enough to spark my magic alight.

Nash arrived beside me, toting the bag and breathing hard. He didn't ask questions but stilled and listened with me. He'd been a soldier and knew about assessing terrain that might hold an enemy.

As I gazed into the growing blackness, I faced the possibility that I'd never see Mick again.

I'd promised to marry him, to be his mate in the dragon

way, and also in the human one. To pledge myself to him alone, which hadn't been as difficult as I'd feared. Mick had always been the only one for me.

"Bring him to me," I commanded whatever waited for me out there. "Do it in the next five minutes, and I'll consider being merciful."

Lightning flashed somewhere to the north, beyond the mountains. I smiled as I encouraged the storm to come to me.

I expected Nash to admonish me for being dramatic, but instead, he called into the darkness, "You heard the lady."

"You believe me when I say something's out there?" I whispered.

Nash shrugged. "I don't see anything but trees and left-over snow, but I've experienced your weird shit before." Too many times, in his opinion.

The reply I received was not what I expected. The darkness moved. It was not a cloud or a shadow, but a *thing*.

Coyote told me that the dragon gods had made a mistake with the Phantomwalkers, that the creatures were unfinished. They'd been trying to make dragons but had got the formula wrong, like a bad batch of pottery that had to be discarded.

What rose before us now was what should have been a dragon. It had the bulk of such a being, with wide, leathery wings. But its body was skeletal, its face likewise, and it had a glow in its void-like eyes.

It opened its mouth and belched fire.

I yelped and tackled Nash, taking him to the dirt. Rocks scraped my skin, and my hands landed in a cold patch of snow.

Nash rolled away from me and gained his feet, snatching up the bag as he went.

"Don't worry—I saw *that*," he snapped. Nash held the bag out and growled at the dragon-beast. "If you want this, you won't hit me with flames. You might burn it."

For answer, the creature threw a fireball right at him. This time I was too far away to help.

The fire wrapped around Nash, who stood his ground. It was magical fire, though it could ignite real things, like trees, dead grass, the houses around the park, and Drake's bowling bag. *That* went up like a roman candle.

Nash threw the bag away from him, sending it end over end through the dirt. I ran for the bag, grabbing it and beating out the flames.

Nash stood calmly in the middle of a pillar of fire. The Phantomwalker drew back in surprise—or maybe it was waiting for Nash to crumble into ash. The flames poured over Nash for a few moments then died with a *whump.*

The creature didn't wait around to puzzle out how this happened. It flapped its wings, sending a foul stench over us. Reaching with its talons, it snatched Nash off the ground.

I screamed. Nash was impervious to magic, but if the thing released him from a great height, he'd smash to the ground as easily as any human. He was as helpless up there as Fremont would be.

Wind came to me, and with it, flakes of snow. Another winter storm was hitting the high country.

I set down the bag and reached for the storm, swirls of snow lighting my fingers. I let the Stormwalker magic ground me as I built up Beneath power to strike.

I hesitated. I needed to make the Phantomwalker put

Nash down, somehow, before I hit it. I couldn't risk it dropping Nash if I pounded the Phantomwalker with enough magic to hurt it. Another worry was that Nash's null magic might destroy the Phantomwalker altogether as he hung in its grasp, which would send him plummeting to the ground. Same dire result.

If I got Nash killed, Maya would hunt me down the rest of my days.

"Nash," I yelled. "Hang on."

The Phantomwalker began to ponderously flap away. I shouted at it, waving my arms as though that would make any difference. But if it got away from me, who the hell knew what it would do with Nash?

Lightning flickered over the mountains. I've heard people express surprise when there is lightning in snow, but it happens all the time. A storm is a storm, whether the precipitation drops out in the form of rain, hail, or snow.

I grabbed for the snowstorm, letting the frigid air penetrate my senses. Living in Flagstaff had driven me nuts, because there had been some kind of weather almost every day. However, the volatile climate had also gotten me used to storms so that they didn't always send me into a frenzy.

I twined the wind with Beneath magic but found that tonight, the storm power wanted to take over. The forces inside me recognized the intense weather forming above the peaks of the sacred Diné mountains. With effort, I held in the lightning I wanted to let fly, fearing for Nash.

The creature turned, raked its second talon down, and grabbed for the half-burned bowling bag.

I dove for it, letting the storm magic lash from me. Wrapping a chain of lightning around the bag, I jerked it from beneath the Phantomwalker's descending claw. I tossed the bag aside, using another snake of power to cushion its fall. It landed with a soft thump on a bed of pine needles dusted with snow.

There was nothing in the bag but Fremont's bowling ball, but the creature didn't need to know that. Plus, Fremont might want his ball back.

My save was for nothing, though, because the Phantomwalker shot a pale stream of electricity from its mouth, the same as what had blanketed my hotel. It blew the bag into a thousand pieces.

Fragments of canvas, foam rubber, and hard resin sprayed over me to settle, burning, on the park's damp ground.

Well then. Either the creature knew I hadn't brought the real egg, or it didn't care whether it was the egg or not. Which meant the Phantomwalkers didn't give a crap about what happened to Mick. Or Nash for that matter. Or me.

Despair wanted to take over, but Mick had taught me, during our hours of training, to focus on the problem at hand. Right now, that meant rescuing Nash and getting us out of here.

I tried to tamp down the storm powers as I willed my Beneath magic to build. I needed the Beneath part to kill the creature, with an assist from the storm to catch Nash.

Mick could have done something like this without breaking stride. I had to concentrate.

The storm, intense and highly localized, had other ideas. The Stormwalker in me liked it, wanted to grab the growing blizzard and dance on its icy flakes. I broke into a sweat despite the cold, trying to ground myself and launch an attack at the same time.

The creature, done with its task, wheeled away, carrying Nash with it.

"Stop!" I roared.

I started running, tripping over tree roots, and sliding on patches of ice. Then I gathered myself and leapt into the air.

Sometimes I could levitate on my magic, as Gabrielle did, though I couldn't always control it. If a storm was robust enough, I did amazing things, but the hell if I knew how. This storm was pretty wild, so I hoped …

I landed flat on my face, spreadeagled in the mud. *Damn it.*

A hot breeze from strong wings blasted over me, melting the snow under my hands. The odor that came with it wasn't the horrible stench of the Phantomwalker, but one that held fire and warm smoke, the kind you welcomed on a winter night.

A dragon, black as soot, streaked above the trees after the Phantomwalker. Not Mick—Drake. Another dragon who shimmered with iridescent light—dark greens, blacks, and purples—charged after him. Titus.

"No!" I yelled. The Phantomwalker would destroy them as easily as it had the bowling bag.

I scrambled to my feet and sprinted through the park, trying to keep the dragons and Phantomwalker in sight.

Drake and Titus flamed the creature, who shrugged it off. I kept running until I tumbled right over a metal railing into a concrete pit, flailing until I hit bottom.

Not a pit, I realized as I struggled to my feet, but the skateboard ramps. This space was clear of trees, and I had an unobstructed view of the dragons fighting overhead.

"Grab Nash!" I screamed, hands cupped around my mouth.

I couldn't tell if they heard me, but I could wait no longer. Lightning played at the top of Mount Elden, going for the antenna farm up there. I grabbed it and redirected it toward the Phantomwalker.

The Phantomwalker screeched when the lightning hit it, then it roared with the keen of a category five blizzard. I wound my Beneath magic through the storm, building it into a massive ball of white fire.

"Look out!" I yelled at the dragons, and then I let my magic fly.

The Phantomwalker tried to swoop away, but I'd been ready for that. With the precision of a heat-seeking missile, the incandescent ball struck the Phantomwalker full in the chest.

It let out a piercing shriek that must have shattered every window in the neighborhood before the cry gurgled to nothing. The Phantomwalker hurtled toward the ground but exploded in midair, pieces of it flying over the trees to land with a boom in the parking lot.

The bulk of the creature above me dissolved into thousands of tiny bright lights. The lights became powdery ash that drifted down to coat the trees, the bed of the skateboard park, and me.

Nash, released from the non-existent talon, plunged toward the ground, heading right for the concrete on which I stood.

CHAPTER TWENTY-TWO

I flailed out with my magic, grabbing for Nash.

I missed.

That was because the black dragon swooped in and snatched Nash out of the air just as my bolt of light reached him. The dragon flapped hard to gain height, and I fell on my butt on the freezing concrete.

More magic coiled inside me, seeking release. So it had done years ago, when it had blasted out and caught an outbuilding on my school grounds on fire.

I really didn't want to burn down any houses or the ponderosa pines in this little park, so I let the power fly straight up into the air. The ball of fire rose and rose into the blackness, until it burst like a firework.

With any luck people would think someone was doing a display, which was highly illegal in this town. That meant cops might arrive soon.

I tried to climb to my feet and couldn't. The storm, which had burst briefly over the mountains, now flowed west, moving toward Williams to wreak havoc there. My

Stormwalker power eased out with it, leaving the Beneath magic sparking and crackling inside me by itself.

A man walked out of the park's darkness and leapt lightly into the skateboard pit.

It was Titus, not wearing a stitch. He gazed down at me with eyes that were luminous gray, then reached a hand to help me up.

"Don't touch me," I warned him.

Titus misunderstood. "I mean you no harm, Janet."

"No, I mean don't because I might kill you without meaning to. I'm not exactly in control right now."

"Ah." Titus took a respectful step back. "If you are physically unharmed, then I will let you rise when you are ready."

"Appreciate it." I struggled to tamp down the Beneath magic that wanted me to kill the dragon then flatten the trees and the houses beyond, regardless of how many humans resided in them. "What the hell are you doing here, anyway? You can't fight these things."

"We received word from Colby that you went off to foolishly meet the Phantomwalkers on your own. You took Colby out of action but gave no such command to us."

"Because I didn't think you'd be stupid enough to try to fight an enemy you can't kill," I snapped at him.

"Mmm." Titus nodded as though I'd said something wise. "But you and your null-magic human bringing a decoy to meet with an unpredictable enemy is intelligent?"

"Fair point," I said grudgingly.

"Also, you were having trouble rescuing the null-magic human. So, our arrival was fortuitous."

"It was." I had to concede that too. I had counted on

Nitis to back us up, but I guessed he either didn't get my message or decided not to respond for reasons of his own.

I heard bad language being snarled under the trees before Nash stalked out of the darkness. The flashlight on his phone illuminated his muddy body and blood-streaked face. Drake, as clothes-less as Titus, followed at a discreet distance.

"Drake dropped me about six feet," Nash informed me, which explained his muddy state. "Though, since I could have fallen fifty, I appreciate the save."

Nash nodded stiffly at Drake, who gave him an equally stiff nod in return.

"Sorry, Nash," I said. "The plan was for you not to get hurt."

"Doesn't matter," Nash answered. "We figured out what they were up to."

I stilled. "We did?"

Nash's expression was grim. "This was a diversion. For us. They knew you'd never give up the egg. So what did they need us not to see?"

Titus answered. "Perhaps they are taking Mick deeper into hiding."

Not what I wanted to hear. I put a hand down to push myself up, and it sank into cold, black mud.

Sirens erupted on the road above us, the Flagstaff police coming to see what was going on. Nash reached for me.

"No," I said quickly. "I'm a live wire."

"Don't be stupid." Nash grabbed me under the arms and hauled me to my feet. "We need to go."

I tried to push away from him, but Nash had more physical strength than anyone human I knew. He held me firmly, and all my Beneath plus residual Stormwalker magic flowed straight into him.

I endeavored to contain it, but to no avail. Nash's body lit up like a ghost on its best haunting night. Snakes of electricity popped from me through him to reach for Drake and Titus, who evaded them with dragon grace.

Then the null magic in Nash clamped around for my out-of-control entwined power and swallowed it whole. The fury inside me died, and the light winked out.

I scrambled away from Nash. The reason I'd not wanted him to drain my pent-up magic wasn't because I worried it would hurt him—I knew from experience it would not—but because it always made me horny. Whenever Mick helped ease me down, it was a wild and wicked time.

Nash, as irritating as he could be, was a hot, fit man, and the turbulent Beneath goddess inside me sometimes didn't care how she calmed herself.

But I loved Mick, my dragon-man with the hot blue eyes, Maya was my friend, and Nash was … Nash.

The goddess in me looked for the dragons, but they'd gone. Either they were sensible enough to fly the hell out of here before the cops showed up, or they were avoiding the weirdness that was me.

A surge of watery fear erased the vestiges of the Beneath goddess's needs. Mick had been taken somewhere by these creatures, and if they killed him, it would destroy me. The Phantomwalkers had killed Cesnia, I was certain, who by all accounts had been one hell of a dragon. What was to say Mick could withstand them any better than she could?

And *where* was Nitis? Was he in truth one of the Phan-

tomwalkers himself? Had he really destroyed them whenever he'd fought them or only pretended to, so I'd
trust him?

I needed to talk to Grandmother.

"Let's get out of here," I said breathlessly to Nash.

"Don't run," Nash commanded as I started jogging in
the direction of our vehicles. "It makes you look like you
were doing something illegal."

Was blasting a phantom with lightning, watching a
bowling ball be destroyed, and wildly tossing magic around
illegal? Probably. I'd buy Fremont a new, nicer ball even if
he insisted it wouldn't be necessary. It was only right.

Fat flakes of snow, no longer blown by the stiff wind,
drifted lazily under the downward-facing lights of the
parking lot.

There was enough illumination to show me that Nash's
new truck had been caved in by one of the Phantomwalker's falling limbs, probably a wing. The wing had disintegrated, and a thick dusting of pale ash coated the wreck of
the pickup.

Nash emerged behind me. I heard his sharp intake of
breath, then his language blistered the air.

He wouldn't blame me for being captured and nearly
killed, for letting us spring an obvious trap, or for his fall
when Drake let him go. But this—another of his beloved
trucks ruined during the adventures of Janet Begay—this
was going to be all my fault.

Add a new vehicle to my bill along with a custom-made
bowling ball. This was turning out to be an expensive night.

———

NASH HAD TO RIDE BACK TO MAGELLAN ON MY
motorcycle, where he clung to me and grumbled about my
driving. He'd insisted on pausing at a twenty-four-hour
truck stop on the freeway before we departed so he could
purchase a motorcycle helmet, since I didn't have a spare. It
was very late, and when we entered, truckers stared at us in
our unkempt state.

"Bad night for driving, isn't it?" the young man at the
cash register said. He was Hopi, with a sunny nature and
big smile. "We have showers for twelve bucks if you want
one."

"No, thank you," Nash said. He handed over his card
for the helmet, and the young man rang it up.

"Be careful out there on the road. Nice bike," he said
to me.

"Thank you." I smiled, trying to be friendly in return,
though I was so exhausted I could barely see.

"You folks have a nice night," the young man chirped.

"You too," I said.

Nash grabbed the helmet and strode out the door. I
lingered to slam down some cash and grab a granola bar
that I stuffed into my mouth as I hurried after him. As
scared and tired as I was, working magic like that made me
ravenous.

Mick and I usually wound ourselves together for a while
after a night like this then went out for a huge breakfast. I
blinked back tears, choked down the granola bar, and
started up the bike to head east to Magellan.

We made it home in the small hours of the morning,
dawn not far away. The hotel was quiet, the party done, the
saloon closed. Hopefully all the guests were snug in bed. I

did not see Gabrielle or Colby, which probably meant they were tucked in as well.

Cassandra and Pamela had remained—they had their own room if Cassandra worked late. They were still up, Pamela regarding me with impatient eyes. Cassandra had the egg next to her in the upgraded bowling bag. I heard nothing from inside and so deduced the little dragon was asleep.

Elena and Grandmother were awake... their voices emanated from the kitchen.

Nash sank into a chair, for once showing exhaustion, but I found the energy to stride through the lobby and slap open the kitchen door.

"Where is Nitis?" I demanded.

Grandmother looked up at me from where she sat on a chair watching Elena chop peppers for the morning's omelets. She appeared fresh and lively for a woman who'd been awake all night.

"I do not know," Grandmother said without worry. "I am not his keeper."

"You asked me to trust him. He wasn't anywhere near when a Phantomwalker found us, and we barely survived."

Elena paused her knife to survey me up and down. "You did, though, didn't you?"

"Yes," I said in exasperation. "Thanks to Drake and Titus. Nash would have been a smear on the sidewalk if not for them."

Elena returned to chopping, her hand a blur as the knife rat-a-tat-tatted on the cutting board. "There is your answer."

"You're saying Nitis sent them?"

"I don't know," Grandmother answered stubbornly. "Why don't you speak to the Firewalkers about it?"

I couldn't, because they'd flown off who knew where. "I asked you this before, but I have to ask again. Who *is* Nitis? Where did he come from? How do you know he's on our side?"

"I don't think he's on anyone's side," Grandmother said. "He showed up one day, cawing at me, so arrogant. He was irritating, but I saw no reason to drive him away."

"Even though you knew nothing about him?" It wasn't like Grandmother to simply accept someone without years of watching them in suspicion first.

"He's not an evil creature," Grandmother answered. "I can tell that. We're not like you young people who 'gurgle' everyone on the computer the minute we meet them."

She meant look them up on the internet, but I didn't correct her. I doubted I'd find much about the real Nitis there anyway.

I hoisted myself onto a stool at the counter and buried my face in my hands. "I'm no closer to finding Mick."

"Aren't you?" Elena asked.

I peeked at her through my fingers. She put fragrant peppers, chopped into perfect quarter-inch cubes, into a bowl and squeezed lime juice over them.

"They could have taken him anywhere." Despair again seeped through me, and in my tired state, I couldn't fight it.

"Not anywhere," Grandmother said. "They'd want to be close enough that you can bring the egg to them."

"That doesn't mean they'll honor their bargain to release him," I returned. "Why do they want the egg so badly? What harm can one baby dragon do?"

"They grow up to be big dragons," Elena said. She

added chopped onions to the pepper mixture and stirred it into a fragrant relish. People came from miles around to try her salsas. "This baby is supposed to kill Mick when he's older, remember?"

"According to Nitis. No one else seems to know that legend."

Grandmother at last looked uncomfortable, as though realizing she might have trusted Nitis a bit too much.

As I'd observed before, Grandmother was lonely. Dad had finally left home for the first time at age fifty-five. My aunts dropped in on Grandmother every day, taking it in rotation, and Gabrielle stayed there on occasion, but otherwise, she was alone. Like Carl Jones, she had no desire to leave her little house for a big apartment complex for seniors.

Nitis hanging around must have assuaged her feelings of being neglected. Everyone in her family was busy living their own lives, while she went on by herself.

"I'm sorry, Grandmother," I said.

Grandmother focused her dark-eyed stare on me. "For what?"

"Everything, I guess."

She frowned. "The entire world's unfairness is not your fault. It is vain of you to think so."

"I'm trying to apologize for leaving home, Grandmother. Let me at least say sorry without being scolded."

"You needed to leave home," Grandmother said, as though surprised at my contrition. "Your powers were going to hurt someone, and you had to learn to control them. Your father and I had taught you all we could. You needed Jamison Kee to guide you, and then Mick, and others you met along the way. If you'd stayed home, you'd have burned down our house at some point. I knew that, and Pete did too."

"Oh." Dad had cried when I'd left—at least, he'd gazed at me with sorrow in his moist eyes. Grandmother hadn't been happy, though she'd gone with me to the BIA office to do the paperwork for my scholarship to attend NAU. The whole family had joined us that day, in fact.

"We got along fine without you," Grandmother informed me. "The universe does not revolve around you, young lady." Her favorite line when I'd been an uncertain teenager.

I swallowed. "Then thank you for letting me go. Knowing you and Dad were there, in that house, was my anchor. I knew I could always go back home, to eat your wonderful stew, and walk with Dad and just be quiet with him."

I was crying now, silent tears streaking down my cheeks. Elena tore off a paper towel and handed it to me.

"You couldn't have come back if you'd burnt our house down," Grandmother said, ever practical. "The pictures you sent to your father and me were nice."

After college, I'd earned a living taking art photos, beautiful black-and-whites, and some in color, of the natural beauty of the world. I'd started in the Indian lands, and then took more around the country after I'd met Mick.

I longed to return to my photography, but I hadn't had much time, what with saving the world from every creature that wanted to destroy me, my family, dragons, whoever, and then getting ready to marry Mick.

Elena turned to the stove, heating oil in a pan. A stack of tortillas rested by her elbow. "What do you want us to do?" she asked over her shoulder. "You came in here to berate us, so you must expect us to do something to help you."

"I need to find Mick." My heart wrenched. "What do I do?"

"Start looking," was Elena's brief answer. She sliced the tortillas into strips and tossed them into the hot oil, where they sizzled with a satisfying aroma. "Where would be the most likely spot?"

"They wanted me to bring the egg to Canyon Diablo," I said.

"That place is full of ghosts," Grandmother said. "Trashy ones. It was a wild town in its day."

"I'm not sure they meant the ghost town as much as the canyon itself." I scrubbed hands through my dirty hair, trying to put aside my fears, and *think*. "Which covers a lot of ground." I hopped from the stool and paced, my thoughts turning to plans instead of panic.

Vistas.

The whisper of the mirror in my pocket, which was followed by a faint tinkle of glass in the saloon, startled me. I pulled out the shard.

"What?" I glared into the mirror. My angry dark eyes blazed back at me. "What vistas?"

I abruptly remembered it babbling about the scenery when Carl had taken off on Mick's motorcycle. Why was it bringing that up now? It wouldn't unless it was significant, right? Then again, the mirror could be off in some dreamy delusion.

"Waves in the rock. Too many shadows." The shard jumped in my hand, and the mirror in the saloon jangled again. "The danger followed him there and decided to stay."

CHAPTER TWENTY-THREE

I shook the mirror impatiently. "Stop with the histrionics and tell me exactly what you mean."

"He went all over, and they followed," the mirror continued in its melodramatic whisper. "They silenced me ..."

I shoved the thing back into my pocket, knowing I wouldn't get anything intelligible out of it for now. Either it was too afraid to be concise or had been compelled to tell me nothing.

"Is Carl asleep?" I asked. "I need to talk to him."

Grandmother nodded. "Finally, you believe old people have something worth saying."

"Do not include me with *old people*," Elena admonished Grandmother as she removed crisp, fried tortillas from the pan with a pair of tongs. "Carl is asleep but said he was an early riser. That is why I'm already making breakfast."

"The sheriff's grandfather is smart," Grandmother said. "Probably more than is good for him." She liked to say that about people, especially me.

"Thank you," I told them both sincerely. They'd made me realize I needed to stop weeping and start acting. "If that's migas you're making, Elena, will you save me some?"

"Mmm." Elena frowned at the pan, where her next batch of tortilla strips were spattering. "If you are here during breakfast hours."

She would never let herself be caught doing anyone a favor. "You got it," I said.

I swung around and headed out of the kitchen, hearing both women clucking in disapproval behind me.

I gave the mirror a soothing pat as I passed it in the saloon, then hurried into the lobby. Nash was still there, growling at someone on his phone to come and pick him up. From his tone, I'd guess one of his deputies. If he spoke like that to Maya, she'd hit him with a pipe wrench or dump him altogether.

I moved quickly past him into my suite. Once safely inside, I made myself peel off my muddy clothes and stand under the hot shower, letting the water's warmth ease my muscles.

Tears leaked from my eyes as I rinsed my hair, but I washed them away. I didn't have time to lose it right now.

I knew that the knots inside me wouldn't unclench until I brought Mick home safely. Then, I wouldn't let him out of my sight until we were wed. After that—

I accepted in my heart that our life together would bring more of the same predicaments we were in now. We were dangerous people, and dangerous things happened to us and around us. Someone out there would always try to exploit our powers or want to kill us because of them.

With those happy thoughts, I finished my shower, brushed my teeth, dressed in clean clothes, and went back out to the lobby. Cassandra sat at her post, as neat and tidy as usual, the bowling bag at her feet, while Pamela ate breakfast in the saloon.

Elena had served the migas there, buffet style. Layers of eggs, peppers, cheese, and tortillas, warmed in a serving tray, and a stone bowl of fresh salsa reposed next to it. Both dishes were already half empty.

I scooped up a portion of migas and strode to the table where Carl sat, devouring a mounded plate of food.

"Spill," I said to him as he munched. "When you took Mick's bike, where did you go?"

Carl's eyes brightened as I sat down. He swallowed noisily and took a loud slurp of coffee.

"Mick's ride is nice," he said. "Shame the cop caught me, though he turned out to be cool. I'd never have done anything to that motorcycle. It's a piece of art."

"You've ridden before?"

"Of course I have." Carl snorted before he masticated another mouthful. "Had a Harley when I was about your age. It's how I met Nash's grandmother. Ellen. She was a beauty. All black hair and blue eyes, biggest smile you ever saw."

He cleared his throat, blinking, and took a more subdued sip of coffee.

I'd love to have said something like *Nash speaks fondly of her*, but Nash had never mentioned his grandmother, or Carl, or even his own parents. I knew Nash had a brother because the first case I'd investigated when I'd come to Magellan had marginally involved him. Never met the man, though.

"I'm sorry she's gone," I said in sympathy.

"Not as sorry as I am, that's for sure. Lost my kids too.

I'm stuck with two grandsons and a granddaughter who all think work is the same as entertainment, and that entertainment is a waste of time. Nash had it bad in the war, that is true. But if you think he's cold now … *Shew*."

"So I've heard." I pulled Carl back to the topic. "Tell me where you went on Mick's motorcycle."

He shrugged. "Up north somewhere."

"How far north?"

"I wasn't paying attention. Out in the middle of nowhere."

"What did this middle of nowhere look like?"

Carl threw down his fork. His eyes flashed, and for a moment, I saw exactly where Nash came by his stubborn crankiness.

"I don't know, sweetie. Why don't you ask your tribal cop friend?"

Oh, I'd ask him, as soon as I figured out where he was. He was another person who'd not showed up to save us at the cute little park in Flagstaff.

Carl's aura, which was a clean gray with a few blue streaks in it, now had a more shadowy gray. I recognized the taint of a compulsion spell and sent him a little smile.

"Stay right here, okay?"

"I'm eating," Carl snapped, sounding so much like Nash I flinched. "I'm not going anywhere 'til I'm done."

I took a bite of Elena's wonderful dish, nipped to the lobby, and beckoned to Cassandra. "Can you help me with something?"

Cassandra clicked a few more keys on her computer then rose without question. I grabbed the bowling bag, and led Cassandra to the saloon.

Carl was still shoveling in his food. Cassandra sat down

at the table with us, her eyes widening as she regarded Carl. She was better at seeing auras than I was, so the spell must have been more obvious to her.

Carl swallowed his mouthful. "You sure are pretty, Ms. Bryson. I know I'm not supposed to say that to a lady, but that's stupid. You *are* pretty. I'm old. I know nothing's ever going to happen between us, so take it as truth."

"Thank you," Cassandra said graciously. "You are very kind. Do you mind if I just …" She lifted well-manicured fingers and carefully touched Carl's forehead. Her brows went up. "Oh, my."

"How bad is it?" I asked in a low voice.

"How bad is what?" Carl demanded. "Do I have a tumor, or something?"

"A spell," I said. I wasn't certain whether he'd believe that, but Carl deserved the truth. "Don't worry. Cassandra will remove it."

"Huh?" Carl took another sip of coffee. "Whatever."

Cassandra closed her eyes and whispered a few words. Carl pretended to ignore her, but his gaze flickered to her in curiosity.

The darkness I'd sensed shrouding him suddenly flared high. Cassandra gasped and jerked her hand away.

"You all right?" Carl asked in concern.

"What happened?" I asked at the same time.

"It's strong." Cassandra drew a shaking breath. "It wasn't one mage who put this on him, but a collective. They don't want him telling you about *something.* I'm sorry, I can't discern what."

"Don't talk about me like I'm not here," Carl said in irritation. "I get enough of that from doctors when Ada takes me for checkups. What are you blathering about?"

Cassandra gazed at him with her cool eyes. "Someone put a spell on you, Carl. They don't want you telling us what you saw or did at some point the day before yesterday, when you went joy riding."

"What are you talking about? I don't remember anyone trying any woo-woo magic crap with me. I rode around until that cop caught me and dragged me home, is all. He's a fun guy, I have to say. Nothing like my grandson."

"Do you think Coyote did this?" Cassandra asked me.

I shook my head. "Doesn't feel like him, plus I don't know why he would. Carl, I suspect you met up with the Phantomwalkers. I'm guessing they tracked Mick's bike, which has his aura all over it. The mirror won't tell me where it went either."

Carl stared at us, coffee cup hovering. "Phantom whats? Seriously, you are crazy, the pair of you. Good-looking, sure, but nuts."

"Can you remove it?" I asked Cassandra.

She drew a breath. "Maybe. It will be difficult. These are serious powers at work."

I knew a spell was bad when a witch as strong as Cassandra wasn't sure she could break it.

"Where's Nash?" I asked Carl.

He shrugged. "Maya just picked him up. Nash told one of his deputies to come fetch him, but Maya intercepted him. I like *her*. She's nice to me and she doesn't act insane."

"You haven't seen her when she's really angry," I told him. "I'll call her. I think we're going to need Nash."

———

As predicted, Maya was not happy when I made my request for Nash to return to the hotel. I didn't bother phoning him directly, because there was a good chance he'd reject the call when he saw my name pop up on his cell.

"He needs to sleep, Janet," Maya snapped at me.

"Can't he sleep after he helps his grandfather?" I asked. "I'm not sure what else to do."

Maya became instantly solicitous. "Is Carl okay?"

"Someone put a nasty spell on him that even Cassandra can't budge. Nash might be able to."

"I'll bring him over," Maya promised. "I have to warn you, though, he's livid about his truck."

"I didn't do it," I said quickly. "Not directly, anyway. Wouldn't he rather have his truck wrecked but his life saved?"

Maya unbent enough to chuckle. "With Nash? Probably the other way around. He gets things into his head, you know? We'll be there."

Maya hung up without a goodbye.

While waiting for them, I took stock of my resources. I tried to eat more of Elena's breakfast, but my stomach was clenched, and I couldn't tolerate the food. I promised myself I'd feast when we found Mick and brought him home safely.

For help, I had Gabrielle and Colby, who were still in the bedroom Cassandra had given them at the top of the house. There was Cassandra for strong magic and Pamela if I needed a good fighter. I had the mirror, which was likely also fighting a compulsion spell to keep me from seeing Mick. I had Nash, who maybe could negate the spell on both the mirror and Carl.

I returned to the kitchen to check on the other two

resources I had. Grandmother was still there, sitting in a chair at a small table, daintily nibbling on breakfast, while Elena chopped more peppers with fierce precision.

As I entered, Elena scraped up the sliced peppers with her knife and dropped them into a bowl. "Still here, are you?" she demanded.

I bit the inside of my cheek and held on to my patience. "If I need your help rescuing Mick, can I ask it of you?"

Grandmother's fork rattled to her empty plate. "Of course we will help. Your Firewalker has proved himself to be a good being, many times over."

"Not *you*, Grandmother," I said before I could stop myself. "This is way too dangerous."

"Do not tell me what to do, Janet Begay." Grandmother used the hard tones I so well remembered.

Elena said nothing, but her glare spoke volumes.

I fumbled for an explanation. "These Phantomwalkers don't seem to be hurt by Earth magic. I don't know if you could hold them off, Grandmother."

"I didn't intend to fight them with magic," Grandmother said indignantly. "That is not my way. But I can do other things. We will find Mick and bring him home, as we have done before."

Not her way, she claimed. I recalled how, not long ago in Las Vegas, she'd helped a Beneath-magic goddess banish an entity back into the oblivion it had come from. Before that, she and Elena had closed a vortex in the middle of a hotel room in New Mexico.

I decided not to bring up either instance. "Please, stay safe. And keep Dad and Gina safe too." I knew Grandmother would only stay home if she chose to, but she did feel an obligation to protect others.

"What about the egg?" Elena asked. "It remains here?"

"No." I'd thought long and hard about that as I'd showered. "I'll have to behave as though I'm truly willing to exchange it for Mick. They knew I wouldn't bring it to the first drop, so they didn't bring Mick either. I have to be sincere. That's why I'm asking for help. It's not just for Mick."

"We *will* help, Janet," Grandmother said. "Now, stop fussing and get on with it."

I opened my mouth to argue, then decided to save my energy. I nodded at them and scurried out of the kitchen.

Dad and Gina were breakfasting in the saloon. The bowling bag, which Gina must have retrieved from where I'd left it with Cassandra, sat firmly under Gina's chair.

I started toward them but before I reached their table, I spied Maya's shining white pickup pull up out front. I waved to Gina and Dad and headed for the front door.

Maya hopped out of her truck, clad in shorts, a loose T-shirt, and sneakers with thick socks folded at her ankles. She preceded Nash, who looked as though he'd had time to shower and iron his jeans, into the lobby.

"Where's Carl?" Maya greeted me.

I gestured her into the saloon, where Carl was finishing up his meal. He'd gone back for seconds of the migas as well as a heaping portion of roasted potatoes.

"Maya," he sang out. "There's my girl." He stood up and enfolded Maya in the hug she offered him.

"You all right?" Maya rubbed Carl's shoulders as they came out of the embrace. "Janet says you're under a dark spell, but she's always spouting that kind of bullshit."

Carl cackled with laughter. "She told me that too, but I'm just fine. Good food here." He rubbed his belly.

Maya had at one time been a huge Unbeliever, one of the few in the town of Magellan, where the paranormal was real. She'd come around after witnessing things she couldn't deny, as well as helping me win a few battles. Now, I read worry in her eyes as she tried to reassure Carl.

"Nash," Carl called to his grandson. "You look terrible."

"Thank you." Nash glowered at him. "Sit down. If Janet says something's wrong, then it's wrong."

High praise from Nash, who also had been one of the biggest Unbelievers around. Small wonder he and Maya had fallen for each other.

"You both are nuts." Carl plopped into his chair and folded his arms, his smiles gone.

Nash turned to me. "What do I do?"

"Touch him," I said. "That's probably all he needs."

Nash took the seat I'd previously occupied. He studied Carl, while Carl gazed stubbornly back at him.

"He looks fine," Nash said.

"Yes," I agreed. "But trust me."

Nash's quick scowl reminded me that his most recent favor had dropped him in mud and wrecked his new truck, but I could see he believed me. He reached across the table and laid a hand on Carl's arm.

Carl regarded Nash's hand, tanned and scarred, without concern.

Then Carl gasped. His body jerked, his face twisted, and then he released a scream of unimaginable pain.

CHAPTER TWENTY-FOUR

M aya lunged for Nash. "Stop!" she shouted.

I caught her by the shoulders. "No." When Maya turned to me in fury, I eased my grip into a soothing caress. "Let Nash finish. Please."

Maya jerked from me, but she subsided.

I too hated seeing Carl locked in pain, his face squeezed so tightly it vanished in a sea of wrinkles. His moans became faint, sound now barely escaping him.

What I found in his aura explained his agony. Red streaks swirled through the shadowy gray, darting, stabbing, swooping. The streaks and shadows encased him in a mesh net, similar to the one that had surrounded the hotel. I sensed the granite-hard magic of the Phantomwalkers entwining to keep out not only Earth magic but Beneath as well.

The Phantomwalkers were adapting.

They didn't know what to make of Nash, though. He was unique.

The gaping dark nothing that was Nash's null magic

seeped into Carl. Carl desperately tried to break his grip, but Nash tightened his hold, just enough to prevent Carl from moving.

My rage at the Phantomwalkers rose. Carl was an innocent they were using in their need to capture the egg and destroy dragons. I'd been feeling a little sorry for the Phantomwalkers for being discarded on the heap of failed god experiments. They'd been rejected, and were only trying to survive, after all.

My pity evaporated as Carl struggled. I understood why the Phantomwalkers hated and feared Mick and other dragons, who had the life they'd been deprived of. I could even understand their need to get their claws on Cesnia's kid, who would grow up to be another dragon to oppose them. Or perhaps they meant to raise him and brainwash him into helping them erase all other dragons. Not that I was going to let them do either one.

But using Carl, a harmless human, simply to slow me down, seriously pissed me off. They could have left Carl alone. So what if he'd blundered into their secret places in the desert? They could have done a baffling spell to make him go a different direction.

Instead, they'd deliberately messed with him in order to thwart me, and that, I wouldn't put up with. They made the evil goddess deep in my psyche want to come out and play.

I watched the void of Nash's negative field pull on the black and red mesh, Carl's body writhing as he fought. Carl grabbed Nash's arm with his other hand, trying to pry Nash loose.

A hand pressed down on both of theirs. I recognized Gina's work-worn fingers holding Nash and Carl together.

Gina had a small amount of shaman power, but

nothing that could destroy entities such as the Phantomwalkers. Hers was the quiet magic of rock and water, sky and breeze, the warmth of the sun on the soil.

I saw the spell in Carl eagerly reach to ensnare her.

"No, Gina, let go," I said in alarm. "It's too dangerous."

Gina regarded me calmly. "The sheriff needs to finish."

Nash, who'd frowned at their collective hands, said nothing. He wasn't actively working against the spell trapping Carl's aura, because Nash didn't control what was inside him. The null magic acted whether he willed it or not.

The threads of red and black began to slowly, but inexorably, flow from Carl into Nash. As Gina's pressure kept their hands together, the spell streamed faster and faster out of Carl to bury itself into Nash's body.

Carl shuddered. He let out a sharp wail when the final ball of darkness wrenched itself out of him and dove into Nash.

Nash immediately released Carl, and I yanked both Gina and Carl away from him. Nash pressed his balled fists into his abdomen, the cords on his neck standing out as he struggled.

In agitation, Maya moved toward him, but I stopped her with a raised hand. No one could help him at this point.

The hot threads wound inside Nash, trying to gather themselves, while Nash silently fought. The compulsion spell struggled mightily to continue its existence, but Nash's null field closed around the mesh like a moray eel snapping up its prey.

The spell shuddered once and then abruptly winked out.

Nash slowly released his breath and unclenched his fists.

When he opened his eyes, he found the rest of us regarding him in consternation—Maya, Gina, Carl, Pamela, Cassandra who'd come back in to help, Dad, who'd stayed at the table guarding the egg, and me.

"Did we get it?" Nash asked.

"Yes," I said around a breath of relief. "You did."

"Shew." Carl put his hand to his heart, but it was a dramatic gesture only, not an indication he was ill. "What the hell was that?"

"Compulsion spell," I said.

"Comp— what?" Carl peered at me in disbelief. "I said you were crazy, even if you're cute. What are you talking about? I thought I was having a stroke."

Maya crouched next to his chair. "It's part of the weird shit Janet gets mixed up in, dragging the rest of us along with her."

"Not on purpose," I said quickly. "You all right, Nash?"

Nash regarded me with his usual steadiness. "I need some coffee, but yes." His left cheek and forehead were abraded from our earlier adventure, and slow burning anger filled his eyes, but otherwise, he looked normal.

"I will bring coffee," Gina announced. She disappeared into the kitchen without another word.

I pulled a chair next to Carl, opposite where Maya knelt. The two of us crowded him, but he didn't look unhappy about it. "Where did you go riding on Mick's bike?" I asked him.

"Toward Monument Valley," Carl answered right away. "Turned off on some back roads, where there's nothing for miles. Great day for a ride. Found some awesome rock formations you'd never know were there from the main highway. I used to hike out in that area when I was younger, but I'd forgotten. Lots of memories in those little creeks through the sandstone."

Waves in the rock, the mirror had said. *Too many shadows.*

"I know where Mick is," I said, and hauled myself to my feet.

———

I BANGED ON THE DOOR OF THE ROOM CASSANDRA HAD given Gabrielle and Colby. I supposed they were officially a couple now, or Cassandra would have found them separate ones.

"Good morning," Gabrielle sang as she opened the door. She was dressed in jeans and a black top, the shower running in the bathroom behind her. "Isn't it a beautiful day?"

I recognized the signs of a woman falling in love with a dragon.

"Come help me rescue Mick?" I asked her. "I figured out where they're holding him. At least, I hope I figured it out. We need to hurry, in case they move him."

"Got it. Colby, sweetie, we're going," she shouted to the bathroom.

"What?" I heard Colby's rumble through the door. "What did you say?"

They were a couple, all right.

I left them and hurriedly descended the stairs. Carl, Nash, and Maya were in the lobby—Carl rubbed his head and grumbled about a slight headache.

"Carl, you're riding with me," I said. "Nash, we'll need you."

"No transportation," Nash said curtly. "Your demonic friends saw to that."

"Maya, will you let him borrow—"

"No." Maya cut me off. "If he goes in my truck, I'm driving him."

"It's too dangerous," Nash snapped at her. "These things are huge and deadly. Stay here and take care of my grandfather. Who is also not going." He scowled at Carl, who scowled right back.

"I'm the only one who knows where *to* go," Carl told him.

"You can draw us a map," Nash countered.

"Nope. I'm gonna—"

Carl's rebuttal was interrupted by a high-pitched scream in the saloon, one only the magical in the room could hear. The mirror was keening, as though the compulsion spell was being ripped from it too.

At the same time, I heard a shout.

"Janet!"

It was Gina. I abandoned the argument and sprinted to her, my heart banging with fear.

The Horribles had come down to breakfast. Instead of sitting and inhaling Elena's pastries while conducting a shouting and squealing conversation, they'd converged on Dad and Gina.

Their eyes were glassy, their movements jerky and zombie-like. Gina clutched the bowling bag to her chest, searching for an opening to run. Dad stood, grim-faced, in front of her, ready to defend his beloved wife from the determined horde.

I saw the grimy shadow of another compulsion spell in

their auras, which were usually bright and innocent. The Horribles were egregiously annoying but not evil.

Whether the spell came from the vestiges of what Nash had pulled from Carl, or through the mirror, or in an encounter between the Horribles and more Phantomwalkers, I couldn't say.

I only knew that if they grabbed the egg, I'd have to stop them before they destroyed it. Murdering humans wasn't my thing, but it might be the only way.

Pamela, who'd leapt to her feet, appeared ready to start the slaying. Changers had a simple outlook on life. Cassandra, behind me, was chanting a counter-spell, but it would be a while before she finished. Same with anything Elena and Grandmother, who'd emerged from the kitchen, could do.

Like Pamela, I also preferred to keep things simple. I dove between Allie and her sisters, lunged past my father, who quickly stepped out of my way, and grabbed the bowling bag from Gina.

The Horribles turned and converged on me. In a few swift twists, I slid free of them and sprinted for the lobby. The family ignored Gina and Dad and ran after me.

"Carl, let's go!" I yelled.

Carl, quick on the uptake, instantly hotfooted it behind me. "I *knew* those people were zombies."

I didn't have time to explain. Nash turned to confront the mob, but Maya pulled him firmly toward the front door. I was barely aware of Cassandra and Elena following the Horribles, both murmuring countering magic.

I led Carl at a run through the door to my suite, slamming and locking it behind us. The Horribles hit the door so hard the wood creaked.

"This is creepy," Carl said as he followed me down the narrow hall and outside through the rear exit. "I love it."

I hurried to my motorcycle, which I'd left parked in the shadow of the hotel, and thrust the bowling bag into the saddlebag. The bag jiggled, and I opened the zipper enough to give the egg inside a reassuring pat.

The egg seemed warmer than it had before, or maybe that was my imagination. I swore I felt a tingle through my fingers and hoped it wasn't about to hatch, not right now.

I handed Carl the helmet Nash had bought in Flagstaff and swung on the bike. Carl hopped up behind me with the agility of long practice.

"They're coming," Carl announced.

The Horribles must have broken into my suite because they were streaming out the back door Carl and I had used. The compulsion spell hadn't let them figure out it would be easier to go through the lobby and around the building. Spells like that made a person single-minded—they'd die trying to get through one door when there was an open window beside it.

Oh well, more repairs.

I started up the motorcycle and peeled off, my back wheel sending a load of dust and gravel over the Horribles. They yelled their rage, continuing to lurch after me as I skimmed around the hotel to the front parking lot.

Maya had her pickup waiting where my property joined Barry's. As soon as Carl and I whizzed past, she slid into place behind me, and we bumped from the dirt lot onto the smooth highway.

The Horribles ran after us, but they could only move as fast as human beings were able, and none of them were in very good shape. They barely made it as far as the paved road before they halted, fists waving.

I hoped the compulsion spell wore off as soon as their quarry—me and the egg—were out of reach. I also hoped they didn't remember anything about it. I couldn't afford to comp their entire stay because they were accidentally ensorcelled.

"Keep an eye on them," I yelled at my side mirror. "Help Cassandra de-spell them if she needs assistance."

"Aw, you're no fun, honey. I like them better this way."

"Do it."

The mirror heaved a grating sigh. "The Phantomwalkers got to me too. Sorry, babe. Spell broke out of me when it jumped to our favorite family."

"It's all right. Do you remember where you went now?"

"Yep," the mirror said brightly. "How about you let me drive?"

"That's okay. I want us to get there alive."

I raced along the empty highway northward toward the I-40, the freeway on which I'd tiredly ridden home earlier this morning. I had much more energy now, though I'd not slept at all. My determination to find Mick fueled me.

At Winslow, I headed west, putting my head down and speeding as fast as I dared. I swerved around clumps of eighteen-wheelers and past cars apparently determined to make Los Angeles in record time. Behind me, Carl yelled his approval.

Maya kept up. Glances into the rearview showed her truck behind me, Nash stiffly in the passenger seat. Not long after we passed the road to Meteor Crater, another motorcycle zoomed next to mine. Colby, his hair braided to keep out of the way, gave me a thumbs-up. Clutching him around the waist and grinning at me, was Gabrielle.

Everyone was excited about this situation but me, and probably Nash. My stomach was cramped, my fears high. I was taking a big gamble on Mick being where I thought he was, and I had no idea what I was going to do when I found him.

One thing I would *not* do was give the Phantomwalkers the egg. Nor would I sacrifice Mick for Cesnia's kid. I was going to rescue them both.

I just hadn't figured out how yet.

Traffic thickened as we skimmed into Flagstaff. The exit that took me to the north-bound road rose over train tracks where a long-haul freight train clanked into town beneath us, its horn mournful.

I swung onto the 89, heading back into Navajo country and open desert. We descended out of the mountains to dry, dry land, the soil and rocks changing from black to a distinctive reddish pink.

Traffic was sparser here, but plenty of RVs and cars made for the North Rim, Page, Horseshoe Bend, and Lake Powell. My destination was in a slightly different direction, but for now, we followed the vacationers.

Colby stayed with me, our pair of motorcycles often side by side, with Maya tailing us. I kept an eye out for any sign of the Phantomwalkers, but I saw nothing. Either they didn't like to be out in the daylight, or they were waiting to ambush us. I was pretty sure my second hunch was right, now that they knew we were coming.

We lost traffic when the road split to the North Rim, but plenty of cars still headed to Page, the only town of any size for miles around.

A bit beyond this turnoff, I halted on the side of the road. Sand lapped from the desert beyond onto the black-top, but scrub and grasses dotted the land, attesting to winter rainfall.

Colby drew up next to me, and Maya scooted her truck as far onto the road's shoulder as she could.

I removed my helmet, stretched my stiff legs, and turned to Carl. "Where?"

Carl scanned the area. "Should be a little bitty road up here somewhere. Takes off that way." He pointed to the east, where hills rose and fell. Flashes of green showed where creeks flowed in between dust and scrub.

"Are you sure you remember where it is?"

"Of course I do. I'm not senile." Carl softened his tone. "My wife and I used to ride all over this place when we were younger. There was only so much to do in Flag on a weekend in those days." He chuckled. "Not much now, either."

"Let me know when we get there," I said.

"Roger that, young lady."

"Want me to fly around?" Colby raised his voice over the rumble of his bike. "Scout the area?"

"Please keep your dragon ass on the ground," I said firmly. "I don't want to have to rescue two of you."

"His dragon ass is staying right here," Gabrielle assured me. She leaned into Colby's back, and I saw a spark of magic crackle in her fingers. Alarming, but I knew she'd keep Colby safe.

"Watch for my turn," I said.

Colby gave me a thumbs-up. Maya nodded through her open window, though I wasn't sure how much she or Nash had heard.

I settled my helmet, and we were off again. This should be a wonderful drive, with smooth red outcrops on one side of the highway and glimpses of the Colorado River and the beginnings of the Grand Canyon on the other. The deceptively flat plains occasionally dropped into deep crevices, bridges sailing over them.

Carl tapped me before we'd gone more than five miles. He pointed off to our right, at a dirt road that meandered into the desert.

I signaled to my friends and swung my motorcycle onto the track. Colby came behind me, and Maya maneuvered her truck to follow. I worried that we'd encounter washes or rocky rises that would hinder her, but Maya drove confidently. Her pickup was good for off-roading, I knew, as she sometimes had to drive out to remote ranches to do electrical repairs.

My bike abruptly began to shudder. I stared in alarm at my dials, then realized it wasn't the motorcycle itself. The jerks came from the egg jumping in the saddlebag. It sensed something that excited it, but I couldn't know if that something was Mick, or it was simply ready to have a go at the Phantomwalkers.

Following Carl's directions, I skimmed down into a valley, the road taking us behind the rocky hills that lined the highway. I was glad we could be somewhat hidden, because any tribal cop or patroller on the highway might otherwise spot us taking off across the open ground. We weren't doing anything strictly illegal, but we'd attract attention and possibly followers.

I breathed easier when we were well beyond the hills and descending once more. I had a feeling I knew where Carl was taking me.

Waves in the rock, the mirror had said.

I discovered I'd been right when Carl pointed again. I left the road, which had shrunk to a mere dirt lane, and drove down a tiny track. Red sandstone walls rose on either side of us, stretching into a long box canyon.

I drove carefully over ruts and tree roots, the motorcycle wobbling. At the very end of the canyon, a sandstone slab towered about a hundred feet above us, closing off the way.

Dark hollows dotted the base of the cliff, and more appeared in the walls around us. Water that trickled through these rocks over the millennia had carved out narrow, curving passageways. Openings in the sandstone ceilings admitted fingers of sunlight that turned the walls inside into bands of exquisite colors.

I halted the bike, turning off the engine. Colby shut down beside me. Maya hadn't been able to get her truck around the last narrow bend, but she and Nash walked toward us from there.

Silence filled the space, wind sighing from the top of the rock walls.

I studied the entrance to a slot canyon which I sensed held more than a pretty hiking trail. *Too many shadows,* the mirror had also said.

I'd always known there was something eerie and evil about this particular canyon, though I'd not thought about it much after I'd left home. Perhaps the Phantomwalkers had holed up here for centuries, perhaps it was as sacred to them as the mountains were to the Diné, or volcanoes were to dragons. Maybe it was their home base, a place well hidden from humans. It might simply be a gateway, like Cesnia's wall had been to her true lair.

Regardless, I felt them in there, watching, waiting in rising anticipation.

From beside me, the mirror hissed. "They're *here*."

CHAPTER TWENTY-FIVE

I couldn't simply run into the canyon, yelling, hands blazing with Beneath magic. I needed a strategy, to line up my troops in the most effective way.

Colby had to stay out of the line of fire, but he could distract the Phantomwalkers, and maybe help Mick escape. Gabrielle and Nash would be with me in the front. Maya and Carl should stay in the truck. They'd be safer, and Maya could race the two of them to safety if need be.

Of course, none of that happened.

Gabrielle swung off Colby's bike and charged into the narrow crevice in the sandstone. "Eat hot death, dirtbags!" she shouted.

Colby rushed right after her.

Nash, who'd clearly also wanted a plan of attack, growled his frustration. He carried a toolbox, which, typical of Nash, was meticulously organized. Ropes, crampons, flashlights, small cubes that would become rain gear, and little packs of rations were all carefully packed into their own compartments.

He pulled out a flashlight, then shouldered a coil of rope and added a grappling hook to it. Smart. The rocks around here could open in sudden fissures, pretty to look at but deadly to fall into.

"Grandad, you stay—" Nash broke off as Carl jogged toward the slit in the rock after Colby. "Get back here! Stay with Maya."

Carl turned at the entrance. "You aren't the only one who saw combat, son. This isn't the jungles of southeast Asia, but I know how to avoid the enemy."

"You were eighteen," Nash argued.

"Doesn't matter. It's something you never forget." Carl started forward again and slipped into the darkness.

"See what I put up with?" Nash muttered, his face tight.

"We'll catch up to them and toss them out," I said. "Then you and I and Gabrielle extract Mick."

"Agreed."

When Nash thought I made sense, things were truly precarious.

I lifted Fremont's bowling bag from my motorcycle and tightly clenched its handle. Leaving it in the truck would be better than bringing it with me but not with only Maya to guard it. I couldn't put her into that danger. I hefted the bag, ready to defend the egg with all I had.

Maya was the only person who showed any astuteness for the situation. She remained by my motorcycle, cell phone in hand. Before we could start for the canyon, Maya strode to Nash and threw her arms around him.

"Come back alive, or I'll kill you," she promised.

Nash's face softened as he cupped her cheek and pressed a kiss to her lips. He said nothing, but their eyes met in understanding.

I glanced away to let them have their moment, and when I looked back, Maya was trotting in the direction of the truck, her sneakers stirring up puffs of dust.

"I love seeing the two of you happy," I told Nash as he joined me.

I got a scowl in return. "It's none of your business. Stay behind me."

Nash strode into the cave before I could say another word. I rolled my eyes and followed him.

We stepped from bright morning sunshine into cool shadow, the sounds of breeze and birdsong abruptly shutting off.

Slot canyons are nature's sculptures hidden deep in the desert. Many of them lie on Navajo lands, accessible only through a tour booked with a Diné company. They'd closed them off fairly recently to keep their beauty from being destroyed by vandals or too many visitors.

Some, like this one, lay far from the tourists' radar, remote, alone, unvisited. Only those who ventured far off the beaten track—and didn't get caught—would have found this place.

I'd learned about this canyon from exploring the land as a child with my father, and as I say, I'd never liked it. Carl had discovered it in his younger days as well, when there were fewer hikers seeking the dwindling wilderness. The Phantomwalkers might have been dormant then or saw no reason to drive either of us away. After all, we weren't dragons.

No matter what this canyon was to them, the Phantomwalkers were now luring me into a well-baited trap. But that didn't matter. I had to rescue Mick, even if he was being used as a dragon-shaped piece of cheese to attract me, the unruly mouse.

I couldn't hear Gabrielle, Colby, or Carl up ahead. The sound of Nash leading the way was all that came back to me, his footfalls thudding in the sand.

Nash's flashlight shone on the sharp curves of the canyon, stone that captured the beauty of the land and froze it forever. Sunlight shone down on us from cracks above, varying the colors of the walls from pink to purple to deep violet to light red.

Nash vanished around a tight corner. I followed a few steps behind him, but when I rounded the bend, I found only another curve and no Nash. I hurried, pattering to keep up.

After the next corner, the canyon straightened into a narrow passage, sunlight showing me empty sand and stone. Nash wasn't there.

I didn't dare shout for him. I pressed outwardly with my senses, searching for auras, but I found none.

The dragon egg jiggled inside the bag, as though it also knew we were alone.

My heart beating swiftly, I pulled the shard of mirror from my pocket and opened its chamois bag. "Hey," I whispered. "Where are they?"

"Gone," the mirror whispered back. "And here. They're all around us."

"Not helping. Where's Mick?"

"In the deepest shadow."

Still not the most lucid answer, but I took the warning seriously. This canyon was a magical place, not only for its splendor but also for the deep cloak of earth magic that embraced it.

Dragons—Firewalkers—were earth magic, very much so. Phantomwalkers, created at the same time, were as well. I couldn't defeat them with my Stormwalker power alone.

I recalled the night Mick had dragged me from a fight in a roadhouse bar in Nevada to the cheap motel across the highway. My opponents had thought he'd planned to teach me a lesson, and I was terrified he was too.

Mick had stood six feet away from me in the motel bedroom and told me to give him my best shot.

I'd fired him with all the lightning from the thunderstorm that had been booming around us. He'd flared with electricity, spreading his arms to light up like a firework. For one horrified moment, I'd thought I'd killed him.

Mick had absorbed all the lightning, a large bolt of it diving down his throat, and he'd laughed. Then he'd taken me to dinner.

Dragons could devour my storm magic for breakfast— or in that particular case, an evening snack. Logically, Phantomwalkers would be able to as well.

Fine. I'd give them a dose of the other side of me, and this time, I wouldn't hold back.

I drew a breath, hugged the bowling bag against my side, and strode onward.

Around the next corner, the crack overhead closed, and the light faded. I conjured the tiniest spark of magic between my fingers, enough to keep me from tripping over any errant rocks, and continued.

I could feel them around me, as the mirror had said. Were they a piece of the cave wall? I recalled the rock thing that had attacked Mick in Cesnia's lair. This entire slot canyon could be a Phantomwalker, or a collection of them.

In that case, I was already inside their collective throat. Not a happy thought.

They didn't attack. I walked alone, in silence, deeper into the cave.

I knew from experience that this slot canyon had an exit on its far end. It came out through a narrow opening above a steep drop to a wash about five feet below it.

As I walked farther and farther in, my small light showing the way, I realized that the canyon I'd explored as a girl with my dad and this place were no longer the same. Had the Phantomwalkers bent the rocks around us to their will, or taken them over somehow? Or was I in a shadow world of the Phantomwalkers, as I'd guessed?

The bag jumped harder in my hand. Warning me?

I rounded another corner and stumbled to a halt when bright light flooded my face. I screwed my eyes shut and flung up my hand, ready to blast whatever had come at me.

"Oops," Carl said, and the light grew less intense. "Didn't mean to night blind you."

I cracked open my eyes to find the older Jones with his back against the dark wall, Nash's big flashlight now pointed at the ground.

"Are you all right?" I asked him. "Where's Nash? Gabrielle and Colby?"

Carl shrugged. "Nash ran past me and gave me his light. I never caught up to your sister and her boyfriend."

This did not bode well. "You can get out if you go back the way I came. Keep your hand on a wall, and that should guide you to the entrance."

Carl regarded me in annoyance. "No shit, Sherlock. But I'm not going back. My grandson's in there, with who knows what else? Besides, I can light your way."

"Signaling to everything in there that we're coming."

"They already know." Carl shrugged. "We've given away our position, so let's use whatever advantages we have. Sneakiness only gets you so far, then you need tactics to win a battle."

"I don't have any tactics," I confessed. "That is, I started to form them, then everyone ran off."

"Good thing you found me." Carl grinned and gestured with the flashlight. "Let's do some planning."

———

As strategies went, it wasn't the best, but we didn't have much choice. First, we had to find the enemy before we could engage them.

I told Carl my theory that the Phantomwalkers were part of the stones themselves, but he shook his head. "If that were true, we'd already be dead."

He was likely right. I reasoned that the others were still alive, only hidden from me. I could hope that they'd already found Mick and would come bursting out with him any moment. Any moment, now …

In the meantime, Carl and I executed our plan. I had Carl stay put, then I walked forward with the bag, rounding a couple of corners but keeping Carl's flashlight behind me in sight. I didn't want to lose him as well. I tiptoed to a niche in the rock and placed the bag there before returning to Carl.

Did I really think the Phantomwalkers would fall for the old fake-egg-in-the-bag trick again? Probably not, but it might distract them. All I needed was for them to move their attention from me for a few moments.

I breathed a sigh of relief when I found Carl where I left him. He held the flashlight in one hand and cradled the egg I'd wrapped in my jacket in the other.

Now to wait.

I wasn't certain what I expected. For the Phantomwalkers to gleefully rush to the bag and run off with it, guiding the way to Mick? They'd proved to be more canny than that.

What I heard as Carl and I waited, hunkered together in the dark—flashlight off, magic extinguished—was wings.

Not the giant ones of dragons or the skeletal ones of the Phantomwalkers, but the feathery rustle of a bird that had flown into the canyon through one of its openings. A bird-sized bird, nothing massive about it.

Carl and I ducked instinctively as the avian zipped over our heads and landed next to the niche where I'd left the bag. I crept forward, Carl at my heels, and we peered around the corner.

It should be dark in that tunnel, but a shadowy-gray glow surrounded the bird. By that light I saw a large crow with white head feathers among its sable ones.

Nitis hopped on top of the bowling bag and used his strong beak to pry open the zipper. He bent to peer inside it, his head disappearing in an almost comical fashion as he rummaged. His big legs remained planted on the bag, while his tail feathers stuck straight up into the air.

The crow emerged from the bag, shook out his plumage, cocked his head, and pinned me with one black eye.

"Wish I had my slingshot," Carl whispered in my ear.

Nitis's head cocked the other direction, clearly hearing him. He jumped down from the bag, opening his wings to soften his landing, and started toward us with that arrogant strut crows had.

I heard another flutter, and a second crow sailed past us, landing with more grace in front of Nitis. She planted herself there and let out a hoarse caw.

I abandoned all thoughts of hiding and raced forward. "No!"

The first crow grew larger, his black wings smoothing into his sides to become arms. His feathers and beak receded until Nitis stood before us in his human form.

The second crow squawked in annoyance and flapped past him into the darkness.

"Stop her," I cried, my Beneath magic light flaring. "Why did you let her come?"

Nitis faced me, folding his arms across his bare chest. *"Let her?"* he asked me incredulously. "Ruby Begay?"

My grandmother walked out of the darkness. Unlike Nitis, she was fully clothed, wearing a long velvet skirt and a blouse, as though she'd dressed up for an event. She tapped her way forward on her formal walking stick, the one embedded with turquoise and silver.

"What are you doing here?" I demanded of her. "This is dangerous!"

"Is it?" Grandmother asked. "But putting a bag with a rock in it and pretending it's the egg isn't dangerous?"

I made a noise of exasperation. "I was trying to draw them out. Which you both have put an end to."

"Yeah, way to ruin a plan, dude," Carl said to Nitis. "Do you have anything to cover that up with?" He waved his hand at Nitis's groin. "It's nothing I want to see. Why women like those, I have no idea."

Nitis ignored him. "There is an easier way to make them reveal themselves."

Carl snorted. "*Reveal themselves*. You're certainly doing that."

Grandmother shot Carl a look of vast disapproval. "It is simple." She raised her cane and brushed it through the air. "Come to us. *Now*."

CHAPTER TWENTY-SIX

The walls moved.

I realized after a sickening heartbeat that I was wrong. It was the patterns in the stones that undulated, while the sandstone remained still.

Horizontal lines, which represented unimaginable time as layer upon layer had formed this place, began to spin through the walls. Lights flashed, too fast for me to see what emitted them.

Skulled faces appeared in the stone, similar to those on the beings that attacked us in Many Farms. They were images in the stone, like projections on a screen, but at the same they time reached bony fingers from the wall.

A hand snatched at the jacket I'd wrapped around the egg that Carl still held. He jerked back, and I grabbed the egg from him, jacket and all.

"Show me Mick," I shouted. "Or you get nothing."

Another projection appeared beside the Phantomwalkers. A flat and dimensionless dragon glared at me, its eye huge and full of fury.

Was this Mick? Or an illusion? I reached for Mick's aura, finding it dark and smoky with crackles of fire, but I sensed it from far, far away. Either Mick was trapped deep inside this stone, or they were showing me a projection of him from somewhere else.

"Mick," I raised my voice, hoping he could hear me. "Mirror."

Mick snarled, the sound deepening as a streak like lightning crackled across his image. His rage increased, then with a snap, he was gone.

The lightning had been too much like a whiplash for my liking. "You better not have hurt him," I told the Phantomwalker images.

They ignored me.

If Mick could get to the mirror and open a channel, I could try to wrest him free, using my Beneath magic enhanced with the mirror's power. I wasn't certain if they'd taken the mirror from him or destroyed the shard entirely, but even the tiny pieces would be helpful. But only if Mick could get to them.

The Phantomwalkers began to speak in their weird, many-voiced chorus. "If you desire your Firewalker's freedom, you must sacrifice."

"Sacrifice?" I demanded. "Sacrifice what?"

I thought I knew, but I wanted to keep them talking until I figured out a way to safely get Mick out of their clutches.

"Sacrifice only works when it's sincere," Nitis rumbled behind me. I wished he'd become the giant badass crow and attack them, but he stood calmly, keeping to his human form. "Janet is not the egg's mother. The sacrifice would be much greater if she were."

The Phantomwalkers regarded Nitis with contempt, but I sensed some puzzlement from them. They were single-minded creatures—*get the egg and then kill them all*. They hadn't expected Nitis to start a debate.

"Cesnia sacrificed herself," I said, turning things over in my head. "You all tried to make the same bargain with her, didn't you? The egg for Cesnia's life. Except, she'd never agree to that. She was his *mother*. She died so her child could live."

Tears wet my eyes. Cesnia had been amazing, according to the other dragons. Even the council respected her. My heart burned with regret that I'd not been able to meet her, and also that Junior had been deprived of a wonderful mother, who'd committed the ultimate sacrifice to save her child.

I was going to obliterate the Phantomwalkers for that.

"She had a choice," Nitis said quietly to me. "Is that a choice you can make?"

I studied him, this man with enigmatic black eyes. I still didn't know truly who Nitis was. A god, a demon? Why did he have so much power over the Phantomwalkers when dragons did not? Was his magic otherworldly? More like Beneath magic than Grandmother's shaman power?

And why the hell had he let Grandmother follow him? Nitis had implied he couldn't stop her, but yes, he could have, if he'd truly wanted to.

"Grandmother," I said. "Why don't you stand over there with Carl?"

Grandmother sent me a withering glance and stayed where she was. Carl had left his place against the wall when it became full of skull-faced phantoms, but he folded his arms and gazed back at them stubbornly, not about to run.

"Make the sacrifice," the Phantomwalkers intoned.

I had promised many people I'd never allow my Beneath magic to prevail. I understood why they wanted to restrict me—what was inside me was incredibly dangerous. If I let myself, I could unmake a large part of the world.

I had learned, via a long, difficult process, how to tame my powers. I now could ground myself with the Earth magic I'd inherited from Grandmother's family and impede the Beneath magic when it wanted to take over.

There was no storm outside, none near that I could feel. There weren't any close enough that I could bounce through the mirror, as I'd done when we'd fought in the gym at Many Farms. A beautiful, sunny spring day wafted a soft breeze over the lands above.

I turned to Carl and again handed him the jacket-covered egg. He hooked the flashlight onto his belt and took the egg, grim-eyed, holding it close.

Then I silently told the Beneath magic to get ready.

I faced the Phantomwalkers who separated themselves from the wall to hover above me. "I love Mick. I'd do anything for him, even die for him. But you're not getting the egg." I spread my arms. "Free Mick, and take your best shot."

I sensed the Phantomwalker's glee. They'd rid themselves of my threat, I could imagine them thinking, and then destroy everyone else without hindrance.

Except, I had a stinger in my tail.

"No." Grandmother was somehow in front of me, her walking stick raised at the Phantomwalkers. "Don't trust them, Janet."

"The sacrifice is not yours to make," Nitis told me. I

sensed a darkness in him, one growing as he advanced on us.

"You asked me if I was willing," I said. "The answer is: Yes, I am."

Nitis regarded me steadily. "But it is false."

I tried to signal him with my glare to shut up and let me do this. Nitis remained stubbornly beside Grandmother, both of them being extremely obtuse all of a sudden.

Nitis was right, of course. I wasn't truly offering myself in exchange for Mick's freedom. I was laying a trap because I was going to eradicate the Phantomwalkers.

Destroying them completely was the only way Mick, the rest of the dragons, and the egg would be safe. I knew Cesnia would have done what I planned if she'd had the benefit of hell-goddess power to aid her.

"Then why were you going on about choice?" I asked Nitis in growing exasperation.

"To make you understand." Nitis's voice expanded to fill the cave. "You do not have the powers you believe you do. You are dangerous, but in the end, you are too nice, Janet."

My brows rose. "Too nice?" I don't think anyone had ever said that about me in my entire life.

"There is not enough evil in your heart," Nitis went on. "If there was, you'd have killed the Phantomwalkers by now, and me as well. You'd have sent Drake away with the egg in the first place, to his death and the egg's. You do not have the malevolence it takes to destroy."

Nitis had grown taller and shadowy-er through this speech. I swallowed, chilled.

"And you do?" I asked.

"Yes." Nitis smiled, all that darkness coalescing into his

expression. "Why do you think I have been so successful thus far?"

Shit, shit, shit. Grandmother had let this man into her house, and into my hotel. He could have ripped our wards away by now, leaving my friends and colleagues and everyone I loved sitting ducks.

The question of what Nitis was suddenly didn't matter. It only mattered that I had another enemy to fight.

"Grandmother, get away from him."

Again, Grandmother sent me her obstinate look. "I do not like to be ordered about."

"For your own safety. Carl, help me."

Carl, who understood danger when he saw it, moved to Grandmother. He cradled the egg tightly, keeping a sharp eye on the Phantomwalkers and on Nitis.

Carl wouldn't be able fight them, though I guessed he'd valiantly try. If either Nitis or the Phantomwalkers went after him or Grandmother, I'd make sure the attackers would die instantly. I was evil enough to do *that*.

As Carl reached for Grandmother's arm, many things happened in rapid succession.

The walls rippled again. This time a string of glowing lights followed the colorful lines of sandstone. It ripped my concentration from the Phantomwalkers, which I thought was what they intended, then I realized they were startled too.

The stone began to shift and melt, and then a ringing sound like the most beautiful music I'd ever heard filled the chamber. Rock groaned, and pebbles broke from the ceiling to ping to the ground.

A finger of sunlight stabbed down from above. The

walls were changing, I realized, moving back to their original configuration.

Which meant something had broken the hold the Phantomwalkers had over this place.

Nash came charging around the corner, a pistol in his hands. He had it pointed at the ground, finger off the trigger, but the sight of the gun made me jump.

Gabrielle plunged in from another passage, Colby on her heels. Gabrielle threw a ball of white-hot fire at the Phantomwalkers, yelling at the top of her lungs.

"I don't *like* being shut in," she shouted as the Phantomwalkers scattered.

"She does not," Colby confirmed in a calmer tone.

Undulating lights flowed through the rocks again, followed by a glowing starburst, like a million glittering fireflies bursting out of the stone.

The mirror in my hand squealed. "I did it!"

Mick's huge dragon head again appeared on the flat face of the rock as if projected there. The dragon body expanded to fill the space, writhing and moving, but still trapped.

Abruptly, Mick's dragon fire exploded out from the tiny piece of the mirror's light. The flames struck the Phantomwalkers, who again scattered in confusion.

The fire didn't hurt the Phantomwalkers, though it disorganized them for a few crucial seconds. In those seconds, I tried to shove Grandmother and Carl into the tunnel that would take them to safety. They wouldn't budge, of course.

I lost track of Nitis, who'd become a crow once more. He flew past me, the rippling lights illuminating his feathers.

Gabrielle blasted the Phantomwalkers again. A few screamed and fell away, but the rest of them regrouped into one giant, skull-faced, tattered-sheet, no-legs entity.

That being let fly a white-hot arrow of crackling power right at Carl, still holding the egg, and Grandmother huddled next to him.

Sacrifice. A real one, not a lie to lure the enemy into a trap.

Yes, I would let myself be killed for the woman who'd given up a good part of her life to raise me. Yes, I'd sacrifice myself for Carl, an innocent human trying to enjoy his remaining years, and yes, I'd sacrifice it for a baby dragon.

I launched myself into Carl and Grandmother. They tumbled out of the way, both objecting, Carl cursing. I landed in the path of the deadly magic that had aimed straight for them.

I expected to frizzle into dust at any moment, too rapidly for any last words. I only hoped that Gabrielle and Nash could get the others out of here and save Mick.

The strike never landed. A massive span of black wings stirred up dust, and a crow with a crown of ebony and white feathers spread himself over me.

The shaft of Phantomwalker magic struck him full force. Feathers exploded as the body of the crow crumpled with the blow. Grandmother screamed.

I waited for Nitis to rise, to laugh in his slow way, and to obliterate the Phantomwalkers.

Instead, he died.

The large black bird fell heavily to the ground. His dark eyes sparkled once, a croak left his throat, then his eyes filmed over, and his head dropped to the dust.

"No!"

The word wrenched itself from Grandmother, a drawn-out wail of grief. She ran at the Phantomwalkers, her walking stick lifted high.

I saw another figure superimposed upon her, a young and stunning woman with long, soot-black hair. Her upright body contained haughty pride, a woman sure of her strength.

Ruby Begay held the cane in strong hands. She threw her head back, keening a song I didn't understand, as she'd done the last time she'd fought the Phantomwalkers. The turquoise in her cane glowed, surrounding her in a blue nimbus.

The lights in the walls responded. They apparently had nothing to do with Mick, who was still struggling to break free, because the glow rippled over him as well.

The collective Phantomwalker drew back from Ruby's song, but they didn't want to touch the illuminated walls either. The wavering lights began to fill every space of sandstone, including the ceiling, meeting the sunbeam that stabbed through it.

Carl had landed heavily, but he'd kept hold of the egg. He stared in wonder at the battle of luminosity above him, while the egg jumped and danced in his arms.

Gabrielle, after an open-mouthed gape at the young Ruby Begay, drew her arm back and threw a basketball-sized flash of Beneath magic at the Phantomwalkers.

It hit them, and they screamed.

"Three pointer," Gabrielle yelled, fists in the air.

I gathered my own magic, ready to end this.

The lights in the rocks swirled together in a riot of blue-white. I paused, my body hot with adrenaline, the Beneath magic poised to explode.

If I destroyed this cave, what would I also kill? Were the lights another manifestation of the Phantomwalkers? Or an ally, who was trying to help us?

"What are you?" I demanded of the swirling radiance.

Laughter shimmered as the glow danced—female laughter. *Sacrifice*, it whispered.

In the next moment, the glittering lights inside the rock burst outward. Gabrielle yelped and ducked, Colby pulling her to safety. Nash hit the dirt, and Carl crouched down, shielding the egg.

Mick burst from the wall. He launched himself upward, his dragon too huge for the space, and broke open the ceiling. Dust and rock poured down on us, coating the air.

Mick winged for the sky, then he disappeared.

My body sagged with relief, the magic that had been building in me sliding away. I fell against the wall, my knees buckling until I slid to the floor.

Mick was all right. He was free.

He hadn't flown away for good, I knew. Mick would be back, ready to do whatever it took.

The wall behind me was warm. The feminine laughter embraced me, soothing down my crazed Beneath magic.

As good as the contact felt, I struggled. I needed the Beneath magic to destroy the Phantomwalkers. Gabrielle, as strong as she was, couldn't do it by herself.

Through all this, Grandmother continued her song. As long as I'd known her, she'd seemed elderly to me, though I realized she must have been only fifty or so when I'd been born.

Now I saw the young woman that was Ruby—the capable, intense, magical being who would become the matriarch who kept our family safe and together.

I hadn't stood a chance against her.

Nitis remained a clump of black feathers on the ground. All the magic dancing in the air didn't stir him.

The lights whirled around and around the cave. I heard the laughter build, and then the string of luminescence became the outline of a massive dragon.

A white dragon, shot with iridescent blue. She stayed inside the wall, not breaking free as Mick had, because of course, they'd already killed her.

"Wing Dancer," Colby whispered. "I thought they were legends."

Before I could ask what a Wing Dancer was, Carl cried out.

My jacket had fluttered to the dirt, as though wind had blown it. As I watched in astonishment, the egg leapt from Carl's grasp. It launched itself into the air, aiming for the blue-white dragon, but before it could reach her, the egg fell.

The baby inside must be trying to fly to its mother, but trapped inside the egg, its momentum would only take it so far.

The blue of Grandmother's magic snapped off just before the egg plummeted through it. Gabrielle tried to send out a snake of Beneath magic to catch the egg but was too late.

I didn't bother with magic. I hurled myself across the dirt floor and slid like a home-base stealer into the other wall. I opened my arms, and the egg landed straight into them.

"I got you, kid." I held the egg, unbroken, close, breathing hard, the emeralds and gold scratching my skin.

The egg wriggled and wobbled, and I lost my hold. The

oval rolled onto the ground at my feet, then it abruptly exploded into a thousand jade, gold, and bejeweled shards.

As I shielded myself from the flying debris, something landed hard on my chest. It said, "Gnahhhh."

Baby dragon fire whooshed out all over my sweatshirt, burning it to cinders.

CHAPTER TWENTY-SEVEN

Cesnia's kid was blue.

Bright cobalt blue with eyes that changed from green to gold to red to black in the space of an instant. Titus's eyes varied color, though not so rapidly, but neither he nor Drake were blue.

I'd have to think about that.

The small dragon flapped on my tattered shirt, gazed into my eyes, and shouted, "Maaaaaa."

Then it wrapped its little dragon wings around me and held me tight.

The luminescent dragon in the wall went crazy. She swirled and danced, her laughter echoing. A wing came down the stone behind me, the closest she could reach.

I sat up, pried Baby Blue from me, and held it nearer to the wall. The little dragon hopped from me to land vertically on the stone. Gripping the sheer wall with its claws, it tried to hug the white dragon as it had done me.

"Janet!" Gabrielle's warning screech tore me from the touching reunion.

I jerked around to see that the Phantomwalkers had broken apart again, spilling around us to strike.

I grabbed Gabrielle's outstretched hand and wrenched myself to my feet. Gabrielle's enormous power came to me with a slap, bubbling like an impatient volcano. That was my sister.

Another hand found mine. I looked down to see slim but strong fingers, skin the same color as mine, gripping hard. The young Ruby Begay gazed at me with Grandmother's eyes, her defiance and beauty a heady combination.

Nash had finally convinced Carl to retreat along the passageway, with Colby protecting them.

We three ladies lifted our hands. My voice and Gabrielle's joined Grandmother's, though I had no idea what we were singing. Ruby's magic surged through me, joining mine and Gabrielle's into a force that could shake down mountains.

We threw this power into the Phantomwalkers, who screamed, writhed, and began to smoke. Without discussion, the three of us pushed them back into the wall, where they did not want to go.

Cesnia tore herself from her child and swirled to meet them.

Janet. Cesnia's voice, musical and sweet, whispered in my head. *Take good care of her for me.*

Her?

I didn't dare snap my gaze around to the little blue dragon who wailed when Cesnia swirled away. With a few flaps of tiny wings, the little one launched herself up, and landed, out of breath, on top of my head.

The Phantomwalkers, in glee, drew together to shoot a

streak of light straight at Baby Blue.

"No you don't!" I yelled.

I directed our collective magic to bat the lightning out of the air before it reached us. The bolt slammed into the ground, sending up an explosion of rubble. Then, my fury joined by Grandmother's and Gabrielle's, we threw the Phantomwalkers into the wall.

Cesnia closed on them with dragon-focused rage.

Dragon fire and their magic hadn't been able to dent the Phantomwalkers, but Cesnia had moved beyond such things. Perhaps, in her ghostly state, she had become like the Phantomwalkers herself, no longer purely dragon. She might have the power to destroy them all.

Go, Cesnia commanded me. *I will do the rest.*

I jerked my hands from Gabrielle and Ruby. "Time to leave. Cesnia's going to eat them, and we should be elsewhere."

Gabrielle understood the gist if not the entirety of what was going on. She bravely seized Grandmother's shoulder and tried to turn her around.

Grandmother shook her off. She dropped to her knees to the floor, her cane falling away, and lifted the dead Nitis into her arms. Grandmother shuffled into the passageway, leaving her cane behind, her form shrinking into its older version as she went.

Gabrielle grabbed the cane and ran after her.

I stood for a few seconds longer, Baby Blue still on my head, and met Cesnia's glittering gaze.

Thank you, Janet.

The words touched me like a cool breath of air. Blue cried out and Cesnia dipped a glowing wing down, trying to reach her. I held the little dragon to the wall, letting Cesnia and Blue touch one last time.

Cesnia nodded at me, her eyes glittering with light, and made herself pull away.

Blue seemed to understand. She climbed onto my shoulders, clinging to me as I retrieved my jacket and the bowling bag and walked down the dark, dry passageway. I felt Blue twisting her head to keep Cesnia in sight as long as she could, before we turned a corner, and darkness swallowed the cavern.

Behind us, a dragon roared with all the rage, pain, and grief the Phantomwalkers had caused her. The cave we'd just left filled with fire.

I heard screaming, the thin wails of the Phantomwalkers as Cesnia showed them exactly why you didn't mess with a mama dragon.

The cave imploded. Eons of sandstone cascaded like a waterfall into the beautiful slot canyon in which we'd stood. Dust and debris flew after me as I sprinted toward the exit, gasping for breath.

Except, the exit wasn't there. I found, not sunshine and cool breezes, but the cluster of Carl, Nash, Colby, Gabrielle, and Grandmother examining the blank wall that stood where the way out should have been.

"What the hell?" I blurted.

"The entire canyon has changed," Nash said, tight-lipped. "Nothing is where it was."

The Phantomwalkers had moved reality once we'd gone in. Maybe the entrance had been part of their otherworld, luring us to them.

"Colby," I said. "Can you blast a way through it?"

"Eventually." Colby ran his hands along the stone as

though testing it for weakness. "But we'll all get a little singed."

Blue drew in a large breath and belched a stream of fire. It was small, almost cute, but barely warmed the stone. It would be a while before she grew into her dragon might, I guessed.

Which brought up the question, who was going to raise her. Me? Watery panic lashed through me.

Drake would want her back. Or Titus. Or would they? They hadn't expected the dragon to be a girl. Maybe female dragons had to be raised by females. I had no idea.

The dragon council would want to weigh in, including the ice-cold Aine.

No way was I turning over this adorable and vulnerable little dragon to the council. She'd stay with me until Mick and I figured things out.

Mick was out there. He'd get us free.

The instant I formed that thought, sparks burst under Colby's fingers. He snatched them back, hissing in pain.

He hadn't created the fire, I realized. It came from the other side of the rock. As we stared, more and more rivulets of blue-white streamed into the stone, sparks showering. A very straight white-hot line formed in the sandstone.

Colby jerked Gabrielle back, as Nash did to Carl. Grandmother, still cradling Nitis, retreated more slowly.

I made sure we were all well out of the way before the outer wall gave. Behind us, deep in the cave, came the rumbling *booms* of the cavern collapsing.

A large chunk of stone crumbled away before us, letting dust and sunlight stream in. Framed in the opening stood Mick, bare in the sunshine.

Next to him was Maya, in armor. Not armor, I realized after one startled moment. She'd donned a welding jacket and helmet, gauntlets on her slim hands. She pulled off one glove to turn off the flame on her plasma cutter, lifted her face shield, and glared at us.

"Well, are you coming out of there?" Maya demanded.

We complied in a hurry. Mick bathed me in a wide, warm smile, his face and body abraded, his hair a dusty muss.

"Hey, baby," Mick said tiredly. "Miss me?"

For answer, I flung myself into his arms. Blue climbed from my head to his, where she settled down with a contented *blurp*.

Nash and Maya started arguing right away. Maya stomped toward the truck, with Nash after her. Gabrielle and Colby bumped shoulders then hurried off to find Colby's bike.

Behind us, the solid monolith of the sandstone hill and the slot canyons it contained crumbled into oblivion. Rock and dust hurtled into the clear sky as rumbling shook the earth.

Mick hustled both me and Grandmother forward, taking us past the bulwark of the box canyon and into the open desert.

Boulders rattled down the canyon walls to settle where they'd lay for the next decades, maybe centuries. Dust floated on the air to coat us all in pinkish powder.

The surrounding mountains held their stance, refusing to bend, but I knew that the slot canyon, the sculpture of nature the rocks had hidden, was no more.

Cesnia had saved her child for good.

After that, all was silence, except for the quiet sobbing of Ruby Begay, who knelt on the desert floor, cradling the body of Nitis, and weeping.

CHAPTER TWENTY-EIGHT

The drive back to the hotel seemed to take forever. We broke the journey in Flagstaff, gathering in a large parking lot at a strip mall to stretch our legs while Colby went into a sandwich shop and bought us all lunch.

Mick wore clothes Colby had kept stashed on his bike. Colby was more compact than Mick, so the shorts and sweatshirt were a little tight, but at least they covered Mick enough to not get him arrested.

I'd ridden in Maya's pickup with the little blue dragon, who kept wanting to break her way out and explore the wide world. I had to hold her pretty tightly. Mick rode my motorcycle, and he looked so weary I wanted to cry.

Next to me in the truck was Grandmother, again an exhausted, elderly woman. She didn't leave the vehicle but held Nitis, still the form of a normal-sized crow, wrapped in a towel Maya'd had in the back. She didn't speak.

Questions whirled through my head as we waited for Colby to return with food, but no answers came. Were the

Phantomwalkers gone for good? How had Cesnia done what she did? What the hell was I going to do about Blue? And how would I console Grandmother?

I hadn't realized what Grandmother had felt about Nitis, but then she was the sort of person who never let on that she had softer emotions. She scolded, lectured, and rebuked those she loved the best, very likely to shield herself from heartbreak.

You love someone, but they could leave, die, or not love you back. Sometimes all three. I'd learned long ago that Grandmother was prickly so she wouldn't have to admit she loved. Didn't mean she didn't feel things more deeply than most.

Colby returned with sandwiches, which we all eagerly reached for. Grandmother showed no interest. I hungrily devoured my ham and cheese with chipotle mayo, or at least, I tried to. Blue ate half of it, and also the paper wrapping.

What did baby dragons eat? That answer dawned on me pretty swiftly. Anything they wanted.

We headed out for the last leg to the Crossroads. Nash and Maya were silent in the front of her pickup, and Grandmother and I were equally silent in back. Baby Blue, about the size of her egg, sat on my lap, when she wasn't lurching around trying to look out all the windows.

Maya had explained on the way to Flagstaff that she'd watched the stone walls close once Nash and I had gone inside the slot canyon, and decided she didn't like that. She had a portable plasma cutter and welder in the back of her truck, stocked and ready for her to cut through whatever she needed when called for a remodeling job.

She'd been ready to use the battery on her truck to power it, but Mick had landed nearby, giving her a dragon fire assist. He'd been too tired to blast through the wall himself, but he'd been a good alternative power source for her gear.

Nash had yelled at her for approaching a dangerous situation, and Maya yelled at him for running into one. All normal in their relationship.

Now they sat in tense silence. Only Blue made any noise, she very curious about the truck, those of us in it, and everything we passed.

We at last reached the Crossroads to find the hotel lobby full of people. The Horribles lounged here, there, and everywhere, blissfully unaware that they'd been victims of a compulsion spell. They gaped at me as I entered in my jacket zipped over my bare torso, carrying a turquoise studded cane and a bowling bag that swung of its own accord.

Mick made straight for my suite, me hurriedly following. He continued through the hall and out the back door, to the space behind the hotel without guests around. There, he told me to set down the bag and back away.

I complied. As soon as I retreated a few steps, Blue ripped her way out. She settled down next to my feet, flapping her wings, and cooing in contentment.

Mick constructed a cage of dragon fire around Blue, the bag, and me—a cube of ten-foot walls on all sides. It wouldn't burn her, Mick said, but would keep Blue safely contained until we could figure out what we'd do with her.

He told me to step out of the cage, and after a moment's worried hesitation, I did. The fire didn't singe me at all, but Blue couldn't follow me. She whimpered, then launched herself up and buzzed around the cage, growing happier as she went.

"You're not a dragon," Mick explained when I asked how it worked. "You can go in and out as you please, but dragons and other magical beings can't. It will keep her safe."

Mick then dragged himself inside our suite, spent, and ready for a shower. I wanted to shower with him, hold him, comfort him while he comforted me, and reassure myself that he was all right.

But I needed to find Grandmother.

"Go to her," Mick said as he paused at the bathroom door. "She needs you more than I do right now."

That was true, I realized. Mick was tough. He'd survived plenty of perilous shit before he'd ever met me. Grandmother was grieving.

I left Mick after a brief but promising kiss and headed into the main part of the hotel.

I found Grandmother in the kitchen. Elena held a polished cedar box about the size of a shoebox, where I guessed she'd placed Nitis's body.

"We'll give him a good sendoff," Elena was promising. "For now, he'll have to go into the shed."

Whatever Nitis had been in life, right now, he was a dead bird. The health department would shut me down if we kept him in the walk-in fridge. If we put him in the basement, a hungry Nightwalker might not be able to stop himself having a snack.

The shed, where Mick and I stored our motorcycles, was cool in these months, the best place to lay him before we could hold his funeral.

That we would have a funeral for him was not a question. Grandmother would need to say goodbye.

"He helped us all," I said.

Sacrifice, Nitis had told me. He'd meant Cesnia, and then himself. Both had given up life in all its sweetness so that the one they loved could live.

Grandmother, seated on the wooden chair she always planted herself in when she visited Elena, gave us both a sullen nod. "It's fine."

I went to her. "I have your cane. It's in my suite. Take it whenever you want it."

Grandmother glanced up at me, her dark eyes red-rimmed and moist. "I said, it's fine, Janet. Don't fuss."

Elena and I exchanged a glance, Elena shaking her head.

I took the box from Elena and carried it with reverence out the back door to the shed, which I unlocked. Inside, I set the box carefully on a shelf above Mick's motorcycle.

"Thank you, Nitis," I said softly, brushing my fingertips over the smooth wood.

The box felt a bit warm, but then it had been in Elena's kitchen, where she had the stove and oven running nonstop.

I wheeled my motorcycle into the shed, parking it next to Mick's, then locked everything up. I checked on Blue, peering at her through the mesh of dragon fire. She'd curled up on the dried grass and now let out a baby dragon snore. I'd bring her a blanket in case the night grew too cold.

"Sleep well, little girl." I reached through the bars to stroke her soft body, blew her a kiss, and went back inside.

———

Later that evening, when the sky was streaked with red and fuchsia, Drake arrived.

I spied him standing next to the fire cage from my back window. His long black coat and dark hair moved in the desert breeze.

Blue was awake when I joined Drake, but she wasn't jumping in joy because she recognized her father. Instead, she ignored him to sail around the small cage, making burbling noises.

Drake studied her with the perplexity of a male realizing a child wasn't a theoretical concept but a living, breathing creature he had no idea what to do with. The same expression came over Titus, who walked out of the desert to halt next to Drake.

Drake snapped his attention to me. "Here." He held out a velvet bag that clinked.

"What is this?" I loosened the drawstring and peered at glittering pieces of gold, emerald, and jade nestled inside. "Is that the dragon's shell?"

Drake nodded. "Titus and I dug it out of the hill where it was buried. Colby called me and told me where it was."

"Oh." I studied the pair of them, who both watched me intently. I didn't know why retrieving the shell was important, but apparently it was. I accepted it without further question.

"No sign of Cesnia," Titus said. "Before you ask. She's gone."

The sadness in his voice, and in Drake's eyes, tugged at my heart.

"Colby called her a Wing Dancer," I said, keeping my tone gentle. "What does that mean?"

Mick's voice rumbled behind me. "A dragon who transforms him- or herself after death to assist one they love."

He walked to us slowly, stiffly, though he'd cleaned off the dust and blood that had coated his skin.

"That's a myth," Drake began.

Mick shook his head. "I saw her. If not for Cesnia and the mirror, I'd still be a prisoner."

"No." I set down the velvet bag and clasped his big hands. "I'd have come for you, no matter what."

Mick caressed my fingers with his thumb. "I know you would, but I might have been dead by the time you reached me. They trapped me so deep in that mountain I couldn't budge. What you saw was them projecting my image so you could watch my suffering."

I squeezed Mick's hands as the anguish of that hit me. "I understand why you all loved Cesnia. I love her now too."

"She was a special dragon," Mick said. "A great warrior."

Drake and Titus both nodded, but I knew they weren't thinking of Cesnia's skill in battle.

"I sensed your aura at her island," I said to Drake. "Did you find her there?"

Grief flickered in Drake's eyes. "In her lair. I wasn't certain what had killed her. I built a pyre for her on the mountaintop, then searched for the egg."

I recalled the charred place in the island's forest I'd seen when Mick had landed us there.

I switched my focus to Drake and Titus collectively. "So, which of you is Blue's dad?"

Titus's brows went up, and his eyes turned smoky gray. "Blue?"

"That's what I've been calling her. I don't know her real name."

"You do," Mick informed me. "Cesnia sang it to you."

I remembered the music mixed with Cesnia's laughter. Just as I did with Mick's name, which was a string of magical notes, I now felt Blue's inside me. It shimmered and danced, entwining Blue and me together.

Blue sensed it. She perked up, flying in a tight circle around the cage, chirping in delight. Cesnia had given me a great gift.

"To answer your question," Drake said, "we don't know which of us is the father. We won't know until she grows up enough to tell us."

"Really?" I asked in surprise.

Mick nodded. "That's how it works. The child knows and finds the father if he or she wishes. *If* the male dragon has survived, that is."

"Sheesh," I said with feeling. "Dragons live complicated lives."

Mick rumbled with laughter, and I was happy to see some of the darkness in his expression lift. "They do," he said.

"Until then, I believe Janet is the best person to take care of the young dragon," Drake declared.

While I staggered under the shock of Drake saying he trusted me that much, Titus studied me with dragon intelligence.

"The question is, does Janet want that burden of care?" Titus asked.

All three dragons regarded me with unblinking eyes, Titus's becoming a smoldering black. Blue zinged around her cage a little longer before she hovered in midair, gazing at me through the mesh.

"Maaaaa," she said.

I heaved a long sigh, knowing exactly what I would do, whether I was ready for it or not. No way in hell would I let anyone take Blue someplace like the dragon compound, where the dragon council could get their aggravating claws into her, and I'd never see her again.

"She stays with me," I told them. "I'll figure it out. Mick will have to help me every step of the way. Are you going to be okay with that?"

I put this question to Mick, but also Drake and Titus, who had to decide whether to let another guy raise their kid.

All three nodded readily. Titus sent me a slight smile. "Male dragons are shit parents."

"Great." I glared at Mick. "Were you going to tell me that any time soon?"

"*Some* male dragons are shit parents," Mick said. "I'm willing to give it a try."

The look he sent me both melted my heart and scared me to death. He took my hand again, his warmth filling me with strength.

This beautiful moment was broken by the sound of crunching. We all swung to the cage.

Somehow, Blue had managed to slide the velvet bag, which I'd set close to the cage, beneath the bars to her. I saw a furrow of earth where she'd dug.

The bag was now in shreds. Blue sat on its tatters, happily munching. As we watched, every bit of gold and precious stone vanished into the volatile mess that was a baby dragon's tummy.

———

THAT NIGHT, AS MICK AND I LAY TOGETHER, THE CAGE'S bars lighting us from outside the window, our motorcycle shed exploded into fire and burned rapidly to the ground.

CHAPTER TWENTY-NINE

M ick and I were up and out in an instant, desperately trying to douse the flames with our combined magics—better than fire retardant and many times faster.

Except, our powers had no effect. The shed burned merrily, the stucco falling away, the wood and bricks melting in the inferno.

"Nitis," I whispered.

Our bikes would be toast, but I was more worried right now about the body of Nitis, whose funeral Elena and I had discussed last night. She'd given Grandmother a dose of something to make her sleep, and Elena and I had quietly debated what to do. We'd concluded that we would put him on a pyre—maybe Elena had chosen to jump the gun?

But no, Elena hurried out in a bathrobe, distressed, with Grandmother, even more upset, in her wake. Grandmother had switched to her plain walking stick, which thumped rapidly as she made her way toward the shed.

Gabriella and Colby raced onto the scene, followed by Carl. I heard guests inside demanding to know what was happening and Cassandra's smooth tones telling them to stay put.

Two of the guests, my father and Gina, had refused to obey her and hurried out. Dad, once he saw we were all right, stopped Gina at a safe distance from the flames.

"Who would do this?" Grandmother demanded. "Who?"

Mick had released Blue from her cage, in case she needed to fly to safety. The tiny dragon fluttered about, minuscule streams of fire emerging from her mouth. She moved to me, squeaking in bewilderment.

I spied movement near the railroad bed. Gritting my teeth in fury, I jogged that way. Mick noticed and followed.

Blue bounced in the air behind us. I heard Grandmother also start to walk after me, ignoring Elena who advised her to wait.

"Did you do this?" I yelled at Coyote before I reached him.

In human form, Coyote lounged against a boulder, fully dressed in jeans, button-down shirt, and cowboy boots. "No."

His quiet word quelled my ire. "You weren't trying to release Nitis? Save him the indignity of lying dead in a box?"

Coyote shook his head. "I had nothing to do with this, Janet. Just be glad I happened along when I did. I put your motorcycles over there for safekeeping."

He nodded at the railroad bed. I couldn't see our bikes, so they must be on the far side.

There was no way he could have waded into that

burning shed and out again with a motorcycle, twice. He was a god, but though he might not have been burned, our bikes would have been. Or the gas in their tanks would have blown up.

"Did *we* do this?" I demanded. "Was it a fuel spill or something?"

"Janet," Grandmother snapped at me. "Hush." She gazed at the fire, her face glittering with tears.

I hated to see her grieving like this, but then I realized she wasn't crumpled with loss. She was crying with hope.

The last of the shed collapsed in on itself. The fire licked the final pieces of board, and then winked out. Not even glowing embers remained.

Wind stirred the pile of ash the shed had become.

"We should go inside now, Grandmother," I said gently.

Grandmother refused to move. She was staring intently at what used to be our shed, her focus sharp.

Within the ashes, something moved. Nothing living, my brain told me. Nothing could have survived that conflagration, whose heat lingered in the air.

The cinders swirled, picking up speed. As we watched, they spun faster and faster, a tornado-like wind forming in the destruction of our insignificant shed. Darkness streamed upward from the ashes like grains of volcanic sand. Those grains spun in the gale-force wind and coalesced into a giant shadow.

A *whump* of wings sent a huge downdraft across the land, tearing at our clothes and sending my hair dancing. Blue zipped around us, chattering shrilly.

Black feathers beat the air, lifting the body of a giant crow from the powdery ashes. White and black down decorated his head, and his black eyes glinted with power. The crow cocked us a glance then shot heavenward, blotting out the stars.

He circled the desert far out beyond the railroad bed. Blue zinged after him, easily keeping pace.

The pair of them returned while my heart tried to remember how to beat correctly, the crow receding in size as he circled the remains of the shed.

He landed on the ground with a graceful thump, and then rose into the form of a man. Wind tugged his black hair threaded with white, and starlight gleamed in his eyes.

Grandmother cried out in joy. She ran for Nitis, jubilation making her limber.

Nitis smiled at her, spreading his arms. Grandmother reached him, drew back … and whacked him across the middle with her walking stick.

Nitis let out an "Oof!" Then he laughed. The sound was filled with gladness and humor, and I laughed with him for the pleasure of it.

"All right," I said to Coyote as Grandmother and Nitis embraced, Blue dancing around them. "How did you do that?"

Coyote gave me one of his blank looks. "I keep saying, I had nothing to do with it. Nitis isn't your ordinary crow."

"Well, duh." I glared at him. "What is he, then? A god? How did he do that?"

"Not a god," Coyote answered quietly. "A Firebird. Some cultures call him a phoenix."

"Rising from the ashes," Mick said in fascination. "I never knew that was real."

Coyote gestured at Nitis, who'd picked up Grandmother and was spinning around with her. Her voice rose in her usual scolding. "Apparently, it's real," Coyote said.

I saw, superimposed on the two, Grandmother as Ruby, her young self. Nitis flickered red and black, both a glowing feathered being and a handsome man.

Sacrifice, he'd said. He'd done exactly what Cesnia had —let his death come so that those he loved would survive. He'd given Grandmother, me, and Gabrielle, a chance to defeat our enemy and live.

Had Nitis known he'd come back? Or was that the chance he'd been willing to take?

"The second one, I think," Coyote said, as though he'd been reading my mind. I hated it when he did that, but I had to agree with him.

As Blue circled the spinning pair, Grandmother's berating words became the hoarse caws of a crow. The figures of Nitis and Grandmother shimmered, and then two crows rose from the place they'd been, soaring into the sky.

The crow with black and white crown feathers skimmed away into the night, with the second crow shot after him, cawing all the way.

I laughed through the tears stinging my eyes. "If they end up in Many Farms, it will be a noisy night there. Good thing Dad and Gina slept here."

Mick sent me a knowing smile. "If they make it that far."

"Shit, Mick," I said in alarm. "I meant them arguing. Don't put *that* into my head. She's my *grandmother.*"

"So? I'm two-hundred and fifty years old and change." His blue eyes heated. "Age doesn't erase passion."

To be fair, he was right. But such things were different when it was your own family you were discussing.

I knew what Coyote's off-color opinion would be, but

when I turned to warn him not to express it, I found empty air. Coyote was gone, nothing left of him but a far-off yip in the night.

Elena was already heading for the hotel, the others following her. Dad had his arm around Gina, but he turned and smiled at me.

Lights flicked off inside, Elena and Cassandra ordering everyone back to bed.

Blue circled the pile of ash then fluttered down to land heavily on my head.

The mysteries of the world could wait. I took Mick's hand, and we returned to our comfortable nest, Blue burbling sleepily all the way.

———

I WOULD LIKE TO SAY THAT ALL WAS WELL THAT ENDED well, but in the morning, the Horribles were still there. They filled the lobby after they returned from breakfast at the diner, shouting snide comments to one another that contained far too much information for the rest of us.

It had been otherwise quiet when they were out. Colby and Gabrielle had departed after they'd eaten Elena's breakfast, returning with Dad and Gina to Many Farms. Gabrielle's team had the semifinal rematch game tonight. Gabrielle was certain they'd make the finals, and then get all the way to the state championships for their division and win those too.

I sent them all off with embraces and many thanks, promising Gabrielle that of course, I'd be there for the games. I held my dad a little longer than the others.

"I love you, Dad." I thought of how Cesnia had given

up her existence to make sure Blue was safe. My father, in his quiet way, had given up his entire life for me.

Dad started when he heard the words, but he squeezed me back. "You too, my daughter. You keep well."

I wiped my eyes as I released him. Gina smiled at me in understanding.

Then they were gone, Dad's truck sending up a plume of red dust before he turned onto the paved highway.

Mick had retrieved the motorcycles from beyond the railroad bed and was now checking them over and tinkering with them, as he liked to do. Blue hovered around him, pretending to help.

We'd have to build a new shed as well as fix the saloon window. I also needed to replace Fremont's custom bowling ball and bag. I'm sure Nash's truck was well insured, but he might try to ding me for the deductible. This spring had already become expensive.

When I entered the now-noisy lobby, Cassandra, behind her desk, beckoned to me, her expression pained. "They've decided to stay for the whole summer," she murmured, indicating the Horribles. "I explained that the rooms were already booked, but they said they'd stay in tents in the back if they had to."

"Great." I let out an exasperated breath. "Time for drastic measures."

I marched through my hall and out the back door. Blue eagerly flew to me when I whistled. She perched on my shoulder, her scaly snout warm as she nuzzled my cheek.

I walked with her back into the lobby. "All right sweetheart," I told her in a low voice while I scratched under her chin. "Why don't you fly around and wreak a little havoc?"

Whether Blue understood my words or only their

intent, she launched herself from my shoulder in exuber-
ance. She sped to the rafters above the staircase and circled
the large lobby, screeching her small dragon cries.

The Horribles ceased calling to each other and jerked
their gazes upward, jaws sagging as they beheld the small
dragon. Blue darted from corner to corner, fire erupting
from her mouth. She started to dive-bomb the family, first
one then another, sending them scrambling for cover with
window-rattling shrieks.

Carl emerged from the saloon, coffee in hand. He
chuckled as Blue chased the family from one side of the
lobby to the other. The lot of them ended up by the stairs,
shielding themselves from her attack.

I whistled again, and Blue broke off, flapping back
toward me in triumph.

The Horribles emerged from where they'd cowered
beside the staircase, shaking themselves out, and regarding
me with expressions of … delight?

"Is that real?" Allie demanded. "Mom, is that thing
real? Can I have one?"

The others chimed in. "How did you do that?" "Is it
animatronics?" "Oh, he's so *cute*."

Cassandra regarded me in dismay. I opened my mouth
to explain that Blue was not only real but could be terrifying and destructive, when Carl upstaged me.

He walked into the middle of the group, dumped his
coffee down the front of his shirt, and started gibbering.

The front door opened at this point, but my attention
was arrested by Carl, as was that of the Horribles.

"Ew," Yvonne said. "What is the matter with him?"

Carl shook his head from side to side, letting his eyes
grow glassy. "Where am I? Who are you? Is there anything

to eat?" He stared blankly at Allie and let drool ooze down the side of his mouth.

"Ick." Allie quickly hid behind her mother. "Get him away from me."

Elena chose that instant to stalk in from the kitchen. She observed the scene, then stepped forward.

"That's enough, Mr. Jones. It's time for your medication."

Carl tilted his head alarmingly to one side. "Don't need no medication."

"You know you do," Elena said. "He's not always violent," she assured the Horribles. "Though sometimes …"

Cassandra and I watched the performance in a daze. Carl continued to act the stereotype of witlessness, with Elena telling him firmly to come with her.

"Excuse me." A gravelly voice tugged at my attention.

I looked down to find a small man and woman, who'd slipped in during the drama, standing beside me. They had squat bodies, gnarled faces, and thin threads of gray hair on their heads. The man wore a suit that fit his minute stature well, with the woman in a blouse and skirt. She clutched a handbag between her plump fists.

I recognized the pair right away and beamed them a wide and sincere smile. "Welcome back. I thought you weren't returning until your anniversary."

Mr. and Mrs. Goblin, as Cassandra and I called them, had spent some time at our hotel last September. In spite of the crazy danger that had occurred, they'd vowed to visit us again to celebrate their special occasion.

Mrs. Goblin answered me. "We enjoyed it so much we decided not to wait. We can always come then too."

Cassandra regarded them warmly. "Of course you can. We're a little short of rooms, but I'll see what I can do."

"We'll make the best of anything," Mrs. Goblin said. She turned to study Carl, who continued to taunt the Horribles. "Is that young man all right?"

"He's trying to encourage some tiresome guests to go," I whispered to them. "Not that I like to throw guests out," I assured her quickly.

"Why not? If they've overstayed their welcome." Mrs. Goblin beckoned to her husband.

They glided toward the clump of people trying to evade a persistent Carl. None noticed the diminutive Goblin couple until they were in the very midst of the family.

Abruptly, the wrinkled but harmless-looking Mr. and Mrs. Goblin swelled and grew until they were snarling, slavering, massive rocklike creatures. Where their clothes and Mrs. Goblin's purse went, I didn't know, but nothing remained of our polite couple.

They penned the Horribles between them, roaring like beasts from hell. Mrs. Goblin—I think it was her—flailed out with a clawed hand.

Elena didn't change expression. "*This* is what happens when Mr. Jones doesn't get his medication," she announced.

Allie screamed. "I'm getting out of here." She broke free of the group and ran, her sisters after her.

Their three husbands had already bolted, reaching the front door ahead of their wives. The six of them tumbled out into the bright parking lot, bumping into each other as they raced for their cars. The parents of the family hurried after them, the mom turning back at the doorstep.

"You people should be shut down," she scolded us.

"You're getting one-star reviews from us." She streamed out, shouting at the others to wait for their father.

The dad also turned back, he more hesitant than the others.

"We'll send your things on to you," Cassandra told him with a pleasant smile. "And email your receipt."

He fled.

Carl doubled over with laughter. He straightened up, marched to Elena, and kissed her on the cheek. "You're perfect."

Elena frowned at him. "And you're more trouble than my good-for-nothing nephews." She humphed and strode back to the kitchen, but I noticed that her face had softened as soon as she'd turned from Carl.

The Goblin couple, restored to their usual guises, handbag and all, laughed with Carl.

"Very good, young man," Mrs. Goblin said. "Can we join you for coffee?"

"Won't say no." Carl led his two new friends into the saloon, calling to Flora to pour three fresh coffees—his grandson would pick up the tab.

Blue did a victory lap around the now-quiet lobby before landing on top of Jamison's coyote sculpture. I worried that she'd scratch it, but Blue perched daintily, as though knowing how much I treasured it.

I accepted a coffee Cassandra obtained for me and gazed around the hotel as I sipped from the mug.

Inside the saloon, Carl and the Goblin couple babbled and chuckled as they got to know each other. I assumed Carl would remain here for a while, and I welcomed him. The Wiccan couple occupied a table near the cracked window, looking relieved it was quiet at last.

Cassandra returned to her laptop, her efficient serenity restored. Blue dozed on top of the coyote statue. Outside, Mick whistled as he tinkered with the bikes, the sound warming me thoroughly.

I'd marry him in June. So much to do, but for now, I was content to have Mick near, where we could breathe in peace.

There was the question of the legend Nitis had told us about, where Blue might grow up to battle Mick, the dragon lord. But that was something we'd have to work through. Legends and prophecies didn't always come true, or at least, not the way we expected.

Two crows cawed hoarsely at each other in the juniper at the edge of the parking lot. In the kitchen, Elena growled something as her knife began its tapping on her cutting board.

The mirror, in the saloon, started screeching a crooner song, way off-key.

I smiled. Everything was normal at the Crossroads Hotel, all as it should be.

AUTHOR'S NOTE

Thank you for reading!

The character of Nitis and his relationship with Ruby was inspired by a pair of ravens who hang around in a ponderosa pine outside my office in northern Arizona. They constantly croak and caw at each other, yelling, conversing, scolding, or whatever they are saying. They are fascinating to watch. I knew as they appeared day after day that I needed to give Grandmother Begay a friend. And so Nitis was born. I enjoyed discovering all about him as I wrote, and he will appear in more tales.

It was also a pleasure to return to all the characters in Magellan and Many Farms, and to explore the roads Janet rides as I researched for this book. Janet and Mick's adventures continue as they learn how to deal with Blue, and finally tie the knot.

The next novel is ***Shape Changer***, where Janet and Mick meet Pamela's shape-shifting wolf family to help them out with the danger stalking them.

Check my website:

https://jenniferashley.com/allyson-james-books/

for updates on the continuing series. Or join my newsletter:

http://eepurl.com/duRXiv

to be notified when new books and audio editions are released.

All my best,

Allyson James

Feral Heat

Wild Wolf

Bear Attraction

Mate Bond

Lion Eyes

Bad Wolf

Wild Things

White Tiger

Guardian's Mate

Red Wolf

Midnight Wolf

Tiger Striped

A Shifter Christmas Carol

Iron Master

The Last Warrior

Tiger's Daughter

Bear Facts

Stray Cat

Shifter Made ("Prequel" short story)

ABOUT THE AUTHOR

New York Times bestselling and award-winning author Jennifer Ashley has more than 100 published novels and novellas in mystery, romance, historical fiction, and urban fantasy under the names Jennifer Ashley, Allyson James, and Ashley Gardner. Jennifer's books have been translated into more than a dozen languages and have earned starred reviews in *Publisher's Weekly* and *Booklist*. When she isn't writing, Jennifer enjoys playing music (guitar, piano, flute), reading, hiking, cooking, and building dollhouse miniatures.

More about Jennifer's books can be found at
http://www.jenniferashley.com

To keep up to date on her new releases, join her newsletter here:
http://eepurl.com/duRXiv

Made in the USA
Las Vegas, NV
04 August 2024

93366594R00184